W9-BGF-217

SWORDS & SCIMITARS

✦ L.L. CHAIKIN ✦

Thomas Nelson Publishers
Nashville

Copyright © 1993 by L. L. Chaikin

All rights reserved. Written permission must be secured from the publisher to use or reproduce any part of this book, except for brief quotations in critical reviews or articles.

Published in Nashville, Tennessee, by Thomas Nelson, Inc., Publishers, and distributed in Canada by Word Communications, Ltd., Richmond, British Columbia, and in the United Kingdom by Word(UK), Ltd., Milton Keynes, England.

Library of Congress Cataloging-in-Publication Data

Chaikin, Linda.
    Swords and scimitars / Linda Chaikin.
        p.   cm.
    ISBN 0-8407-6728-5-(pb)
    1. Crusades—First, 1096–1099—Fiction.   I. Title.
PS3553.H2427S9   1993
813′.54—dc20

93-8534
CIP

Printed in the United States of America

1 2 3 4 5 6 7 — 98 97 96 95 94 93

Sword Blessing

Hearken we beseech Thee, O Lord, to our prayers, and deign to bless with the right hand of Thy Majesty this sword with which Thy servant desires to be girded, that it may be a defense of churches, widows, orphans, and all Thy servants against the scourge of pagans, that it may be the terror and dread of all evildoers, and that it may be just in both attack and defense.

List of Characters

FICTIONAL

Tancred Redwan, a Norman warrior, scholar, and seeker of truth

Mosul, a Moor and assassin, cousin to Tancred, and his archenemy

Helena of the Nobility, a beautiful Byzantine

Nicholas, a maverick warrior-bishop, friend of Tancred, and Helena's uncle

Philip the Noble, Minister of War in Constantinople

Lady Irene, the aunt and enemy of Helena, the mother of Philip

Bishop Constantine, bishop in Constantinople, enemy of Nicholas

Bardas, a Greek eunuch slave belonging to Helena

Zakeem, a Moor from Palermo and Tancred's faithful friend

al-Kareem, the Moorish grandfather of Tancred

Kamila, the Moorish cousin of Tancred

Derek Redwan, half-brother of Tancred

Walter of Sicily, uncle of Tancred

Count Dreux Redwan, deceased father of Tancred

Rolf Redwan, adoptive father of Tancred

Niles, a serf on the peasant Crusade

Modestine, a French village girl

Wolfric, a brigand Rhinelander

Leupold, a Rhinelander

The Chief Rabbi at Worms, Germany

David, a Jewish boy

Rachel, a Jewish-Christian girl at Worms

Prince Kalid, son of the Emir of Antioch

Rufus, captain of Lady Irene's personal bodyguard

HISTORICAL

Alexius Comnenus, Emperor of Byzantium, 1081-1118 A.D.

Pope Urban II, pope who called for the First Crusade

Peter the Hermit, leader of the peasant Crusaders

Walter Sans-Avoir, a Frank knight and the first Crusader to arrive at Nish

Bohemond I, Norman prince of Taranto

Count Raymond of Saint-Gilles, Count of Toulouse

Roger I, the Great Count of Norman Sicily

Godfree of Bouillon, Duke of Lower Lorraine

Hugh, Count of Vermandois, brother of King Philip of France

Robert, Duke of Normandy, son of William the Conqueror

Emich (Emicho), robber-baron of Leinigen, persecutor of the Jews in the German Crusade

The Goose of Emich

Volkmar, persecutor of the Jews in the German Crusade

Gottschalk, a renegade priest, persecutor of the Jews in the German Crusade

Bishop of Worms

King Coloman, King of Hungary

Governor of Wieselburg

Nicetas, governor of Nish

Adehemar, Bishop of Le Puy and official papal legate on the Crusade

Raymond of Aguilers, a chronicler of the First Crusade

Henry IV, Emperor of Germany

Kerbogha, commander of the Seljuk warriors

"The Red Lion of the Desert," a Seljuk commander

Nicephorus, Emperor of Byzantium, 963-969 A.D.

Basil II, Emperor of Byzantium, 976-1025 A.D.

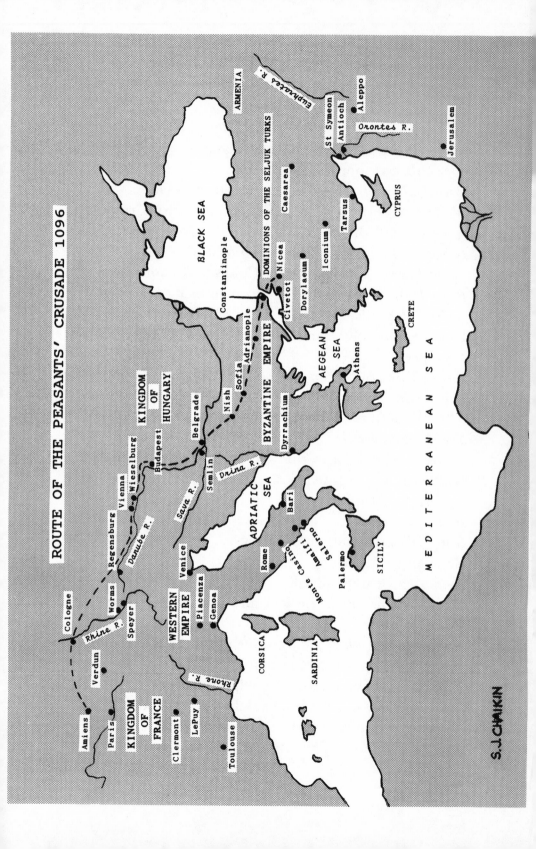

ROUTE OF THE PEASANTS' CRUSADE 1096

S.J. CHAIKIN

PART ONE

CHAPTER 1

Sicily, Redwan Castle, near Palermo

✤ Any moment now, news that Tancred had escaped his castle chamber would bring the sound of alarm. The great walls encircling the fortress castle loomed dark and impregnable. Tancred crouched in the shadows, trying to still the thudding of his heart. If he were going to escape from these walls, he must do it now. He would not be safe hiding in the castle's crannies for long. Norman guards serving his uncle were everywhere.

He knew the castle's environs well, having explored every inch of the fortress when first brought here as the adopted son of the great Norman mercenary, Rolf Redwan. Tancred also knew every twist and turn of the sun-drenched hills of Sicily, the vineyards, and the rugged coastline bracing against the seas of the Mediterranean—the Iconian on the east and the Tyrrhenian on the north.

Knowledge of the castle, first built by the Moors a century earlier, fortified his hope of survival. But for now the castle, with its series of stairs and passages that connected every part of the ancient building, was his prison. No, his place of execution.

He listened, hoping to hear the wings of the falcon. His face felt the wind from the sea . . . for the last time? How many Norman mercenary soldiers guarded the tower walls? Ten, twenty?

He waited. The ancient stone of the castle's inner bailey retained the sun's heat as the sky darkened. High above the arches and along the battlements, a myriad of stars lay scattered like grains of white sand against the blackness.

Above the chiseled flight of steps, a flaring torch reflected on the conical helmet and chain mesh of a Norman soldier on watch. Only yesterday these same mercenaries had been his friends. As a growing boy, they had taught him to use the long Viking sword and heavy armor and to ride the Great Horse of the feudal lords. Now these Ironmen were his jailers, prepared to see him die.

According to Norman custom he would undergo "craven" to prove his innocence in the death of his half-brother, Derek. Had Derek lived, he would have been heir to the Redwan fleet of galleons and the castle with its lands. The Redwan family believed Tancred's desire for the inheritance had caused him to murder Derek.

Few survived craven, the ancient trial by fire, water, or fist. Tancred was certain that his uncle, Walter of Sicily, would see to it that he did not. Tancred's demand that the trial wait until word was taken to his adoptive father in Byzantium had been rejected.

Night deepened. Nothing stirred in the courtyard except a whisper of wind that touched his dark riding cloak. His gaze swept the gate towers on the massive wall.

Waiting a moment longer, he told himself that he must try to escape from the castle. By morning it would be too late to save himself. Perhaps his intimate knowledge of the castle would be advantage enough.

The castle was first built during the Byzantine rule under Emperor Justinian, but had fallen to the Moslems when Sicily was taken in the eighth century. Now it was no longer in Moorish control but was a Redwan legacy, a booty of the Norman conquest of Moorish Sicily. The Christian Normans, bearing the accolade from the church as "Soldiers of Christ," had also established a northern kingdom in Italy and were now engaged in fighting Moorish Spain.

He knew that ancient castles always had more than one escape route. Many had elaborate tunnel systems with passages large enough for horses. They usually led to an opening in the woods where sorties could be made against an enemy and where supplies could pass in times of siege.

All but one of these passages were known to the Redwan clan. If he could reach the alcove within the walled garden undetected, he would come out near a copse by a partially breached donjon.

His hopes soared when he saw the falcon. The fowl circled as though searching for him, and Tancred gave a low whistle. It flew like the wind to his forearm, landing with outstretched wings.

Tancred removed the rolled message from the leather jess of the tiny chapel, the leather hood about its head. The falcon, a silhouette against the silver glow of moonlight, flew to the weatherworn stone arch as the breeze rippled its feathers.

In the flickering glow of a torch, Tancred made out the Arabic writing.

Alzira waits in the copse. Your sword and family heraldry are behind the stone in the alcove. Make haste to the vineyard. Z.

The message was from Zakeem, a Moorish teller of tales, a crafty spy, and a sharp-eyed peddler whom Tancred had known since he was a boy in Palermo. Tancred had met the Moor while wandering the bazaars, which offered everything from eastern intrigue to Byzantine silk.

Zakeem came and went like the falcon; he traveled on his Arabian mare with a freedom that Tancred envied. He had depended on his Moorish friend, who had proved faithful again.

Waiting a moment longer and keeping in the shadows, he made his way to the backside of the stone wall encircling the garden. He leaped, grasped the rough stone, and pulled himself up to lie flat on the narrow ledge.

He lay there, listening to the early sounds of night. A cricket chirped. The darkness below was still and filled with the heavy sweetness of blossoms. Nothing moved. He dropped to the ground, his cordovan boots making no sound.

Darting from the wall, he slipped through the gnarled olive trees to the stone alcove used in ancient times as a cloister for religious meditation. His Norman family avoided the accursed place.

Inside, Tancred ran his hand along the smooth stone ledge. Zakeem had not failed him. His fingers found the hiding place of his Toledo sword; his heart surged with new confidence. Belting on the scabbard, he drew the blade, which reflected the moonlight like a flash of silver.

His hand brushed the rough stone wall, feeling for the arrow loop. Beneath it was a familiar solid slab of stone. Bracing himself, he pushed hard with his shoulder, and the stone moved, opening the way to deep darkness. Steps led down to a narrow tunnel. The air that greeted him was stale. But first, he must find the box. He felt for the candle on the side wall, and lighting it, he worked swiftly.

Using his dagger, he worked to loosen a stone and set it aside. With his fingers he felt inside the enclosure for the small box that he had hidden there. He touched cold metal. Swiftly he drew it out, then stopped, and whirled in the direction of the garden, sword lifted.

A dark shadow loomed before him. He recognized the giant Scandinavian ax man, the captain of his uncle's personal bodyguard.

"I knew the heraldry was hidden somewhere."

"I am innocent of my brother's death."

"That is for you to convince Walter of Sicily. You will soon confront him at the trial. If you are innocent, it will be proven."

"Though I survive, he will not believe. Does he not wish himself to be seignior of the castle and the Redwan galleons?"

"Do you accuse your uncle of your half-brother's death? Was it not your dagger in his heart?"

"It was planted."

"Prove it by craven."

"Craven will prove nothing. I shall find the assassin who killed my brother. And when I do, I shall bring him to the castle to stand trial."

"Words!" he scoffed. "Derek was a full-blooded Norman, and you slew him. Who does not know how you have spent your boyhood with divided loyalties between the Redwans and the House of al-Kareem?"

The reference to Tancred's Moorish grandfather deepened his conviction that the contents in the box must not fall into his uncle's hands. Inside was the family heraldry that had belonged to his Norman father, Count Dreux

Redwan. The solid gold falcon bearing his father's name, and Tancred's as the legal heir, was from the lineage of William the Conqueror.

That his mother had been a Moorish beauty from the Moslem section of Palermo changed nothing, except in the mind of his uncle. Neither was Tancred ashamed of having the blood of the House of al-Kareem course through his body nor of his knowledge of Arabic science and medicine.

"Give me the box. I have no wish to kill a student physician."

Tancred met Ivan's gaze. He did not believe him. The big Norman had never liked him and would try to kill him anyway, claiming it was in defense. The man was one of the best swordsmen among Walter's vassals, but Tancred had trained well at the armory, both with the Norman's long blade and the curved Moorish scimitar.

A breeze rustled through the olive trees and touched his brow. His hand gripped the handle of his sword.

"Hand it over, infidel," Ivan said.

"Here then, have it."

As Ivan reached a great hand to receive it, Tancred strengthened his grip on the sword. Ivan's sword hammered down, and Tancred's came up.

For a moment he thought his move in vain, but the force was missing from the Scandinavian's blow, and his blade slid harmlessly off Tancred's. Tancred did not hesitate to follow through with an upward thrust. Ivan fell to his knees.

A soft footfall came from the garden. Tancred lifted his blade a little, waiting. A moment later, surprised by whom he saw, he lowered it.

Odo, the old one, stood there, his shoulders unbent by

his mounting years. With his monk's cowl thrown back, his silver hair shone in the moonlight.

Odo, his great-uncle, was the castle priest. Devoted to the church, he spent time each day interceding for Tancred's soul. "To save you from the teachings of the Koran," he had said.

He was the last man Tancred expected to see now. He had not noticed the monk about the castle in months and had thought him ill.

"Walter may be my son," said Odo, "but pride does not blind me to his ambitions. He will see you dead. It is not the loss of young Derek that prompts him to see you pass through the ordeal of craven but the knowledge that you are the future seignior of the castle."

Tancred swiftly embraced him. "You have risked your life to come here. You must not be seen, lest Walter also turn against you."

Voices and the sound of running feet told him his warning was too late.

Odo cast a sharp glance over his shoulder, grasping Tancred's arm. "Away! The two of us! We must find Nicholas. I must perform a duty, else I shall never be free. Come!"

"Duty?"

Tancred saw an archer on the wall, but before he could stop Odo from surging into the open, an arrow whizzed. He heard a sickening gasp as the old one stumbled and fell.

A shout followed and another arrow whizzed as Tancred grasped Odo and helped him move to the shelter of the olive trees. The garden would soon be swarming with Norman guards.

A glance at the wound told him there was no hope. Still, he lifted Odo to his feet and made for the passage.

Torches flared up as men came through the gate. He recognized Walter's voice as he shouted to the men.

Tancred darted from the trees helping Odo along. When he reached the alcove, he crawled into the small opening and entered the blackness. Laying the old one down, Tancred shoved the stone into place behind him, sealing out the flare of torches and the sound of running feet.

Breathing hard, he took the precious candle from the ledge and then crawled forward, feeling the tunnel walls closing in about him. He came to Odo, who was gasping.

"No . . . time . . . in my robe . . ."

Tancred placed his hand into his brevet and removed an object wrapped in a dark cloth.

"This treasure . . . captain of bodyguard knew of it, and sought . . ."

Tancred leaned closer to hear the words over the rasping breaths.

"Take . . . to Jerusalem . . . holy site . . . save my soul from eternal flames, and yours . . . I stole . . . when very young . . . go, Tancred."

Tancred felt a wrench of despair. Take a treasure to Jerusalem? Odo did not know the personal sacrifice he was asking of him. He grasped the old man's shoulders.

"Say not that! Anything but pilgrimage!"

"My soul!" Odo gasped, raising his head, his eyes widening. He clutched the front of Tancred's tunic. "Jerusalem," he choked, blood seeping through his lips. "Save me . . ."

Tancred lowered his sweating forehead against Odo's heaving chest, gritting his teeth. He had to decide immediately.

"I will go," he whispered. "For you, I will go. For no one else would I do this."

"First . . . find Nicholas . . ."

Tancred knew Nicholas, the unconventional warrior-bishop, was journeying to Piacenza to attend a church council called by the pope.

"I will go to Nicholas. And I will find the assassin who killed Derek. Then to Constantinople and Jerusalem."

With reluctance, Tancred stuffed the object inside his tunic. He kissed the old man and formed the sign of the cross on his forehead.

"Rest in eternal peace."

The old one made no answer. Tancred knew he was dead.

He would not think of losing Odo now, nor of the quest that he had put upon Tancred. He must concentrate on reaching the opening at the other end, where Zakeem had his horse waiting. He must escape before guards were sent to search the grounds outside the castle walls.

He knew the route through the passage well enough, for he had traveled it on several occasions. The air was bad, but he worked his way forward.

Strange that so small a light as a candle gives so much direction when all about you is black as pitch.

Thinking this, he remembered what Nicholas had told him at the abbey of Monte Casino. "Christ is the Light of the world. Follow Him, and your feet will arrive safely in paradise. Trust not in relics or in pilgrimage to soften the heart of a holy God. Christ is our merit."

At the moment, Tancred would be content to arrive safely in Italy to see Nicholas.

When he pushed on the lever at the end of the passage, the stone slid open on its axis. A black sky, winking with white jewels, welcomed him. The waft of fresh air held the tang of the sea and cooled his perspiring face.

He crawled out, careful to close the opening and then

rearrange the shrubs and vines to conceal the stone. He stood surrounded by an apricot orchard.

When he heard the wings of the falcon, he looked up. A soft snort came from the trees as his horse picked up her master's scent. A moment later Alzira emerged and trotted toward him, head lifted.

With a quick stroke to her neck and whispering something in Arabic, Tancred mounted easily. The horse's shod hooves echoed, followed by the falcon's shrill cry. The cry died away as the bird flew east toward the vineyard.

Tancred rode up the goat-track on the far side of the road, passing a shepherd. Two miles farther he came to a small village in the hills surrounded with groves. He walked the mare until he came to a bend in the dusty track that wound up into an ancient vineyard. The gnarled vines stood stark against the pale horizon, where the faint color of lilac outlined the foothills.

Tancred drew up and for a moment sat alert, looking into the trees and listening, every muscle in his disciplined body tense, his hand on his sword.

A twig snapped. A shadow disengaged from the other shadows and stood in the starlight. Tancred recognized the tough brown face of Zakeem.

"Ah, Great One! The peace of Allah! Or should I say, the blessing of the Virgin?"

"Father of Hypocrites, what news do you bring?"

"Important news, my young friend. An informer has arrived from Spain."

Tancred's heart raced. "Yes?"

"He knows the assassin of your half-brother."

Tancred gripped the reins. "You are certain? It is not a trap?"

"I am certain. Yet take heed. The informer may be watched by others who are enemies of your grandfather."

The lineage of the House of al-Kareem knew its enemies not only among certain Normans but also from
Moorish Spain. Blood feuds between the great ruling families of the past had not died with time nor with Norman
conquest. His grandfather was from the old Berber dy-
nasty of the Almohads, a white people from North Africa
who had come to Sicily in the ninth century and intermar-
ried with the Arabs, forming what was known as the
Moors. Hatred smoldered, even during the rule of Roger
the Great Count. A decade of peace between opposing
forces could swiftly break forth into bloodshed.

"The informer, where is he? How will I know him?"

"He travels from Cordoba with a string of Arabian
mares. Go to the black tent near the caravan bazaar. One
of the horses is of the family of your own Alzira," he said,
patting the horse. "Tonight go not as the son of a Norman.
Go dressed as the son of your mother."

Zakeem returned from the olive grove carrying a bundle in his arms. "Your clothes from the House of al-
Kareem."

Discarding his scholar's cloak, but leaving on the light
coat of chain mesh worn over an under tunic, Tancred
donned the outer tunic of dark-blue wool bound with a
silk sash. The full black trousers were worn by fashionable
young Moors, and he bloused them into the boots that
covered his muscled legs.

Zakeem gathered the discarded pieces of Norman uniform and placed them on his own mare, then returned to
watch Tancred wrap the dark-blue silk turban about his
head. His brown hair, bearing the flecks of sun-ripened
wheat, and the blue-gray eyes he had inherited from his
Norman father, only emphasized his handsome, Moorish
good looks.

Zakeem proudly produced a scimitar. Tancred recognized the deadly curved blade that his grandfather had presented to him on one of his visits. He held it firmly in his hand, remembering. The balance was perfect. He whipped it through the movements from the manual of style so swiftly that the silver cut through the darkness.

Zakeem chuckled. "You were always a better Moor than a Norman."

Tancred slung his sword over his shoulder Moorish-style and mounted Alzira.

"After the meeting at the black tent, let us find a ship sailing to the Golden Horn, master, lest we both lose our heads. Let us sail for Constantinople and find your father."

He had every intention of finding his adoptive father, Count Rolf Redwan, who was in service at the Castle of Hohms near Antioch.

"Not yet, Zakeem. First I must see Nicholas."

Zakeem scowled at the mention of the stalwart Norman priest. "You walk on a bed of coals, master. Be on guard! Is not he a clever man? Are you not the scholar he wishes to enter the monastery?"

"Like a falcon, my friend, I will find contentment in naught else but my freedom. I must tell Nicholas of Derek's death and of the old one, Odo, who was killed tonight."

"Your life, too, will be nothing by morning. Yet I dare not ride with you to Italy."

"A wise decision," murmured Tancred, thinking back to the frowns that came from the abbey monks when Zakeem had appeared at the Christian domain, even though Zakeem had wisely kept outside the gate. Only Nicholas had been able to persuade them that Zakeem had converted and that he wore a turban because he had no hair and was badly scarred.

Whether all this was true or not was somewhat disputable.

"Come," said Tancred. "The meeting with the informer in the black tent cannot wait."

CHAPTER 2

The Informer's Black Tent

✤ The wharf lay dark and quiet when Tancred arrived. Leaving Zakeem on guard, he proceeded to meet his contact. Familiar buildings that remained from ancient times looked like dark skeletons. Some of them, it was said, were constructed by Alexander the Great, others by the Emperor Justinian.

A spring rain had set in. Sweet drops wet his face as a frontal wind came in from the sea. He drew his riding cloak about him and walked his mare toward the harbor.

The rain kept dockside activity to a minimum, and the shores were crowded with merchandise to be loaded or unloaded with the light of dawn. Now the shadowy hulls slept, camels dozed, and their drivers had taken shelter beneath the black and white goatskin tents.

Ahead were Moslem caravans from the regions of the Caliphate of Cordoba and as far south as Tunis and Tripoli. Ships were from all the ports: Alexandria, Venice, Constantinople.

He spotted the black tent of which Zakeem had told

him. He would need to approach with caution. A fire sputtered beneath a shelter of dried date palm branches, sending a delightful aroma of food to his nostrils. He neared, leading Alzira.

A graybeard sat on his haunches by the fire, his head covered. He must have sensed Tancred's presence, for he turned and fixed his dark eyes on Tancred.

Tancred bowed. "Peace on such a night as this. I saw your fire."

The man stood, and with a sweep of his arm to show that Tancred was welcome, he said, "Sit and share my bread."

Tancred stepped under the skin shelter and seated himself on the rug. The Moor ladled several chunks of goat meat onto small round Arab breads and scooped hot bean curry into a metal bowl.

Tancred gestured to the pen of horses. "You know your breeds well. They all appear to be of the blood," referring to the five great Arabian breeds.

The merchant pointed to a mare. "She is by far the best I have."

"From which of the five?"

"Sagalawi." The black eyes measured him.

Tancred was certain the Arab noticed the blue of his eyes and questioned his Moorish ancestry.

The Arab said, "My brother sold another mare to the house of al-Kareem a year ago. Such a horse! I bought her from Prince Kalid of Antioch."

"The mare's name is Alzira," Tancred stated quietly. "She is before you."

The man studied the mare, and a gleam of pride showed in his eyes. "Ah, so it is. Then you are the man I am to meet. Clothes aside, you do not look a Moor."

"I am Tancred Jehan Redwan, son of Safia of al-

Kareem and of Dreux of the House of Redwan. What news do you bring me?"

The Moor ate quietly and for a moment did not speak. Did he truly have information on who had killed Derek?

"Danger troubles you from your own house."

Tancred already knew that. "Walter of Sicily searches for me. Yet the killing of my brother was not of the skill used by Normans. The dagger was dipped in poison."

"I did not speak of the Normans. Your cousin killed your brother."

For a moment Tancred was confused. He had eight Redwan cousins, all of whom swore to see him pass through craven for the murder. But surely none of these had slain Derek. Then he understood.

Mosul, his Moorish cousin. Tancred stood up and stared at the man. "Mosul?" he breathed.

"Yes."

This information he had not anticipated. "Why? What motive would he have? Does he not do well for himself in service to the caliph of Cordoba?"

"He does."

"The informers who told you this, can they be trusted?"

"They are friends of Zakeem. Worthy men, all."

Yet informers worried Tancred. Zakeem he knew well, and this graybeard, he sensed, retained honor. But who among the many spies of Cordoba could he trust? Many worked on their own for a price, while others served men and women of importance.

"You are certain of this?"

"I suggest you speak with your grandfather, al-Kareem." Tancred had wanted to avoid his grandfather's house for fear his presence would give Walter an opportunity to move against him. Even now the house might be watched. He was only a step ahead of Walter's men.

Yet the informer was right. His grandfather would best be able to tell him if Mosul was involved. More importantly, was his cousin in Palermo now?

Tancred took his leave of the graybeard. It was still dark, but the rain had stopped as he rode with Zakeem to the Moorish section of Palermo. They rode with caution through the narrow stone streets.

The houses, with windows screened with alabaster, towered above them. The bazaars were still open, and the street brightly lit with lanterns. A babble of voices filled Tancred's ears.

"If you are to catch a ship to Italy, you must make haste," said Zakeem. "By now Walter has men out looking for you."

Tancred approached his grandfather's house from the alley, leaving Zakeem on guard. It was a fine house he knew well. There were many buildings and stables, which housed well-bred horses. He had kept Alzira there while he attended the medical school in Salerno. Beyond the stables were orchards, vineyards, grass, and a running fountain.

He found his way to the wall of the private garden where colored glass lanterns shone. A female slave sang, her fingers caressing the strings of the qitara.

Tancred stood in the cool shadows outside the wall listening, waiting. He was concerned that he was putting his grandfather at risk. Was he being watched by enemies?

If he were careful, he could accomplish what he needed and be gone before Walter could move.

He jumped, caught the wall's ledge, and pulled himself up. Below in the darkness it was still. He saw no one, not even the slave girl who sang. Beyond the fragrant orange blossoms, light from suspended lanterns fell on the open stone courtyard. To the right stood a colonnade of Moorish arches.

Tancred dropped to the earth. With a whisper of his cloak, he moved among the vines and came toward the lighted gallery and a room that opened off the garden. He paused near the doorway.

Turkish rugs, woven in silk with designs in wool, added shimmers of blue, green, and yellow to the room. Cushions were centered around a low table, which held plates of dried figs, dates, goat cheese, bread, tea, and Arabic coffee.

He was familiar with the room, having come here often to visit his mother's family, to study his Moorish ancestry, and to listen to his grandfather on the teachings of Mohammed.

Tancred's mind wandered back to his boyhood. How often he had sat there supping on fruits and nuts, while his grandfather cross-examined him on the Christian teachings he was learning from Nicholas at the abbey of Monte Casino. Tancred often deliberately baited the two with his knowledge of both religions to see who became the angrier. As a boy he had found it an entertaining diversion when he became frustrated with each of them for scheming to win his allegiance.

"Are not Jews and Christians to be respected as people of the Book, Grandfather?"

"They are," he said grudgingly.

"Why then are both harassed in Jerusalem?"

"Lies! They are not harassed!"

"But Nicholas says the Christians who go to Syria on pilgrimage are oft mocked and sent away from the holy shrines." Tancred smiled and devoured another handful of almonds.

"Nicholas has beguiled you. It is a curse that you must go to that place. You must not go again, Jehan."

"I must go, my Grandfather. Nicholas says that before my father died in St. Peter's Basilica, he made Nicholas swear to train me in the knowledge of the church. It is all written in the archives at Monte Casino."

"So it is," he said grudgingly. "The curse be upon me that you go there. It was I who gave your mother to Count Dreux Redwan. But listen to me, Jehan, you must weigh the words of Nicholas with the wisdom of the Koran."

Tancred enjoyed the fire in the old man's dark eyes. "Yes, Grandfather. There is no ill in learning my father's ways, even as I am learning my mother's. I enjoy the writings, Grandfather. There is a large library at Monte Casino."

"Infidels write those books. They are of Satan. You esteem the few books at Monte Casino? Ha! You should see the great library in Cairo, in Baghdad, in Cordoba! Monte Casino? Bah! You will not learn from Nicholas!"

"I would like to see such libraries, Grandfather. And one day I will. But the Christian Book, Nicholas says it was written a thousand years before the Koran. Is it so? And Nicholas says that Jews are from Father Abraham, like Ishmael the Blessed."

Al-Kareem shifted his weight on the cushions, his brows lowering. "Jews are from the seed of Isaac, yes . . ." His eyes brightened. "But to Ishmael belong the promises."

Tancred reached for a cluster of dark purple grapes. He studied them thoughtfully. "Nicholas says the promises are Isaac's."

"Nicholas, Nicholas. The barbarian Norman does not know of that which he speaks so ignorantly."

Tancred covered a smile. "He says the same of you,

Grandfather. Only he does not become as flushed and indignant as you. He is more difficult to provoke—" He stopped at once, knowing he had given himself away.

His grandfather's eyes narrowed. He drummed his fingers on his robed lap. "Jehan?"

Tancred looked at him with innocence. "Yes, Grandfather?"

"Do you deliberately bait Nicholas as you do me?"

"Nay, Grandfather. I do not know what you mean!"

"You must not be wicked, Jehan."

"I would not be wicked. But, Grandfather, what of Jesus?"

"A good man, a prophet, like Abraham and Moses. Enough for one day. I will close the Koran."

"Nicholas says Jesus is greater than any prophet, even Mohammed. That Jesus is God's Son."

His grandfather hissed under his breath and closed the Koran. "Enough for today, Jehan. Your cousin Mosul waits for you with the armorer. It is time for your lesson with the scimitar. Remember, it is not wise to fill your mind with the insane mumblings of infidels, Jehan. There is only one God, Allah, and one prophet, Mohammed."

Tancred smiled. "Yes, Grandfather. There is but one God."

Al-Kareem smirked. "You are a pleasant child, my son Jehan. You have your mother's smile but the eyes and hair of a Norman. Stay wise, and you will inherit all things."

A rustle of garments brought Tancred back to the moment. He turned. Al-Kareem entered from another room, a big man with a protruding belly. But he still carried himself well.

Tancred crossed the room, and according to custom, kissed both sides of his grandfather's bearded face.

"My informers have explained everything," said al-Kareem.

"Then it is certain? It was Mosul?" Tancred's voice was quiet, for the words of betrayal were painful to speak.

Al-Kareem hesitated, then nodded. "I should have known it would come to this. I should have moved sooner to stop it."

"Known about Derek? But how could you?"

"Mosul was jealous of you even when you were boys. He wished your demise."

That Mosul had been ambitious Tancred understood. As boys roaming the hills of Palermo, Mosul had always tried to best him, and when he failed, he would be morose for the remainder of the day. But that his Moorish cousin would have stooped to such treachery had not entered Tancred's mind.

"I fear he has always shown himself to be imperious," said al-Kareem. "It seems I should have worried more of Mosul and less of you and your Christian Normans. I should have seen the merciless tendencies in Mosul as a boy. Now it is too late."

Tancred's hand tightened on his grandfather's shoulder. "I will find him."

"It will do no good to search for him. He is not in Palermo. He has fled to Constantinople."

"Then I will go there to find him!"

Al-Kareem shook his head as though in doubt of success. "I fear, Jehan, it will not be so easy."

"I must try."

"I expected you to. You have the warrior's blood of two races, both fierce."

"Continue to seek information from your informers, here in Palermo and in Baghdad. If you have news, you will find me at the bazaars in Constantinople."

"Then take my ring, my son. It will open the mouths of the dumb."

Tancred slipped the signet ring on his right hand. "I will not fail. I will bring Mosul back."

Al-Kareem laid a steady hand on Tancred's arm. "Slay him not. Let his punishment come from the house of our Moorish family here in Palermo."

Tancred knew of such judgment. "The House of Redwan will also have something to say of his punishment, my Grandfather. Derek was the firstborn son of Count Dreux Redwan. Justice must be done. And my innocence must be proven. I shall have no life except that of a mercenary soldier unless I return Mosul to Palermo alive."

Al-Kareem watched him with distress. "If you go East seeking him, you risk your life."

That Mosul was without scruples, vain, and selfish, Tancred well knew. His confidence in finding him and returning him to Sicily was like a fleeing shadow. The possibility was slim, and before he sought Mosul, he must first try to locate his father.

"I risk even more if I stay here. Have I a choice? Walter is searching for me. Even this small delay gives him time."

"Yes, yes, it is so. You must leave Palermo at once, Jehan. And now I have lost both my grandsons."

"Nay, I will be back. I will not abandon my heritage but bring honor to both the Norman falcon and the House of al-Kareem."

His grandfather's eyes welled with tears. "If Allah wills, it will be."

"Grandfather, I shall fight for my freedom and my honor. I shall not turn away, doing nothing, accepting the fruits of inaction as divine fate! Evil must be confronted, lest it crush beneath its boots the skulls of those who sit indolently before its advance."

Al-Kareem's mouth turned up. "And to think I worried that Nicholas and his relics would turn you into a recluse within a monastery."

Nicholas! Tancred suddenly remembered his other mission. He must see Nicholas not only to keep his vow to the old one but also to explain his situation.

He stood up from the cushion, anxious to be on his way to southern Italy, the kingdom of the Normans.

Nicholas was anything but a gentle recluse. A stalwart bishop at Monte Casino, he would have much to say about the deaths of Derek and Odo.

Little did his grandfather understand the mind-set of Norman-appointed priests, monks, and other clerics. The Normans believed one should carry a Viking sword in one hand and the cross in the other. They used both without a wink of the eye.

Nicholas was an expert swordsman.

A slight movement in the doorway that opened onto the flagstone courtyard caught Tancred's eye. He whirled. It was only a slave. Tancred was about to turn away, when something about the sullen expression of the man's mouth and the wary way in which he proceeded to light a lantern that had gone out, stopped him. He gave the slave a measured look.

His grandfather followed his gaze and shook his head. "Be of no concern."

"I do not remember him. He is new?"

"He has been with me for a year now. He is a deaf mute. His duties bring him where I would not trust others."

Tancred's instincts told him otherwise. They warned

him to be cautious, despite his grandfather's confidence. "You are certain?"

"A friend in Cordoba sent him."

"You also have enemies there. Mosul knew them all well."

"I am certain of this slave."

Tancred was not but said no more. The slave, noticing Tancred's level gaze, walked away on slippered feet. Tancred didn't like the situation. Restlessly he paced, aware of too many slaves moving about, busy in their duties but too close.

He considered his position. He had his sword and scimitar, his fast mare, and his loyal friend Zakeem. Zakeem also knew his way about the bazaars and would prove invaluable. There also were the informers and guards who served his grandfather in Palermo, but he hesitated to involve them further, fearing Walter would turn against them.

Al-Kareem walked across the room to a table and returned with a book in his hand, a handwritten copy of the Koran. "Take it with you and you take wisdom."

Tancred would admit to no one that his heart asked questions for which he had yet to receive answers. He felt the need to search further for truth. He knew the Koran, but he also wanted to know more about the Bible, although copies were not available for private use.

He had stayed at Monte Casino for several years as a child, the only place he knew where he could find complete copies of the Old and New Testaments. Tancred knew nothing of Hebrew, but he had learned Greek from Nicholas and used Latin at medical school.

He accepted the Koran, embracing his grandfather. One day he would also study the Scriptures for himself. Perhaps the answers to his many questions were neither in

Rome nor in Mecca, but in the great Royal Library at Constantinople where he could have complete access to the Bible.

But for now he knew he had already stayed with his grandfather too long. Both the instinct of the hunted and the intelligence of a scholar told him he must go.

The house he had loved as a boy now began to close in on him. He longed to be astride Alzira, racing through the forests that would lead him to Nicholas.

"I will send word of my whereabouts," he said to al-Kareem.

"Go in peace. And do not forget the blood of the woman who bore you."

"That, my Grandfather, I promise I will never do."

The loitering slave was not to be seen in the garden when Tancred left by way of the wall. Was he truly a deaf mute? Tancred could not help thinking how the position might allow the man to spy unhindered. But perhaps he was too suspicious.

As he joined Zakeem, he heard retreating horse hooves on the narrow street.

"Did you see who it was, Zakeem?"

"A slave, master."

Where had the slave gone? Would he deliver information he had overheard? Soon now Walter would be on his trail.

Zakeem must have seen Tancred's frown as he mounted, for he offered, "Would you want me to hunt him down?"

"No, Zakeem, let him go. There is no time. By now he has fled down some alley. Tell my grandfather he has a spy in his service. I must ride on."

"Where to?"

"To find passage on a ship to Italy, then Constantinople."

"Then I will find you there, master. I go by way of Moslem Spain."

"Take care, Father of Spies!"

CHAPTER 3

Constantinople, Queen City of the Byzantine Empire

❖ The waters of the Sea of Marmora, azure blue, gently lapped against the granite foundation of the private summer palace belonging to Helena's absent uncle, Nicholas. She stood between the white columns of the open marble pavilion looking out toward the sea.

The setting sun was crimson against the horizon on the purple hills of Asia. Who could guess that beyond the Bosphorous, Moslem Turks waited with scimitars to battle the barbarian knights from western Europe over control of Jerusalem.

Helena's eyes were riveted on the Greek dromond at anchor in the harbor. The fast vessel was preparing to sail for Italy in the morning, where the emperor's emissaries would call on the Latin pope. They would request mercenary knights to come fight the Moslem Turks who were infringing on Byzantine territory.

Her heart thudded as she gripped a letter, concealing it from the eyes of slaves. Would her Uncle Nicholas be at that important council at Piacenza, Italy?

Oh, he must, thought Helena. And her eunuch slave Bardas must be aboard the dromond with her letter to Nicholas.

Helena had more on her mind than the call for a Crusade to liberate the Christian shrines in Jerusalem from the Seljuk Turks. However, the Crusade would afford her uncle the perfect opportunity to return to Constantinople without arrest.

Within the walls of the Sacred Palace, and even in the seclusion of the women's quarters, plots and counterplots hatched as women, eunuchs, and courtiers sought to better their own positions.

Helena's enemies in the palace bought and sold information that put an end to her power, but she too had learned the Byzantine art of intrigue.

Girlish fancies, best left to banquets, had died when her mother was arrested by the Imperial Guard. Accused of plotting against the emperor, her mother had been incarcerated in a women's monastery until her reported death the year before. The story of her mother's fate, dark as it had sounded to her, might have been accepted by Helena had she not heard by way of paid informers that her mother did not die of fever.

Suspicious of her aunt, Helena had begun further inquiries. She discovered that her mother may yet be alive, not in the monastery, but as a slave. Where? In Egypt? Tabriz? Baghdad?

Nicholas must be informed. She must get the letter to Bardas tonight before the dromond sailed. But Bardas was late.

She felt certain that her aunt, Lady Irene, had used intrigue against her mother, bringing about this despicable destiny. And if that were so, what about Helena?

As heiress to the Castle of Hohms near Moslem-held

Antioch, she was unable to claim the castle until first provided with a husband. Irene and Bishop Constantine would arrange the wedding. Already many men in Constantinople and elsewhere, including the Seljuk Turk Prince Kalid, son of the Emir of Antioch, were making their interest known to her guardians.

Antioch . . . the Moslem Turks . . . the Western Crusaders . . .

The moon rose, pale and golden, while the warm wind stirred across the sea, touching her skin. She listened again for the chariot wheels in the courtyard that would announce Bardas's arrival. But nothing stirred except for the water that lapped against the seawall of the St. Barbara Gate.

Helena paced. She had reason to fear ever since her arrival in the Sacred Palace. Intrigue was the mother's milk of the Byzantine culture, as necessary to the populace as the games at the Hippodrome or as the daily occurrence of religious phenomena at the Church of St. Sophia and the Church of the Holy Apostles. Intrigue poisoned the Byzantine's intellect. Skilled in clever machinations, without scruple, Constantinople was the hotbed of subterfuge.

But this was no time to let fear master her. Helena would use her own informers to thwart her aunt. Impatience goaded her into trying to locate her mother now, yet no choice remained but to wait. She must not betray her intentions to her aunt and the bishop.

First her informers must make inquiries into her mother's whereabouts, and that would demand time. She must be cautious and wait for Nicholas to arrive with the Western barbarians. He would help her. But first the letter . . .

She turned her thoughts to Nicholas. Her affectionate

memories of the stalwart Greek bishop, bearing sword and chain mesh, heartened her. During her childhood, Nicholas had served the patriarch of the Eastern church until he was accused of heresy and removed from his position. Without ceremony he had been sent to a Byzantine stronghold on the northern coast of Italy called Bari, where the Greek language and culture prevailed.

Her letters from Nicholas were few and precious. She knew she had Irene to blame for that. Irene feared Nicholas, but the reasons for this apprehension Helena had been unable to discover.

A robed eunuch brought in a tray of sugared fruits and wine and set them down on the low marble table for her. He bowed.

"Mistress, a message arrived from Lady Irene. Her plans have changed. She arrived in Constantinople an hour ago from the Castle of Hohms. You will dine with her and her son, Philip, tonight."

Helena's decision came with cool resolve. There was no time to lose. If her aunt were on her way to the palace, then she dare not wait for Bardas. As soon as the slave disappeared, she sped across the marble floor, her silk skirts trailing her. Snatching her marten-lined cloak from the gilded footstool, she slipped past the columns and down the broad steps toward the courtyard.

She would risk taking a chariot to the harbor of the Golden Horn to deliver the letter to Bardas. She might even meet him on the way. Her eunuch slave must be aboard that Greek ship with her letter before it sailed to Italy.

Nicholas was friendly with the barbarian Normans of Sicily. What better way could he show his face again than in the company of one of the feudal princes' large armies, sent for by the emperor himself?

CHAPTER 4

Piacenza, Italy
March, 1095

✠ The big Greek eunuch stood watching the Latin bishops arrive at the cathedral.

Bardas glanced at the mud streets, the buildings that paled into insignificance compared to the illustrious Greek empire of Byzantium. He sniffed his disdain as he scanned the bishops and priests who were arriving in Piacenza from all over Italy, France, and Normandy.

So this was the West, the land of barbarians. What possible good could these men of ignorance and heresy do for the grand and glorious emperor in his struggle with the Seljuk Turks?

Bardas stood erect, his face hinting of his inward disdain. One hand grasped the hilt of his jeweled scabbard, the other rested on his hip. His shaved head glistened in the morning sunlight. He wore black trousers with a sash of gold and a circular cloak about his shoulders. His marble brown eyes scanned the delegations on their way into the chamber, searching for the church prelates from

Monte Casino. He was at a disadvantage since he had never seen Nicholas before.

In the crowd, he caught sight of the insignia announcing the monastery of Monte Casino, followed by a Norman delegation from southern Italy, some on foot, some on horses. An old man with long white hair was being carried on a litter.

Bardas stepped from his place beside the mud street and approached the old man. Out of respect for his mistress and because the bishop bore Greek blood, he bowed at the waist.

"Oh, Favored of the Saints. Oh, Blessed Friend of the Virgin. Peace to you, Nicholas, uncle of the beautiful Helena of the Nobility. My mistress has sent me from Constantinople with an urgent letter."

Bardas drew a sealed document from his belt, bearing a red ribbon, and extended it to the old man.

The man on the litter scowled, scanning the slave up and down with horror. "Who art thou? And why has your mistress not demanded you clothe yourself? It is indecent to be marching about half naked like some barbarian from the East!"

Bardas, stunned by the insult, stepped back. With a grimace, he stared down at the frail man, who appeared unintimidated. The old cleric grabbed his staff and poked it harmlessly at Bardas's bare chest.

"Did not the Almighty clothe Adam and Eve with skins of animals? Art thou any better?"

A chuckle of amusement came from those behind the litter. Bardas turned his indignant gaze in that direction and saw several rugged men astride strong horses. The one who looked the most amused was some manner of cleric. He was leaning his arm across his saddle, watching Bardas. The man had a bold look and a smile that one might expect to see on an adventurous mercenary. "And I," snapped the old man on the litter, "am not Nicholas." He gestured a frail but impatient hand in the direction of the man on the horse. "There is Nicholas of Monte Casino. Now step aside, thou art in my way!"

Bardas, indignant but at a loss for words, did as the old man told him and bowed at the waist. The procession moved on in the direction of the cathedral.

Not until Bardas watched them disappear through the door did he realize the man on the fine horse had not ridden on with them. Bardas turned toward him.

Nicholas smiled. He wore a clergyman's habiliments, with a dark cloak trimmed with fur. His wide-brimmed black hat sat on a sturdy head with black locks that were faintly tinged with gray. Beneath his cleric tunic, he wore a chain mesh shirt. He had done so since nearly being thrust through with a German lance in St. Peter's Square the night Rome was sacked and burned.

He had stumbled into the Vatican to find an eight-year-old boy taking refuge under the altar. The boy, a handsome child with gray-blue eyes, hair the color of sun-ripened wheat, and a wit that amused Nicholas, was named Tancred Redwan, the youngest son of Count Dreux Redwan of Sicily. Tancred's father had been slain in the battle for Rome.

The mesh shirt Nicholas now wore was fine, supple chain that would turn aside all but the most direct dagger thrust. But the metal did not gleam openly; after all, he was a bishop.

He had left his sword and scabbard in his small chamber, but a dagger was kept at his left boot top, for he was left-handed. A smaller dagger of infidel Moorish design was worn in a wrist-sheath strapped along his forearm underneath the mesh. The knife was a birthday gift from Tancred, a joke shared between them.

"I am Nicholas. I assume you serve my niece Helena. What news do you bring me?"

He had deliberately spoken in Greek, and Bardas, who was won over at once, bowed and extended the document.

"Your servant, Master Nicholas. I have come aboard the same ship as the Byzantine delegation sent by our illustrious emperor."

"You said the letter was urgent?"

"Your niece, my mistress, wishes above all the known world that you come to Constantinople."

"Does she indeed. And how does she fare?"

"All things are explained in the letter, Master Nicholas. I dare not utter the words aloud. I shall tend to your horse until you are free to leave the council meeting. I shall wait for your orders."

The Piacenza council was called into session by the pope to take up church matters, including hearing the scandalous accusations of Praexda, the disavowed wife of King Henry IV. But the pope was also expecting the prestigious arrival of the Byzantine emissary sent by the Eastern emperor to ask for military aid against the Moslems.

The call for mercenary soldiers from the West was not sudden, nor was it the first contact between Emperor Alexis and Pope Urban. Through Nicholas's contacts in the Greek church in Bari, he was aware that the emperor had frequently asked for aid by way of letters written to Urban and to certain feudal princes, who were known for their military prowess. But now that Urban was established on the papal throne, the time was conducive to respond to the appeals.

The meeting was well underway when Nicholas, having read Helena's letter, entered the chamber through the listening gallery. He was grave, his mind on several matters at once. His primary concerns were his niece's safety and her suspicion that her mother, Adrianna, yet lived but was a slave.

Some ten minutes later, seated in the gallery, his eyes swept the Byzantine delegation. He did not remember the minister of war from his days in Constantinople, and he watched as the Greek solicitously addressed the pope with famed Byzantine eloquence.

Nicholas's lips turned into a thin smile. He knew the Byzantine mind. The request for support to bolster the emperor's defense of the Eastern churches and of the Western pilgrims journeying to Jerusalem was politically based, although expressed in the religious dialogue the West would most likely respond to. To think as a Byzantine was to scheme, to hire one enemy to dispose of another, only to reject them both in the end.

The emperor had once hired Seljuk Turks to fight the Normans, who were then at his empire's gate. He was not above hiring Normans to defeat the Turks, who now were on his doorstep.

Nicholas tapped the edge of the rolled parchment against his chin and thoughtfully turned his gaze to a handsome young man in a purple cloak standing just behind the minister of war. He recognized the Greek official as Philip the Noble. That Helena was determined to marry him troubled Nicholas. Philip was anything but a pious representative of Constantinople. He was under the rule of his cold and calculating mother, Lady Irene, and Bishop Constantine.

Nicholas tensed. His gaze left Philip to rivet on Constantine, who stood in the delegation. He was a shrewd man with high ambitions—and was Nicholas's enemy.

As though some instinct had alerted the other man to Nicholas's presence, Constantine looked up into the gallery, his shrewd black eyes confronting Nicholas. Startled to see him among the gathered bishops, Constantine lifted his head a little.

Nicholas's hand brushed against the dagger in his boot. He slowly stood to his rugged height, looking anything but a humble and pious bishop, and stared back at Constantine with a slight curving of his mouth.

No, Constantine, you do not see a ghost, he thought. *The night you left me for dead on the Golden Horn, I was yet alive. Just barely.*

Constantine's mouth formed a hard line of concealed consternation. But the anger in his eyes revealed he nursed no regret for the past. The sight of Nicholas, though unexpected, was met with disdain and a lack of fear. Constantine was no soft and overweight cleric but a man of dangerous skills, a man that Nicholas knew would be a match with the sword.

Nicholas maintained his smile and placed the wide-brimmed black hat on his head. He drew his cloak about his broad shoulders and, for a moment, continued to watch Constantine.

The Byzantine stared back, then turned his head away and walked out of the stone chamber with the conclave that followed after the pope.

Nicholas watched until they disappeared through the velvet drapery. The council meeting had adjourned. There was a stir in the gallery, and below in the chamber, a discussion broke out among the clergy.

Seated next to Nicholas, Turill, a frail old man with silver hair, both friend and colleague, leaned toward him.

"Well, well, Nicholas, you know the Byzantines. What think you of all this display?"

Nicholas turned to the archbishop, who was nearing his eighty-second birthday. The eyes, now partially blind, were nevertheless clear to behold.

"Think?" said Nicholas. "My dear archbishop, the veiled promises brought to Urban are disguised in the rich Byzantine garb of intrigue." He smiled. "What else?"

"Intrigue you say. Well, well. I thought so myself. A handsome troop they were though." His old eyes twinkled. "The lord pope was impressed by your Greek brothers. He has called for another council to be held in Clermont in November. Not only are the bishops to be there but also some of the feudal lords, Count Raymond of Saint-Gilles and perhaps the brother of the King of France."

Clermont, France, was the pope's homeland. But Nicholas believed there was another reason for choosing the land of the Franks for the meeting. France, the land of the gallant spirit of Charlemagne, held restless knights only too anxious to draw sword.

He had heard good things of Count Raymond. It was boasted that he could put fifty thousand knights on horses. This did not include the five men who surrounded each knight. Nicholas thought the number to be exaggerated, but it would be a formidable army nonetheless. One the pope might count on for a Crusade to the Eastern empire.

Turill sighed and gathered his robes about him, as if the dampness troubled his bones. "Clermont in November will be wretchedly cold. I would think the lord pope might at least wait till spring to sound forth the crusading trumpet."

Turill left the gallery, and Nicholas stood thinking of Helena and the letter she had written. Was her information accurate? Could her mother be alive?

The possibility brought a frown. Adrianna was a virtuous woman, faithful to his brother, Andronicus. Bishop Constantine had prompted the emperor to arrest her for treason. If she were alive, then she must be found.

Perhaps the time had come for a return to the city of his birth. Not only to see Helena but also to visit his friend Count Rolf Redwan, the seignior of Byzantine forces at the Castle of Hohms near Antioch.

He decided to send a message to Tancred Redwan at the castle in Palermo. He had not seen him in a year, and he wondered how the young scholar-warrior fared. Perhaps he could interest Tancred in making the journey with him. It had been some years since Tancred had seen his adoptive father, Rolf Redwan.

Perhaps, thought Nicholas, *it would be wise to travel east in the company of one of the feudal princes.*

The Norman knights serving Bohemond would be a worthy legion to attach themselves to for the two-month journey.

But first there was the pope's second council at Clermont. Just what would the Latin head say? It would be a mistake to sanction such a Crusade in the name of Christ.

Nicholas made up his mind. He placed Helena's letter inside his cloak. He would return.

Clermont, France
November 28, 1095
Nicholas tarried on the steps of the somber gray cathedral, watching the bishops, archbishops, and abbots set out on foot for the open field outside the eastern gate of Clermont. It was the last day of the council meeting, which had gone on since the eighteenth.

Aside from settling several church matters dealing with controversial subjects—several of them long-standing, including King Philip's adultery—the council meeting had not differed from those that had gone before.

One matter that caused some stir among the church prelates was the abduction of a fellow bishop named Lambert. Nearing Provins, Lambert had been seized by a robber-baron. It had taken the threat of excommunication from Pope Urban for the baron to free the bishop. The only other mentionable stir was the death of old Durand, Bishop of Clermont. The responsibility of arranging for the entertainment of all the delegates in his city seemed to have been too much of a strain on him, and he had died on the night of the first council meeting.

Nicholas sighed and glanced up at the dismal sky. Rain clouds marshaled their forces, and dampness was in the chill November breeze.

More than likely they would all be rained on before it was over, he thought as the huge crowd gathered in the open field to hear what the pope would say.

He had promised "a very important announcement."

Nicholas was grim and in a cynical mood. He knew what the announcement would be, for he had spoken with his good friend Adehemar, Bishop of Le Puy. Pope Urban had come to Clermont with a well-prepared speech to raise an army to make war on the Moslem Turks holding Jerusalem. The emotional response to the call for a Crusade was already agreed on: *Deus le vult!* God wills it!

Count Raymond of Saint-Gilles had agreed to raise an army. He was sure to be joined by other strong feudal princes across Europe.

Nicholas had no doubt that the Normans too would journey to the east when the news of the authorized Crusade reached them at the siege against the seaport of Amalfi in southern Italy. Bohemond was there, and Nicholas knew him well enough to guess he would go.

Still scowling to himself, Nicholas mounted his fine horse and rode toward the field. The pope's speech was already underway when he arrived. Urban's voice, raised with vigor, was sweeping through the great throng, carried along with the November wind. Clerical robes of black and crimson fluttered, mingling with the nobles' garb of fur-lined cloaks.

"The kingdom of the Greeks is now dismembered by them and deprived of territory so vast in extent that it cannot be traversed in a march of two months."

Nicholas knew that he spoke of the infringement of the Seljuk Turks into the territory of the Byzantine Empire. But it would take more than the misfortune of the Greeks, whom the Western knights disdained as effeminate warriors, to arouse their interest in a Crusade a thousand miles from home, knowing they would endure great hardship and personal loss.

Nicholas stroked his black mustache and glanced at the faces of those present. They listened attentively, expectantly. Bishop Adehemar sat close to the platform. Nicholas knew why he was there, and what he would do at the end of Urban's speech.

Now Urban was appealing for unity of brotherhood among the Christians of the Latin church and the Eastern church, who were "all sons of the same Christ and the same church. . . . It is charity to risk your lives for your brothers."

Nicholas's smile was cynical beneath his mustache. It would take a miracle indeed for the pope to interest barons and knights who battled each other as fellow Christians to rescue Greek Christians. Knights did not groan easily over the sufferings of others.

Nicholas was surprised to hear the pope's next exhortation, addressed directly to the Frank barons in attendance. The harsh but forthright accusations of the pope caused Nicholas's dark brow to lift. Urban's words, like arrows, whizzed across the field to penetrate the armor of those barons gathered.

"You, girt about with the belt of knighthood," came his ringing voice, "you are arrogant with great pride; you rage against your brothers and cut each other to pieces. You, the oppressors of children, plunderers of widows; you, guilty of homicide, of sacrilege, robbers of another's rights; you who await the pay of thieves for the shedding of Christian blood as vultures smell fetid corpses. Let, therefore, hatred depart from among you, let your quarrels end, let wars cease, and let all dissensions and controversies slumber. Let those who have been accustomed to make private warfare against the faithful carry on to a successful conclusion a war against the infidels, which ought to have begun ere now. Let those who once fought brothers and relatives now fight against barbarians as they ought."

Nicholas scanned the rugged faces of several barons standing nearby. They were grim; one stirred uncomfortably. Another scowled.

"Let the Holy Sepulcher of the Lord our Savior, which is possessed by unclean nations, especially move you. And remember also the Holy Places that are now treated with ignominy and polluted with filthiness. Reflect that the Almighty may have established you in your position for this very purpose, that through you He might restore Jerusalem from such abasement. And some of you have seen with your own eyes to what abominations the Lord's sepulcher has been given over. And yet, in that place rested the Lord; there he died for us; there he was buried.

"Most beloved brethren, if you reverence the source of that holiness and glory, if you cherish the shrines that are the marks of His footprints on earth, you should strive with your utmost efforts to cleanse the Holy City and the glory of the sepulcher by every means in your power."

Nicholas felt a cold plop of rain splatter against his face. He lowered his wide-brimmed hat and turned up his collar.

"Jerusalem is the navel of the world; the land is fruitful above all lands, like another paradise of delights."

Urban went on to explain that to pray at the Holy Sepulcher was the best of all Christian pilgrimages. The Crusaders were to be "fighting pilgrims," "*militia Christi*," who would open up the route to Jerusalem, which had been obstructed by the Seljuks, and would liberate the holy city. The feudal wars of princes and barons were sinful, but they could become soldiers of Christ by going on the expedition.

By wresting the Christian shrines in Jerusalem from the infidels, Crusaders would gain God's favor. An indulgence for sins was to be granted to all who went, with no regard for honor or money.

Nicholas's dark eyes were riveted on Urban. The faint smile that once touched Nicholas's lips was gone. What was this? Did he hear the pope correctly? Forgiveness of sins?

"The possessions of the enemy will be yours, too, since you will make spoil of their treasures. Wrest that land from the infidels, and subject it to yourselves, that land which, as the Scripture says, 'Flows with milk and honey.' "

Nicholas tensed. The pope said that France was too narrow for the barons and their knights. Nor did it abound in wealth, and it did not furnish enough food for its cultivators. So the barons devoured one another.

Nicholas had little doubt that the migration of landless

barons and knights, troublemakers, would relieve pressure and promote peace in the west. But conquest, plunder, the forgiveness of sins—could this be said to be of God? Nevertheless, he knew these promises would be tempting incentives for the fighting knights. God was on their side, they were told.

However, the poor, the old, and the feeble were not to go, for they would cause more trouble than the good they could do and would be a burden to the princes. If any peasant insisted, he was permitted to go, but only if he received permission from his feudal lord. Nor were priests or clerks to go without permission from the bishops or abbots.

Nicholas could see that the pope wanted the clergy to filter out unarmed peasants who were not qualified to be "*militia Christi.*" Now he thought he understood the reason for the cloth cross that Bishop Adehemar would introduce after the pope's speech.

Nicholas's uneasiness grew. Urban insisted that all who went to Jerusalem take a solemn vow to pray at the Holy Sepulcher, and the cross they would take on the journey east would be worn as a sign that they had taken a vow to follow Christ.

The cross, thought Nicholas, *would be similar to joining a religious order.*

Since the journey was long and filled with hardship and sorrow, the vow to pray at the sepulcher was to bind the Crusader so he would not turn back without having to face the consequences.

The "sword of anathema" threatened all who would falter and turn back. If any man who had accepted the emblem of the cross decided to turn back, he would be regarded as an outlaw forever unless he changed his mind and returned to Jerusalem to fulfill his vow. Only unforeseen illness or lack of means to journey would be accepted by the bishops or abbots as a valid reason to break the vow.

Nicholas listened as the pope's words rang out.

"And if those who set out thither should lose their lives on the way by land, or in crossing the sea, or in fighting the pagans, their sins shall be remitted. This I grant to those who go, through the power vested in me by God. Let those who have been hirelings at low wages now labor for an eternal reward."

Nicholas did not move. But the response from the those gathered sounded throughout the field with a tumultuous cry: *"Deus le volt,* God wills it!"

Nicholas turned to look at Adehemar, Bishop of Le Puy. As he had expected, Adehemar stood from his seat and was kneeling before the pope's throne, begging for permission to join the expedition. Since the pope had spent time with Adehemar before coming to Clermont, Nicholas was certain they had already discussed the expedition. Nor did Nicholas believe that Adehemar's gesture was spontaneous.

Adehemar, with great emotion that Nicholas believed to be real, tore red cloth from his clerical garb and with it formed the first red cross.

The field was a tumult of echoing cries: "God wills it!"

Hundreds surged forward to be blessed by Urban. A cardinal, whom Nicholas recognized as Gregory, fell on his knees and loudly repeated the confiteor. All around him, Nicholas heard the masculine voices repeating the prayer. Pope Urban pronounced the absolution. He bade his audience to depart for home in peace. The bishops and abbots in attendance were to return to their respective districts and abbeys to preach the expedition with enthusiasm.

Nicholas did not vow. He had already decided to journey to Constantinople after receiving the urgent letter from Helena. Nevertheless, he was disturbed.

"Deus le volt!" was a cry instigated not by holy God but by Urban, with the backing of the bishops, certain feudal princes, and the Emperor Alexius Comnenus.

Nicholas had studied the Greek New Testament for too long to accept the promise of forgiveness of sins by going on a Crusade. He knew he could be excommunicated if he openly challenged that doctrine. But Scripture was clear: Forgiveness of all sin was by trusting in the merit of the finished work of Christ on the cross.

He made his way through the crowd on the field to find his horse. The rain was falling, and men were already taking apart the platform on which the pope's throne had sat. The result of his speech, however, could not be as easily dismantled.

Taking the cross on the Crusade was met with greater zeal than even Urban had expected. The news spread like fire. Those going east were to be prepared to leave by the Feast of Assumption, August 15, after the harvests were gathered. Thereupon, they would journey to Constantinople to wait outside the great walls of the city until all of the feudal princes arrived with their army of knights and footmen.

CHAPTER 5

Genoa
January 1096

✤ The late afternoon sky was wild with thunderclouds when the Venetian vessel set anchor in a driving rain at Genoa. A ramp was run out, and Tancred led Alzira off the ship.

The shores, even on such a day, were crowded with heaps of merchandise and throngs of merchants. Tancred wasted no time in saddling Alzira. Donning a heavier woolen cloak with a hood that covered his helmet, he mounted and chose a narrow street leading inland toward France.

Feeling the eyes of strangers, he glanced back. A mercenary soldier stood alone in the street watching him. Spies and thieves abounded.

He took the trade route used by merchant caravans and pilgrims. Groups of traveling friars and monks were a common sight along the roads through Italy and France and were usually guarded by soldiers serving an abbey.

Many abbeys were extensive, similar to walled towns, and were usually full of pilgrims, knights, merchants, the poor, and the sick. The monks were mostly honest, hard-working men, helping to counter the war-like influence of the baronial lords and territorial magnates. If the monastery were vast and wealthy, the abbot would keep mounted knights for travelers' protection as well as for the monastery itself.

A monastery with a thousand monks, a hospital, and a learning facility needed a great deal of food to feed itself, needy visitors, and guests. And such a vast amount of food was a sort of wealth worth stealing.

A group of friars stopped when they saw Tancred, taking in his chain mail under the dark tunic and his scabbard.

"Hail and well met, Soldier of Christ. Do you go to join the army setting forth on the expedition to free Jerusalem? They are gathering at Le Puy."

"I seek one among them. A Norman bishop from the abbey of Monte Casino. His name is Nicholas. Have you heard of him?"

"Who has not heard of Nicholas!" The monk pointed his staff down the road behind him. "But you are several days from Le Puy. If he has not yet left, you will find him staying in a small cottage belonging to the chronicler, Raymond of Aguilers."

Le Puy would be a natural gathering place for enthusiastic Crusaders. The town was a major center of pilgrimage in France, and it was also the bishopric of Adehemar, the appointed papal legate of the expedition to free the holy land from the Moslem Turks.

"People are gathering from hundreds of miles around to join the expedition," said the monk.

"When is the official starting date, do you know?"

"August fifteenth for the barons and their knights. But God's poor follow the good Peter; there is much impatience among them, for they are anxious to reach the Holy City. When we left, there was talk that they would gather at Amiens."

God's poor? No doubt the monk had the peasants in mind. Amiens was the start of the journey that would lead them across Europe to Constantinople. It was popular to follow the route that the revered Charlemagne was reported to have used for his legendary pilgrimage to Jerusalem.

Did the peasants intend to travel without the protection of the feudal lords?

Tancred rode well into the night, hearing the thunder grumble in the mountains. It was deep night when he rode off the trail, choosing a small cluster of trees away from the wind-driven rain. There was grass for Alzira, and finding some dead branches, he made a small fire. He untied from the back of his saddle the rabbit that he had taken with his bow earlier that day and roasted it.

Eating in the stillness, he listened to the sighing of the wind amid the branches. Hunched over his small fire, his mood turned cynical.

What mocking hand of fate was this that had robbed him so unexpectedly, and with such complete devastation, of everything he had counted dear?

Fate. Nicholas would scoff at the idea. He would probably say God was on the move, a resistless force of holy energy with a plan, a purpose, and a war to win.

Tancred, too, knew the arguments against the impersonal force called fate. The sovereign God rode the saddle of history, and He commanded the flaming horse of events to ride the four corners of the earth. Both time and chance were brought together to accomplish His grand purpose.

But what of himself? It was one thing to gaze out at the

starry universe and see omnipotence at work, but it was quite another matter to see with the eye of faith the footprints of Deity walking amid his shattered dreams. His well-laid plans lay in a pile of ashes. A fickle gust of wind would carry them off into oblivion.

The future—no, that concept was too broad—his future. What lay ahead for Tancred Jehan Redwan? Did it matter to Omnipotence whether he took this path or that? Did fulfillment wait to greet him at the end of his road, a road that led to where?

I am blessed just to be alive, he thought.

If he could find Mosul and vindicate himself of Derek's death, dare he ask more?

The passing days brought him west into the kingdom of Burgundy and the land of the Franks. The country was open although patches of woods and thick growth had sprung up along streams.

He remembered the medical school at Salerno he had attended only months ago. Would he ever walk its learned halls again?

By late February he reached the river Rhone in the Auvergne region of France. He followed the northern bank where the woods grew thick. Rain had fallen in a steady drizzle for days. Lightning danced white across the black sky, and the brooding thunder echoed as he rode through the trees. Rain splattered against his winter cloak.

Toward the gray afternoon, when shadows deepened, he saw a small village consisting of a cluster of simple cottages, bleak and silent. He had ridden since before dawn, and night was coming swiftly.

He hesitated to continue riding. Beyond the cottages, on a small rise, stood an old inn built of heavy timber, looking sullen against the clouds. A curl of smoke hovered above the roof, and the smell of roasting meat drifted to him.

He saw no one. Among the peasants, superstition ran high. When the last ray of sunlight ebbed, the shutters of the small houses would close, and the doors would be bolted, not to open again until the wicked things of the night retreated with the dawn.

Everyone knew that those travelers who feared God journeyed by day and were behind their doors or within the common inn when the sun darkened. Only vagabonds or wicked creatures, be they beast or spirit, prowled the autumn night by foot or on horseback; some declared that they rode on the backs of werewolves.

Tancred was aware of the superstitions, and he knew he must be cautious. Strangers were looked on with distrust. Emotions could be strange masters. Belief in the haunting of the woods and bogs included tales of wandering spirits of the restless dead, igniting fear of dark curses from the nether world. Omens were seen everywhere by those who wished to see them: a croaking frog, a sudden windstorm, the coming of autumn, or an unusual stranger.

Among the ignorant, such beliefs could even mingle with a strong adherence to the name of Christianity, forming a conflicting mixture of light and darkness, truth and error. Frightened villagers often crossed themselves or tied pouches about their throats for safety.

The contents were secret, but he knew they included herbs, barks, and sweet-smelling flowers dried in the summer sun. Why these would protect a soul from a dark curse, he could not guess, except that they were said to have been blessed.

On this windswept night, which sent dead leaves chasing each other across the countryside, the garb of a priest would have brought him a welcome among the villagers. But emerging from the woods on the back of the cold wind and riding on the sleek auburn horse, he appeared some ghostly warrior, easily surmised to be on a mission of personal vengeance. His coat of chain mesh was covered with a tunic of woolen cloth, and he wore a black hooded cloak.

Weariness called for every muscle in his body to rest, and the wind nagged him forward toward the dingy inn with its breached stone wall. He heard voices, causing him to stop. Behind him, some wet branches snapped under running feet.

Unexpectedly a disheveled girl bolted through the trees followed by the shout of pursuit. Confronting Tancred astride Alzira, she froze, terror-stricken, as though wondering if a warrior from the dark abode had come to block her escape.

The wind distorted the voices gaining on her flight. He drew his sword.

"Mercy, monsieur!" She fell to her knees in the mud and rotting leaves.

"Do not be afraid."

"Please! I must not be taken!"

"What have you done?"

"Would it matter if nothing?"

"It should."

"Not with him!"

At that, an angular figure in a soiled monk's tunic stumbled out from the trees holding a torch, followed by two lanky boys in knee-length tunics and hose that were worn thin. The sight of Tancred astride the horse stopped them as solidly as a stone hedge.

The eyes of the lads bulged. They gaped at the majestic horse and its shining mane as it pawed the earth as if guessing their awe.

Tancred's interest fixed on the rope held in the monk's hand.

"What do you intend with that?" he asked.

"That," the monk said irritably, "is my business."

"Three men chasing a girl? I make it mine also."

"Girl? Witch, that is what she is, filled with devils! You dare interfere in the work of God?" he challenged.

"The work of God I have reverence for, but—"

"Be gone, stranger. I shall see to this punishment."

Tancred continued as though he had not been interrupted. "But the malice burning in your blood convinces me this pursuit is not of God's design."

The monk stepped forward as if to order his arrest.

Tancred ignored him and spoke to the girl. "You have sorely distressed the monk."

"Yes, monsieur."

"What heinous crime befits so great a stir on a night like this?"

"He accuses me of breaking the Truce of God."

The Truce of God was a church ban imposed on all fighting and stealing. It was effective from the ninth hour on Saturday until Wednesday evening and also during Lent and Advent.

"She is a born thief," the monk declared. He pointed a finger at the girl. "How many times have I caught you stealing my goose eggs? Ten? Twenty?"

"The goose is mine!" she whined. "You had no right to take her."

"The goose belongs to the abbey. Madame bestowed the gift as she lay dying," the monk argued.

"But the eggs belong to your stomach," suggested Tancred dryly. "Are not the abbeys in Norman-controlled Italy commanded by the bishop to minister to the hungry, the sick, and strangers? Is there not enough charity to spare a goose egg?"

The monk's eyes narrowed. "What is your name?"

Tancred gave a slow smile. "You may call me Priest Redwan."

"You add to your sin, sir knight. And you will pay for this interference in the justice of God."

"Ah. The justice of God. A profound subject. May I suggest you go back to your abbot and tell him to expound its meaning to his befuddled clerics?"

The monk stiffened. Angrily he motioned for the boys to lay hold of the girl, but their eyes were fixed on the blade that Tancred held.

"The sun sets, darkness comes," Tancred suggested to them. "Go home. Leave the monk's vengeance undone."

They backed off until they reached the trees, then turned and fled as though werewolves were at their heels, leaving the monk to face Tancred. "You will pay for this," he warned.

"If justice were done, your judgment may be more severe than hers."

The monk took in Tancred's fine but wet clothing and the well-blooded mare. "I know not who you are, nor what arrogance owns your tongue. But beware. You will answer for this impious treatment!"

He swung about on his heel and walked through the trees, his footsteps dying away over the crumpled leaves.

The wind struck against Tancred, and the rain came again. He lowered his blade and looked down at the girl. He could not tell what she looked like, for she was too dirty.

"Where do you stay? I will take you there."

"Since Madame died, I am alone."

"Madame? The owner of this famed goose?"

"Yes. She died of sickness." She cast a nervous glance over her shoulder. "If I stay here, the monk will burn me for a witch. A woman was burned last Michaelmas."

"Have you someone else you can trust? A friend?"

"No, but there is a monastery a half-day's journey by foot. That is where I came from. Madame brought me from there when I was small. There are women there. The abbot is a good man. He is the one who gave me to Madame long ago. He knows I am no witch," she said defensively. "I was on my way there when I ran into you. I thank you, monsieur." She gave a clumsy bow.

He returned a more elegant bow of his head. "At your service, mademoiselle. I am Tancred Redwan. And you?"

"The abbot gave me the name Modestine."

"A winsome name."

Under her disheveled hair, matted with dirt, her alert gaze watched him with a sudden awe that made him cautious. He realized the simple compliment, meant only to comfort her, had sparked her interest.

She boldly scanned him. "You do not wear the church tunic. You truly are a priest?"

If he said no, she would hound him. "Yes and no."

"I do not understand, monsieur."

"You need not. It is enough that I said so."

"I shall be yours."

"No."

"A servant to tend you?"

"No. I ride on alone. Understand?"

Her eyes fell.

"Tomorrow I will take you to the abbot."

She looked up, troubled. "Tomorrow! I must escape tonight! You do not know the monk. He will return. Oh, yes, he will! With more to help him."

Tancred suspected it might be so, but his eyes were fixed in the direction of the inn, now hardly visible. He sheathed his sword. "First, I eat. Then I need rest. After that I will consider."

The mention of food appeared to numb her anxiety. "The host killed a pig today," she whispered as though she bestowed on him a great secret. "I watched from the trees. By now, master, it is ready to be served with mulled wine."

Tancred felt his irritation rise. "I am not, nor do I intend to be, your master."

Her eyes admitted that she wished it so.

He reached to lift her up, ignoring the uncleanness of her garb and hair. *She ought to be thrown in the river for a quick washing*, he thought, turning away his face. It was amazing how westerners rarely bathed. The Redwans had learned cleanliness from their wide travels in Sicily and North Africa, and the house of al-Kareem had taught him the best of Moorish culture.

In her eagerness to claim the position beside him, he heard the faint crack of a shell, and a yolk splattered on his boot.

She kept her head bent, refusing to meet his eyes. "I am repentant, monsieur."

"Yes, damsel, I am certain, enough to go on pilgrimage."

Her eyes widened. "To Jerusalem with you? Oh I would! I would! They gather now to go!"

"No."

They rode toward the dark inn.

"Your mistress died of sickness?"

"Very wicked it was. Her body felt like fire. And her skin turned black."

Plague had called on Europe since 1083, followed by

sweeping floods in France and the Rhineland that destroyed the farmers' crops. Drought came the next year, and famine followed. Even in the best of times the peasants lacked adequate provisions. Their meals consisted mainly of ground chestnuts, made into a gruel, and roots. If the barons and lords of the land for which they worked were generous, they had meat at Michaelmas. Hungry peasants were in every village and outside the walls of the monasteries, beggars.

No wonder the pope's call to the feudal lords to rescue the Holy Sepulcher at Jerusalem was also greeted by the common people with zeal. Not only was the forgiveness of their sins promised, but also, on the dispersion of the Moslems occupying Jerusalem, a feast of fat things.

What meager existence did they have here? What future? What justice? And by what measure of truth could they judge the reality of the promises? They had little knowledge of Scripture, and their spiritual teachers pronounced the expedition a command from Christ. If one was to follow Christ, one must follow the church.

How did the unlearned peasant, or for that matter, even a feudal lord, know truth from error? The church was the voice of God. Woe to the flock if the shepherds led them to the cliff's edge rather than to green pasture.

"Madame should not have died," she said. "I washed her with blessed water as the monk told me. He is more angry over her death than the goose egg. He blames me. He says I did not follow his orders. But I did, monsieur, I vow I did! And I believed."

"Perhaps it is not the amount of faith we have, but the object of our faith."

"But I had the blessed water!" she argued.

Tancred said nothing.

"I watched him bless it. The monk says that Christ is with him."

"It is more important whether the monk is with Christ. You be the judge."

She gasped. "Are you not afraid to speak so?"

"Only a man who wishes to die as a heretic would not fear. But it is also true, if one fears God, he need not fear the lesser. A man may claim anything, but does that make it so? Nor does a questioning mind make one a heretic."

The rain drove against them, and darkness fell over the mud path.

"You must guard your horse," she warned, glancing at him over her shoulder. "Nothing so goodly has been seen here since a group of Normans rode through. A beggar tried to steal from them, and they showed no mercy. They hung him."

Immediately Tancred was alert. "Norman knights? Were they from Sicily?"

"Sicily, I have never heard of, but the innkeeper will know." She smiled wistfully. "Why, once he journeyed all the way to Le Puy!"

She pointed toward the shadow of a barn. "Over there they kept their horses and supplies. And over there," she pointed in the opposite direction to a tree twisted and burned by a recent fire, "they killed the beggar. I did not stay to watch although some did. They say he called on the saints to retrieve his soul and bring it to Saint Peter."

Inside, the common room was dim and dank, and the rain leaked through the thatch roof. Several containers collected the drips with a monotonous plop. The rafters were low, the wood tables with benches, worn. True to the girl's word, a piglet roasted on a large spit in the middle of the room, and a blackened pot of chestnuts was suspended above the coals. Regardless of the dreariness, the smell cheered Tancred with the thought of supper.

A group of traveling serfs and peasants were seated together. As he entered, they turned their heads, their wary glances taking in his habiliments, which marked him a class above.

Tancred took the girl's elbow and steered her to a separate corner of the room. She seated herself and looked over at the men, tossing her tangles with smug satisfaction.

At Tancred's quiet order, the innkeeper brought a chunk of meat and a loaf of bread, scanning him as he did. He gestured to the girl.

"It is none of my business, monsieur, but she is not worthy company for a man such as yourself."

"She is hungry. Bring another plate. And a pitcher of goat's milk."

The girl looked up at the innkeeper and minced a smile.

Wisely, the innkeeper said nothing. He returned carrying the pitcher and two mugs, still eying Tancred cautiously.

"Anything else, monsieur?"

"The men who killed the beggar, were they Greeks from Bari?" he asked evasively, knowing they were not.

"Are you from there?" the innkeeper asked.

The peasant was more clever and cautious than Tancred had given him credit. He decided to take a risk. "I am from Sicily. My family are vassal knights of the Great Count Roger I."

The host scanned him again, then nodded appreciably. "The men were also Normans."

"You are certain?"

The innkeeper smiled, and he eyed Tancred. "I would know Norman warriors anywhere, monsieur. My brother is a mercenary serving the Norman prince, Bohemond, in siege against Amalfi."

"Yes, they are rather ambitious," he admitted easily.

The Normans were respected and feared as the greatest of fighting men. Many hated them, others loved them. Tancred knew there was cause for both feelings.

"You also have the looks, monsieur."

The other men turned their heads to make their own judgment concerning his Norman blood.

Feeling their gaze bore through him, he deliberately removed his dagger and carved a slice of meat for the girl. The physician-like ease of his blade cut through the pig as though it were made of warm butter. The serfs and peasants shifted their eyes away.

Before Tancred could put the chunk on the girl's platter, she snatched it from him with both hands, devouring it. The oozing fat and juice dribbled between her fingers.

He arched a dark brow. There was nothing of beauty about her. Well, perhaps her eyes. They were the color of clear amber. He could not tell the color of her hair. He looked away, making eye contact with the men.

They hungrily averted their eyes from the slab of meat, but one gaunt young serf in thin clothing, big-boned, with ruddy face and corn-colored hair, was bolder, more friendly. He turned on his bench to converse with Tancred, but kept his sunken eyes on the food.

"The Normans who rode through here a week ago all had wondrous swords and halberds. All had horses, and they had a sure way about them. They carried the gonfalon of Count Dreux Redwan of Sicily."

Tancred felt his heart surge but forced himself to remain unreadable. Then his cousins were not with the Normans in the siege against Amalfi. He must be cautious. Had they gone to Le Puy?

The friendly serf turned his shoulder, displaying a red square cross. Tancred saw that he carried a rusty pike. Evidently he believed that once he had "taken the Cross," the crude instrument was all he needed to rid Jerusalem of the infidels.

The serf's brown eyes moistened as he ran soiled, calloused fingers over the cloth insignia. "Blest by the Abbot of Saint Annes. You, too, seek Jerusalem, no doubt. But what of your cross, monsieur?" He gestured to Tancred's shoulder. "I see it not on your noble tunic."

Tancred had heard that all those who took the Crusader's vow to free the holy sepulcher and rid the promised land of the infidels received a cross blessed by a bishop, cut from crimson cloth. He did not question that the ritual was a sincere endeavor to bind the hearts and swords of those who went into a unified army. But it was one more evidence of the Latin belief in the supernatural power attached to objects and relics.

He thought again of the object he must give to Nicholas to return to Jerusalem.

Tancred evaded the serf's question. "Those riding under the gonfalon of Count Redwan, did they say where they were going?"

Tancred's voice, low as it was, found its way to the others. Heads turned in his direction, and a feverish excitement now showed in their eyes.

An old man grumbled through his beard, "Where else, monsieur, but farther north, past Paris to seek the good Peter."

Peter the Hermit. Had his formidable cousins not gone to Le Puy for a sword blessing after all?

One of the other men in the room pointed to an old serf, and his voice held awe. "Old Jacques here, he knows the way to the Seine River, and beyond, to Rouen. He has been there in his youth. He will lead us to the good monk."

The old farmer nodded in agreement, looking proud and worldly-wise. For a peasant to have traveled anywhere outside his village earned the respect of his peers. He sucked on a pipe stuffed with dried grasses.

"I was there as a boy at flood stage. Had not the angels of Michael held back the waters, we would all be drowned men this good day. It was a miracle, it was."

"Tell the Norman here about Peter," the man urged.

The old serf's eyes twinkled beneath his white brows. "They say the good monk has gathered a hundred thousand of God's poor to lead to the promised land."

Tancred understood the peasant mind. "A hundred thousand" could better be reduced to fifteen thousand. Still, it was a large contingent of peasants journeying east to face Seljuk Turks with nothing more than a cross sewn to their garments and blind faith in a land flowing with milk and honey.

The gaunt serf who had earlier displayed his cross to Tancred leaned toward him. "You will join the other Norman knights and seek the Hermit?"

Tancred wondered if his Redwan cousins could possibly be content to join the ranks of a monk on a donkey, followed by a horde of serfs and peasants with their families. If they rode to Jerusalem at all, would they not ride under the bold gonfalon of the formidable Norman, Prince Bohemond, with his army of knights and footmen?

He saw his opportunity to ask more questions of the gaunt serf and gestured to the roast. "Join us?"

He did so immediately, dropping to the bench. "Niles is the name."

"Tancred. The Normans who rode through here, how many were there?"

At once the mood in the inn changed. Niles glanced with caution at the dagger Tancred held.

"Friends of yours?" he inquired quietly.

Tancred thought of the charred tree outside.

"No, enemies."

Niles nodded with understanding. "There were a dozen, maybe more."

No doubt some of the men from the castle at Palermo rode with his cousins, thought Tancred. But he must be certain these men were indeed his cousins. He carved the meat.

"You say they carried the Redwan gonfalon, but did they say where they were from?"

"A strange name it had."

"Palermo?"

Niles pounded his fist on the table. "So it was. Palermo!"

Then they were his cousins. And if they saw him at Le Puy, they would know he had escaped the castle.

"How long since they rode through?"

"Days now. But you do not forget such men, monsieur."

"Their seignior, did you hear his name?"

Niles paused, trying to remember. "Erich, I think it was."

Erich Redwan was Tancred's cousin.

"After the ugly incident, I heard one say that they rode to join Peter the Hermit." He stuffed the hunks of pork into his mouth.

One of the peasants asked, "Do you also seek the good hermit?"

"No."

The peasant gave him a slight scowl.

"We all seek Peter," offered Niles. "Most of us here are

tenants, and the lord who rules the land for the baron has forgotten us. He sends other lords for the harvest and never comes to see how we fare. He has enough and cares not that we want. So we go with the hermit."

"This man, Peter, where does he wait?"

"Amiens, and from there they will cross the Rhine River to Cologne. The good Peter rides through the villages and countryside on his donkey, calling on the people of Christ to follow him to Jerusalem."

"You have a far distance to travel," Tancred warned. "By land, Jerusalem is more than two months from here. You will need strong oxen to carry your supplies, weapons, and much food. There was a famine in the kingdom of Hungary, and it is early in the year. You will journey through Budapest and Belgrade before harvest. If the king does not expect you, there will be no open markets along the route."

They looked at him. The old man said over his pipe, "We will forage, and God will provide."

Tancred scanned the thin peasant. Forage from whom, the poor Hungarian peasants? There would surely be trouble along the Danube River, he thought.

A young boy spoke up. "They say Peter the Hermit's face shines, and his tongue speaks heaven's language. The hairs from the tail of his donkey bring blessings."

The old man nodded and looked toward the fire crackling in the hearth. "A good man he is to lead God's expedition to the land of milk and honey."

Tancred could take no more. Peasants traveling to Jerusalem to fight the Seljuks with nothing but farming implements for weapons. Blessings from the hairs of the monk's donkey!

"Beware," he stated. "Believe not everything you hear, but test all things as to whether they are true. As thistles sprout thickly after a rain, so tales are abundant on the tongue of the unlearned. It is not milk and honey that awaits you in Jerusalem, for the land has been ravaged by centuries of war and oppression. It is the scimitar and arrow of the Seljuk Turks that wait to greet you. They are fierce fighters. You will need more than a few pikes to defeat these Moslem warriors. I have heard of them. They come from a distant land called the Steppes, a lowland not far from Cathay."

At once the atmosphere tensed, as though he had profaned something holy.

"We have taken the cross. It is our armor. We need naught else but faith."

"God wills it," agreed another. "We are a match for any Saracen infidel!"

"Perhaps," said Tancred, "but to trust God, must you march without defenses? Did not Christ Himself say in the gospels, 'A strong man armed keepeth his house?' "

"Where did you learn the Scriptures, stranger?"

"He is a priest," said the girl.

Tancred looked at her, surprised she was even listening, so intent was she on her food.

"You are a priest?" the old man asked cautiously. "Then where are your garments?"

"I am a student physician from the medical school at Salerno. I am not a priest, although I was raised to be one at the monastery of Monte Casino. And you, my friends, will need weapons, strong horses, and armor. I advise, despite your faith, that you do not go to Jerusalem until you have them. It is true that God can deliver by faith alone, but has not Solomon written of the blessing of wisdom and sound counsel? Faith demands a foundation of truth, else it becomes presumption. True faith must act on what the Almighty has revealed, not on our own desires."

"You speak with authority, stranger," observed Niles.

"It is Peter the Hermit who has authority to speak," suggested a peasant with unpleasant eyes. "You, Norman, wear the garb of a soldier, and I doubt not you can use your sword well. But tell us, why should we trust what you say? Did not the voice of truth come from the Council of Clermont?"

"I do not ask you to trust me," said Tancred. "I only ask you to think and consider well. If I were you, I would not be so trusting of the words of this man called the Hermit."

"You speak blasphemy, stranger."

"Against a mere man?"

"Peter went to Jerusalem! There Christ appeared to him. He gave Peter a letter that told the pope to deliver the holy sepulcher and Jerusalem from the infidels!"

"The letter from heaven, you saw it?"

The serf began to rise to his feet, but the old man named Jacques caught his tattered sleeve, holding him back. "What do you know of these infidels?" he asked. "Have you been to Jerusalem on pilgrimage?"

"The Seljuk Turks are strong. If you insist on going east, then go, but at least wait and journey with one of the feudal princes. Go with Raymond of Saint-Gilles or the Duke of Normandy, even Bohemond. At least you will be armed and fed."

"The well-dressed Norman from Sicily is quick with his advice," said the peasant with unpleasant eyes. "I suppose, like the other feudal lords, he wants the treasure all for himself, and so he wishes to discourage men like the good Peter, whose only desire is to see Jerusalem purged of infidels."

Niles stood from the table, as though to avert trouble. He turned to the other peasants in the room. "As for Peter, I heard at the abbey of Ajello that he has already left Amiens for Cologne. They say we will find him near the Rhine River."

"The night is wild with rain," another grumbled, rising and stretching. "Enough talk. Let us get some sleep. And pray the road toward Paris does not become a bog by morning. It will be no blessing to have our cart wheels stuck for another day. We may never catch Peter."

The others, still seated, watched Tancred to see if he dare disagree. He could also have warned them that their meager carts and undernourished oxen would never survive the long journey, but why provoke them further?

Their minds were made up. They would believe as they wished, for all other hope was perishing. He pitied them. The monk named the Hermit did not sound like the manner of liege to lead them to victory across Europe.

The girl reached across the table and caught his wrist. "Monsieur priest!" came her warning hiss.

Tancred became alert. He glanced toward the peasants. They had not moved. What then?

Then he understood. He threw back his seat and was on his feet, sword unsheathed. He grabbed her arm, whirling her behind him.

The door burst open with a gust of wet wind, and the monk stood there with a group of men armed with pitchforks and pikes.

"Arrest the soldier and the witch!"

Tancred's blade lifted. A dungeon, again? Not this time.

CHAPTER 6

A Ruin in France

✤ "By the chimney. There is a side door." It was the rasping voice of Niles.

But even as he spoke, three men with weapons stepped forward to stop Tancred. One leveled a pike at his stomach, while the other thought to disarm him. But Niles grabbed the pot of hot chestnuts and flung them in their faces. The girl grabbed the hunk of meat from the platter and darted across the room.

A quick glance over his shoulder showed Tancred her escape route through the small door. The big man lunged at him, but Tancred deflected the blade. The point jumped, lancing the man's cheek.

Shocked, he reached a hand to his face, then stared at his fingers as though he had never seen blood before. He turned a sickly ashen color.

Tancred felt Niles grasp his shoulder. "Quick!"

Tancred followed, overthrowing the tables as he went. They ran through the kitchen into the black night, wild with wind and rain. The girl was waiting with Alzira and a donkey, which probably belonged to the monk.

She was already on the horse, clutching the hunk of meat in one hand and the donkey's reins in the other. Tancred sprang into the saddle, breaking away, glancing back to see if Niles was coming on the donkey.

Niles sat on the animal, shouting at it, flapping its reins, and digging his heels into its sides. The donkey did nothing.

Suddenly it took off at a swift trot, splattering mud as it went. Tancred raced Alzira forward, feeling the wind and rain in his face, and the girl's fingers clutching the back of his cloak.

"Drop the meat!" he shouted over his shoulder, but she would not.

Niles was far behind. Tancred rode a short distance ahead then waited for him under an overhang of drooping black branches. A few minutes later he heard the donkey coming and rode out to meet Niles.

Soaking wet and shivering, Niles gasped, "That horse, she is worth all the world."

"When your neck is at risk? Yes," said Tancred, amused. He sobered. "Look, I go on to Le Puy to find a friend. The trouble tonight was not yours. There is no reason you must part from your friends. By morning the monk will be gone, he will forget about you."

"Go back and be skinned alive for stealing his donkey? I like not the countenance he bore!"

"It was the girl who borrowed his donkey. But return Modestine and the donkey, not to him but to the friendly abbot not far from here, and I am certain you will find peace. I will give you a gold piece to take with you. Give it in the name of Count Dreux Redwan. The abbot will listen."

"Redwan! So that is who you are!"

"Dreux was my father. He was killed in Rome when I was a boy."

"And those knights who rode through bearing your family gonfalon are brothers?"

"Cousins, and at the moment," he said thinking of Derek's assassination, "I could wish my name were anything but Redwan. But do not ask me why. You must not burden yourself further with my difficulties. If you do, you will find more than a monk on your trail. I thank you for your help at the inn, and I wish you Godspeed."

Before Niles could reply, he felt the girl grasp his shoulder. "But you must not ride to Le Puy tonight," she protested. "Brigands watch the road, even in this weather. A band of merchants was attacked and murdered by them only yesterday. If you ride the road, you will come on the charred ruins of their caravan. They have not yet been buried. We must wait for the light, monsieur."

Tancred noted her use of the word *we*. But what she said made sense, and he was well acquainted with the threat of brigands, who had a penchant for attacking traveling merchants. Nevertheless she was hinting that Tancred, Niles, and she had somehow formed a camaraderie binding their futures. The nearby friendly abbey was the last place she now wished to go.

No matter. In the morning, she will be sent there.

"I know of a ruin not far from here, monsieur. But, it is cursed with devils," she said.

"Do you know of it?" he asked Niles.

"No, I am a stranger to these parts. But do let us go there. Any shelter is better than this rain. My bones rattle with cold."

"Can you show us the way?" Tancred asked her.

She cringed but gestured toward the trees. "Yes, but I

77

warn you, master, witches and infidels are buried there. The ground is cursed."

"It is the living I wish to avoid. And I told you, do not call me master."

They rode forward through the dark woods, hemmed in on both sides by branches. Then they came to a small incline that had at one time been cleared for a castle. The trees were gone, but secondary growth now covered the ground with prickly shrubs and wild vines. He felt her tug at his cloak, then point.

"Over there," she whispered.

They rode nearer. Tancred began to make out the skeleton of a ruinous heap of stones that in ancient times had housed some tribal chieftain. They entered through a broken stone wall covered with moss into a partial chamber with an earthen floor. Portions of the roof and walls were still in place, and they took shelter there from the rain.

Niles gathered pieces of wood and worked to start a fire. When the flames burned hot, the girl drew near.

"Ah!" sighed Niles, holding his hands toward the heat.

But the girl kept her hands hidden beneath her ragged cloak.

Tancred stood before the fire. He would put a quick end to any romantic notions she had.

Pretending arrogance, he stated bluntly, "Well, woman? Remove the chunk of meat from under your cloak! Are you trying to deny us men food?"

Niles looked up at him, masking surprise at the sudden change that had come over Tancred.

Scowling, Tancred scolded her. "By now you have pig grease smeared all over the front of your garment. You could soak for a month and not be clean."

She did not take offense. "I will wash with the herbs of the wild moss," she said. "It kills vermin."

Tancred's eyes narrowed. That she did not jump to her feet and insult him, troubled him. "Well? Heat it on the fire!"

She removed from under her cloak what now seemed to Tancred a disgusting piece of pig. With a proud smile, she held it up.

"You are pleased?" She shoved it toward Niles. "I remembered to bring it."

Niles grinned, anything but irritated. "You are a wise woman. We have food and shelter because of you, Modestine."

Her eyes swerved to Tancred to see if the compliment had altered his mood. He refused to express Nile's sentiment, but simply removed his hooded cloak. He tossed it down. "Wring it out to dry."

She hesitated only a moment, glancing at the meat, then obeyed. Niles maneuvered the slab of meat onto a wedge of bark to heat. It soon began to crackle and hiss as the fat ran.

"It is ready now," she urged. "We must not waste the fat."

Niles evidently agreed. He removed it at once and began to tear off a chunk with his hand, then stopped. He looked up at Tancred, abashed. "It is yours."

Tancred's even gaze looked from Niles to the glowing face of the girl. He felt pity. They had both gone without adequate food for most of their lives.

He gave a gesture of his hand, shook his head, and turned away. "I am not hungry now."

Evidently they were not disturbed by his rudeness. He was a noble, and they accepted without question his position. He wanted to smile. Little did they know he was presently in a far worse situation then they.

He heard them eating. Walking over to the opening of the ruin, he looked out at the rain. "What of you, Niles? Will you go on with your friends to join the man Peter?"

Niles studied the fire. "I do not know, Count Redwan. What you said back at the inn made good reason."

He looked at Tancred, who leaned his shoulder against the wall. "I think you are wiser than we," Niles admitted.

"Not wiser. More experienced perhaps. But learning comes with experience. Any man can learn and increase his knowledge."

"But as you say, Jerusalem is far from here, and I have no horse. I walked from Ajello."

"You have friends and family there?"

"If there are others of my blood, I know them not. I grew up at the abbey near there, tilling soil and planting seed with the monks." Again he scowled to himself. "They were good to me, but a man wants more than that. When news spread of Peter the Hermit and the march to Jerusalem, it awakened a desire to go where I have not been, to see for myself the world beyond the abbey walls.

"The church has offered blessing on those who will take the cross. Land belonging to me! A place to grow my own vines, tend my own pigs. What more could a man want?

"And so I left Ajello weeks ago and arrived here at the same time Jacques came with the others. They said I could join their group, and I said yes." Niles gave him a searching look. "What of you? Will you take the cross at Le Puy and join the feudal princes?"

Tancred hesitated to explain the real motive that took him to Le Puy. The town would be full of men who would know of the intrigues in Sicily, and some would recognize him. If he were to locate Nicholas at the house of the chronicler, it would be wiser to go there by night and to leave in the same way.

"I travel to Constantinople," he said. "My blood father is dead, but I was adopted by another, an uncle. His name is Rolf, and he serves the Byzantine emperor."

Niles looked impressed. "At the abbey, we were told it was the Greek emperor who had sent men to the pope asking for soldiers."

"But you, Niles, what will you do?"

"I would hear your advice."

"Go back to the monastery at Ajello."

Niles lifted his hands, scarred and calloused from the fields, and stared at them in the light of the small fire. "If I do return, I will grow old and die there, and what will I have accomplished?

"With you, it is different," he said dejectedly. "All the world is before you."

"Another man one day sat feeling much as you do, yet for an altogether different reason. He was in despair, not over loss of opportunity, but for failure to find contentment in what he had already accomplished. At thirty-three, he had conquered the entire world of his day. But was he satisfied? Nay. He wept, his soul was empty and parched. Why so? Because there were no more worlds to conqueror! Had there been one more world empire to subjugate, would he then have found peace and contentment? No. The man's name was Alexander the Great.

"Purpose, peace, contentment, love," said Tancred with a sigh, and looked at the embers blazing hot reds and golds. "Do they not elude both great and small? And why so? God has made it so that a man's worth is not dependent on his glory. As Augustine has said, a man's heart is always empty until filled by the One who created it for Himself."

Niles said grudgingly, "I perceive that Modestine is right after all. You are a priest. But you say these words about contentment because you are better off than I."

"Perhaps not. It may be that I am worse off than you."

Niles looked at him, curious, but all Tancred added was, "You are right. I am not you. But I think that if I were, I would go back to the monks."

"You know not what you ask!"

"I do. From the time I was eight until I became a young scholar, I lived, moved, and had my very life enmeshed in the workings of the monastery at Monte Casino."

"But the abbey at Ajello is small."

"Yet you will find more opportunity at the monastery than you will find with Peter the Hermit, in spite of his sincerity. Where will sincerity lead without truth? Will it deliver the blind from the ditch or from a broken neck if he falls over a cliff?"

Niles rubbed his chin, staring at the fire. "You speak well. But opportunity at the abbey of Ajello? You jest!"

"I am most serious. The abbeys are secure, at least. If I were in your place, I would go back to the friendship of the monks. They are best able to help landless men."

"Yes, they are my friends, but I am weary of the field! I would see war."

"War," Tancred scoffed. "You speak like a Norman barbarian."

Niles looked shocked. "You speak so of your kin? I would be proud to be a Norman. Why all Calabria, all Sicily, is in Norman rule."

"You forget England," quipped Tancred. "The son of William rules. And the Duke of Normandy is also a son of

William. He comes now with the Count of Flanders to take up the Crusader's banner. Yes, I am proud," said Tancred. "But there is more than the boast of my father's blood. I am also respectful of the blood of my mother," he said, thinking of al-Kareem. "But I wish none of the Norman wars nor of their clannish infighting. I would heal the wounded, not take his head for my platter."

"But you are a knight!"

"I am many things. God created man with more complexity than to fit only on a Great Horse donned in magnificent armor. I also like to read books. I am grieved I had to leave my collection behind."

Tancred was silent a moment, then he unsheathed his blade, holding it up by the hilt. In the firelight it gleamed beautifully fierce, its metal like silver light.

He spoke softly, quoting from the knightly ballad of the "Song of Roland" from the days of Charlemagne and the birth of chivalry. "Ah Durendal! How white and lovely you are, and your golden hilt so full of relics!"

The song was the heart and soul of the Frank and Norman knights, whose sword, named *Durendal*, was endowed with power from heaven. To be a knight meant a man battled for God as well as for his earthly liege. To be a knight meant a man's armor was his honor, he fought with courage, and whether by life or by death, it was glorious.

Saint Michael was their true liege, for he was the warrior-angel, the one sent from heaven to go before them in battle against evil. And Durendal would strike the foe into submission.

Even now, Tancred knew that knights and soldiers gathered at Le Puy for the sword blessing at St. Michael's chapel.

All was quiet, and aware that Niles and the girl were

watching him, Tancred sheathed his blade and said bluntly, "Yes, if I were in your stead, I would go back to Ajello."

Niles smiled slightly and gestured to Tancred's scabbard. "You tell me to be content to bend the back and stare at clods of dirt all day. But you will ride off to see distant kingdoms, and your uncle waits for you in Constantinople."

"I would not go, but I must. I would rather return to my medical studies at Salerno."

"What would you do if you could finish your studies?" Niles asked.

Tancred looked out at the monotonous rain. "I would return to Salerno until I had learned all there is to know in the West. Then I would journey to Jundi Shapur."

"In Rome?" breathed the girl, her awe showing.

Tancred smiled a little. "All does not center there. Jundi Shapur is in the Moslem East. It is said to be the greatest of the world's universities."

"Infidels?" asked Niles, shocked. "Surely you do not believe it?"

"I do. Why should it be so shocking that there is knowledge in the East?"

"But we are Christians, and they are infidels," gasped the girl.

Tancred shrugged. "Much of what they have learned came from the ancient civilizations of Greece, Persia, and the Jews. And the Arabs have many great scholars. Archimedes for one."

He saw their expressions in the firelight. "Why should this disturb you? Has not the Creator endowed all humanity with abilities to learn, to discover, to excel? Knowledge itself is not the proof of God's favor or acceptance, nor is power or riches. In Jundi Shapur," he said easily, "I shall learn."

"A physician . . . ," Niles repeated thoughtfully.

Suddenly he pulled up his sleeve. "This. It is a curse. I have bled it a hundred times, yet it remains. Can you heal it?"

By now the girl had stopped eating and was staring at Tancred. Evidently the idea that he was a student of medicine held no less awe than her previous conclusions about him.

In the light of the fire, Tancred studied the swelling on Nile's arm. It looked to be an infestation from an insect or a boil.

While the girl followed his orders to heat water, he went on speaking with Niles. "Convince the abbot you wish to learn. To read, to write, to study, to know. These gifts will open doors to you that the sword can never bestow. And once you prove to the abbot that you have a heart to learn, you will find your position far better than most. Many in the church seek young men for the universities at Salerno, Rome, and Monte Casino."

"Why do you boil the dagger?" the girl whispered. "To kill a curse?"

She watched him with rapt attention.

"Cleanliness is ancient in the practice of medicine. It was known by the Jews in the Old Testament Scriptures."

"And Normans?" she asked.

"The Normans are experts in the practice of craven."

"Craven?"

"An ancient Viking custom still held to by my kin. When a man is accused of a crime, he must pass through judgment. The worse the crime, the stricter the judgment. To prove his innocence, he must not only survive, but his injuries also must heal. A man may need to walk across burning coals, but by morning his burns must begin to show improvement, or he is guilty. Or he must plunge both hands into boiling water to retrieve metal. If infection sets in, he is guilty. Or he is bound hand and foot and tossed into the river."

"But how will he swim to the top if he is tied?" she breathed.

"He hopes his liege will remember to pull him out in time," he said dryly.

"And if he does not?"

"It is of no concern, except to his mother or lover. His drowning only proves he was guilty."

Her brows came together. Tancred smiled.

He used his boiled dagger to lance the swelling, treated it with ointment from his pack, and sealed it with a strip of clean cloth.

"There," he quipped to them both. "Your lessons are done for the day."

"And tomorrow?" she asked.

"Tomorrow, I ride to Le Puy, alone. And you and our good friend Niles will both journey to Ajello. What say you, Niles?"

"I suppose you are right. She would be safer in Ajello than here. The monk whose donkey we borrowed will pose no threat to either of us. Especially," he added, "if we return the donkey to the abbot, along with the gold coin Count Redwan has promised us."

That Tancred was not yet a count seemed trivial at the moment. The important thing was that Niles was listening to him.

He found a corner to himself and, unbelting his scabbard, placed it with his other weapons within easy reach.

A few hours of sleep, he thought wearily, and he would

be back on his way to find Nicholas. And now that he had gotten rid of the girl . . .

He lay down, using his bag for a pillow, and placed his hands behind his head. In the darkness, he stared above him, hearing the rain.

"What say you, Modestine?" Niles was asking her. "I think he is right."

"I wish not to be burnt as a witch," she grumbled. "If monsieur will not take me with him, then I have no choice. Monsieur?" she called quietly.

Tancred pretended to be asleep, and after some silence, she did not call again. He heard the two of them talking quietly. From the tone of their voices he guessed they were getting on well together. For the first time he heard her laugh, then try to silence it, thinking he was asleep. Niles too laughed.

It was good, Tancred thought. He had hope for both of them. And his own future? He felt unexpectedly restless.

His ears turned to the slightest sound from the darkness outside. He heard nothing but rain dripping among the ruins, yet the unease persisted. The wood had burned into coals. The girl and Niles continued to discuss their plans to return to Ajello in hushed voices. Tancred eased himself onto his elbow, his eyes riveted to the entrance of their shelter.

He had been too lax. His hand moved toward the hilt of his blade and clasped it. He silently rose to his feet.

Something or someone was moving outside the ruin. He heard a soft but nervous whinny from Alzira.

Now certain that brigands were intent on stealing the horse and donkey, he laid a quiet hand on Niles's shoulder. Wisely, neither the girl nor Niles responded with surprise.

Tancred signaled Niles, who rallied at command by rising to his feet, weapon in hand. He hoped Niles was an expert with his rusty pike.

CHAPTER 7

The Brigands at the Ruins

❖ Lightening played bizarre shadow games against the distant sky, and branches swayed in the wind.

The flashes of light revealed four brigands. One stood guard, a second had the monk's donkey in rein, and two others tried to quiet the mare. Alzira was nervous and uncooperative, backing away and shaking her head.

Four men, but were there others about?

Tancred could not let them take his mare without putting up a fight. He motioned for Niles to take the brigand with the donkey. Could he do it? Niles was not a soldier but a farmer, while the brigands were experienced fighters.

Tancred decided he could not count on Niles to take a second brigand. He must be prepared to confront three.

Easing his dagger from a wrist-scabbard and a second from his boot, Tancred laid them before him on the wet stone. When the moment was right, he must reach them quickly and throw with precision. If the lightening continued to illumine his targets, he had a small chance of success.

He lifted his bow and placed an arrow. The guard would be first since his weapon was ready.

Niles was grim, the rain wetting his face. Tancred gave the signal and stood from the shadows, taking careful aim. He released the arrow, and it slammed into its target.

As the thief staggered forward, Niles stood, drew back his pike and heaved it like a javelin at the brigand leading away the donkey.

Tancred hurled the daggers—one, two—as Niles scrambled to withdraw his pike and finish off his opponent.

Tancred sprang forward, sword lifted, but there was no movement in the shrubs or in the ruin.

As suddenly as it had begun, the fight was over. Two brigands were dead, one mortally wounded, and the other posed no threat.

Niles was scrambling to arm himself with the brigands' weapons and the choice pieces of armor. "They must have had horses too. I shall own myself a horse!"

Tancred said nothing as he retrieved his daggers. He glanced at Niles and did not like the exhilaration on his wet face.

The rain was coming down heavily. The girl appeared from the shadows and, seeing the results, ran to join Niles in stripping from the brigands anything usable.

Tancred walked to his mare and quieted her. A few minutes later Niles joined him.

"Are we safe here for the rest of the night?"

"There may be more not far away. I ride on to Le Puy. I suggest you and the girl start at once for the abbey."

By the time Tancred had retrieved his bag from inside

the ruin and saddled Alzira, Modestine returned leading two snorting horses.

She beamed at Tancred. "Look, monsieur! Look!"

Tancred smiled slightly. "If you ride now, you can be at Ajello by tomorrow afternoon."

Niles ran to look over their booty, and Tancred mounted Alzira. He rode toward them, drawing up.

"You fought well," he told Niles. "I wish you God-speed."

Niles clasped his hand. "Should you ever ride through Ajello, we will be pleased to host you."

Tancred turned to Modestine. She watched him, her expression sullen, her eyes clinging to his. He turned away. Prolonged goodbyes made him uneasy.

"Adieu, mademoiselle."

With that he rode into the darkness toward the muddy road. Coming to a break in the woods, he turned toward Le Puy and would not look back.

When he arrived, Le Puy was astir under the March sun. Barons rode the crowded street with their knights, while hunting hounds barked at the nervous pigeons circling and landing safely on the peak of St. Michael's chapel. From atop their haven, the pigeons looked down on the falcons, which sat on the gloved wrists of nobles, who in turn wore choice displays of armor, fine cloaks, and fur collars.

Tancred rode toward the chapel and the house where Nicholas had been staying with the chronicler, Raymond of Aguilers.

The streets were crowded with every class of people. There were ill-smelling beggars and those of ill-repute. Many of them had taken the Crusader's vow to atone for their sins, believing that going on pilgrimage and fighting the Saracen would gain God's forgiveness.

Tancred rode Alzira around the pigs that were grunting and wallowing in the muddy street. Goats bleated, scrawny chickens and geese squawked and honked, flapping their wings to get out of the way of oncoming horses and mules.

Wherever Tancred looked he saw overloaded oxcarts. Some had already broken down on the pilgrimage route to Le Puy.

The hammering of blacksmiths, who were kept busy with repair work, filled the hot morning air. The shops belonging to the armorers had more business than they could keep up with, and young apprentices dashed about as their cranky mentors berated them for slothfulness.

The talk among the common folk was the same. Jerusalem the golden, Jerusalem the abode of angels, saints, and prophets. Jerusalem, where the blessed stones and dust had been touched by Christ's feet.

Once again Christ was being blasphemed and betrayed, even as Judas had betrayed Him. Did not their Lord and His mother expect them to come to the rescue of the holy sepulcher? To make straight the paths of pilgrimage to the city of cities?

No matter the cost, they would go. And God's poor would be rewarded at last with the earthly blessings of milk, honey, olive orchards, and running streams.

Knights kneeled, taking their solemn oaths, well aware that if they changed their minds having once taken the cross, excommunication awaited.

Tancred noted that nobles and barons were willingly selling their lands and possessions to take the cross. Others signed over their lands to the safekeeping of the church until their return. Wills were drawn up, leaving them to family members should the owner die during the Crusade. The clerics minutely transcribed the sober transactions down to the last bag of feed. The barons and nobles were confident. The church had sworn to protect their lands and families while they were away.

He watched a big, bearded Rhinelander waving his arm, trying to communicate with a Frank peasant about a rickety oxcart that he wished to buy.

Since each feudal lord was responsible to provide his vassal soldiers with needed equipment for the journey, many had already spent themselves into penury to outfit their armies. Others had mortgaged houses, lands, and even that year's crops to buy supplies of weapons and food stuffs.

Tancred saw women and children sitting in wagons loaded with all their belongings, willing to journey with their husbands and fathers. Others would remain behind to work the land.

Each day would begin with prayer, each night the same. Yet fear would haunt their steps as they wondered if their husbands, fathers, sons, and brothers would come home or if they would be buried in the sands of the Eastern desert.

But they were comforted. Had not the pope promised God would protect them? And should any be slain, they were assured immediate entrance into paradise.

The throng was thick, and Tancred dismounted to walk his mare toward St. Michael's chapel. It was built on a pinnacle of lava some 275 feet above the valley floor at Le Puy.

Tancred saw what he was looking for. A cluster of small houses nestled against the foot of the lava pinnacle. The steps to the chapel began among the houses at the foot of the rock.

As he walked his horse, a beggar appeared from the throng and came to his elbow. Pressing a message into Tancred's hand, he was gone again, merging into the crowd.

Caution! Go not to the house of the chronicler. It is a trap. Your Redwan cousins are here in Le Puy to take the Crusader's vow. Walter of Sicily has been seeking you since the night you escaped the castle. He has sent a message ahead by falcons to warn your cousins of your arrival. I will wait for you inside St. Michael's. Come not by way of the steps. A back way winds up the side of the rock. Nicholas

So then his cousins had not traveled toward Amiens to find Peter the Hermit. Riding to the far side of the rock, Tancred tied his mare beneath a small tree where there would be shade, then climbed the steep path that wound up the side of the mountain behind St. Michael's.

The sun was hot on the lava, the wind moist from the rains of the day before. He emerged at the pinnacle, hearing the wind around the rough crags, a cry of birds, and far below, the muffled din of voices.

The view of the Auvergne valley was breathtaking. Castles belonging to the feudal lords and knightly families dotted the distant hillsides. From these castles they would set forth for the East, their swords having been blessed by the bishop and sanctified for holy warfare. The sky was a sharp blue after the rains, and the hills and valley, a rolling display of green.

Tancred turned at the sound of footsteps. Mosul stood there with a dozen swordsmen, their weapons drawn. A smug smile was on his haughty face, his white teeth showing against his bronzed skin.

"Welcome, infidel cousin. I see the slave delivered my message."

CHAPTER 8

Le Puy

✠ He had been a fool to trust the message.

"Where is Nicholas?" Tancred asked.

"Resting in the house of the chronicler. He is not well." Mosul's teeth bared in what was intended as a smile. "At my direction a slave added something to his food last night."

Tancred's hand moved toward his scabbard. Mosul saw it at once and said coldly, "Do not try it, my cousin. You are hopelessly outnumbered. One move, and I will have you tossed over the cliff."

"If you have harmed Nicholas—"

"He is alive. In a few days he will be on his feet. He intends to journey with the Normans to Constantinople. But that is no concern of yours. You will not be here then."

So Nicholas was going on the Jerusalem expedition.

Tancred mentally placed each man's position. There were too many. Mosul had made certain of his advantage.

What did he have in mind, to kill him?

"Does Nicholas know I am here?"

Mosul smiled again. He was darkly handsome with a haughty face, his short Moslem beard neatly trimmed. "No. And where I send you, he will not come looking. You have no way out, Jehan."

Tancred refused to show alarm. "How did you know I was here? That I escaped the castle at Palermo?"

"Zakeem. The fool sent his falcon with a message for Nicholas. My men intercepted it. That you escaped Palermo at all shows your cleverness. But you will not escape this time."

"You will turn me over to my Norman cousins?"

Mosul laughed. "Your Redwan cousins are not in Le Puy. They are still with the Normans in the siege against Amalfi."

Tancred noticed that Mosul and his men were dressed as Norman soldiers. It dawned on him that Mosul had wanted the innkeeper and peasants to think they were Normans from the House of Redwan. Noticing Tancred's appraisal, Mosul seemed delighted with his own cleverness.

"A necessity, my cousin. Surrounded in Le Puy by Normans and Franks, all vowing to collect Saracen heads, what else could we do?"

He glanced at his men, as though helpless, and they exchanged sarcastic smiles.

"Why did you kill Derek?" asked Tancred.

Mosul's dark eyes were cold. "A mistake. He was where he should not have been. I was told you would be the man in the garden."

In the garden. Tancred's mind went back to that night at Palermo. He was to meet his cousin Kamila in the garden, but he had been detained. Tancred's emotions recoiled. His eyes met Mosul's and saw them full of hate.

Mosul had killed Derek because of Kamila.

"Kamila arrived to keep her appointment with you," said Mosul. "You were late. She paced, and I waited. Derek emerged from the trees, and I mistook him for you."

"You were a fool, Mosul. I did not love her. I had come to tell her so."

Mosul dismissed the words with an abrupt lift of his hand. "It matters not now. They are both dead."

Dead. His eyes searched Mosul's. She could not be dead. His grandfather would have known and told him that night in Palermo. Mosul had escaped Sicily before him, and he could not have turned his wrath on her without his grandfather knowing, unless—Tancred's reasoning rammed into a stone wall.

He understood and took a step toward Mosul, but the guards moved to block him. "Father of Lice! You abducted her when you left Palermo."

Mosul shrugged. "I tried to please her. She remained uncooperative."

"You could have let her go back to al-Kareem alive!"

"I took no pleasure in her death. But when she refused me, she became a risk. I could not permit her to return to Palermo knowing it was I who threw the poison dagger. She would go to Walter of Sicily and argue for your innocence. And that, my cousin, I could not have. He will search for you until you die, so will your cousins."

Tancred outwardly remained calm, but inside his anger raged. Mosul had killed the young and beautiful Kamila.

"You will fight me then?" Tancred asked.

Mosul folded his arms and smiled slowly. "No."

"You are a coward."

"Your words mean nothing to me. Why should I risk a

duel? I have everything to gain; it is you who will lose."
He smiled. "Matters have turned to the better by killing
Derek and leaving you alive. For the rest of your days you
will remember what was once yours, and you will drink
those bitter dregs. You dare not return to Sicily, for your
Norman clan will make you face craven. No one in
Palermo or at the Redwan Castle suspects me."

Al-Kareem knew. The informer in the black tent knew.
But Tancred remained silent, for Mosul was vicious
enough to hire men to assassinate them.

"You will suffer knowing that you should have died
instead of him," said Mosul. "And Kamila too, a woman
you wanted, is dead because of you, sleeping permanently
in a shallow grave—"

Tancred lunged at him, but the Moors grabbed him,
holding him back. Mosul walked up and backhanded him.
Tancred tasted blood.

"Use your dagger while men hold me. Show them the
coward you are."

"You will not die so easily, my cousin. I will not kill
you, nor will my men." He smiled triumphantly. "I have
other plans for you. You have been sold."

"Better kill me now," breathed Tancred. "Because if
you do not, I shall find you, if it is the last thing I do."

Mosul gestured to one of his men. "Remove his armor.
And make certain he has no secret weapons."

"Are you soldiers or women?" Tancred scoffed at
them. "If you would choose a captain to follow, why not a
warrior? Mosul is both a coward and a murderer."

"Silence him." Mosul turned his back, adding over his
shoulder, "I shall enjoy owning your Arabian mare. She is
a fine specimen."

Tancred threw himself forward, breaking the grip of
one of the men. He struck his fist into the soldier's mouth,

sending him backward, and hit hard into the belly of another. Stepping back, he drew his blade but felt a crushing blow to the back of his skull. He fought against the darkness sucking him into unconsciousness.

PART TWO

CHAPTER 9

Toward the Rhineland

✛ Tancred awoke with a throbbing head. The earth was moving beneath him, or did he lay on a bed of seawater? His vision was blurred, but after a moment he distinguished a black sky above, sprinkled with stars.

He heard a familiar sound filling the night about him: the creak of cart wheels; the slow, steady plod of oxen; and coming from behind him, the unmistakable sound of horses' hooves and the clink of armor.

He was lying in a cramped position on the bottom of a rickety cart piled with baggage and supplies. With a start, he felt binding chains about his ankles and wrists. At the same moment he remembered the pinnacle of St. Michael's and the heavy blow to the back of his skull.

Did Mosul and his men guard him?

As he struggled to his elbow, he became aware that his Norman clothes were gone. He was wearing a soiled monk's robe. His jaw clamped to control his rage. Mosul had found it humorous to pass him off as a monk.

His hands fumbled, searching for details about his surroundings. Dare he hope that somehow in the confusion Mosul and his Moors might have forgotten to remove a weapon?

It was too much to expect. His Damascus daggers were gone. So was his prized blade with the insignia of the House of Dreux Redwan on the hilt. Gone too, his bow, even his boots. He was barefoot. Tancred said something under his breath.

His satchel! He tried to sit up. He had left his bag tied to his saddle. Inside was the Redwan gold falcon with the inscription of Dreux Redwan, naming Tancred both son and heir. Was that now, like his Arabian mare, in Mosul's hands?

He struggled, but the chains bit into his flesh. Each move sent his brain spinning. He touched the back of his skull. His hair was matted with dried blood. The rickety cart, bumping its way along, was sickening. As he tried to gain his bearings, the ox swerved to avoid something in the road, causing the piles of ill-smelling baggage to topple against him. His hand touched something about his neck.

A cross. But, no, it was not that. He tried to concentrate, to trace his fingers around the edges.

A star? He found himself again overcome by blackness.

He awoke with a start as water slapped his face. A boot kicked his leg. "Wake up!"

Tancred opened his eyes. He was no longer in the cart but flat on his back on the ground. Light was spreading across the eastern sky, and damp tendrils of gray fog hung over a glade surrounded by birch and oak trees.

He looked up at several men who stared down at him. They were knights, but one glimpse told him they were not of the disciplined order he was accustomed to. They looked and behaved more like brigands.

Before moving, he surveyed their armor, for it told much about their background. They lacked the better pieces. Most of it was nondescript, as though collected along the way, no doubt the booty of past battles.

The man who had prodded him with his boot turned and spoke in a strange tongue to one of the others who squatted beside a small fire.

Rhinelanders, Tancred thought.

What were they doing in France? He quickly decided from the cart and baggage they were on their way east to Constantinople.

Could he manage to escape these barbarians?

Tancred caught the familiar whiff of wood smoke and the smell of food cooking. A moment later the man who had been addressed strode up.

Standing wide-legged, he gazed down on Tancred. Tancred was amazed at his size. He looked to be close to seven feet tall, clad in foul-smelling black, with a grimy boot-length cloak.

Tancred's mind did not falter. He was under their immediate control, but escape he would.

Fierce blue eyes stared down at him, as cold and hard as flint. The harsh face was sun-baked, with a thick black beard. His black hair brushed against the shoulders of his chain mesh.

"You get up, Jew!"

Tancred stared at him. *Jew?*

The man gestured his head toward his men, and one of them spat at Tancred as they roughly jerked him to his feet.

Angered, he struck the side of the man's neck with both hands chained at the wrists, knocking the knight to the dust.

The big Rhinelander backhanded Tancred with a force that sent him sprawling.

"Try my patience, Jew, and you will hang on yonder tree, gold or no gold!"

Jew? Tancred wondered again and spat blood. *Gold?*

"You speak in riddles, Rhinelander. I am Tancred Jehan Redwan, son and heir of Count Dreux of Norman Sicily. And when I am free, I will split you open like a ripe melon!"

The Rhinelander gave an evil grin. "Your lies will not deceive us. You are a filthy rabbi."

Tancred gazed down at his robe and saw in the daylight that it was not a monk's robe at all. And the chain about his neck held not a Latin cross, but the star of David.

He struggled to his feet, outraged.

One of the men walked up carrying something, and Tancred recognized his satchel. The big Rhinelander grabbed it and threw it at Tancred's bare feet.

"The sealed document from the Bishop of Le Puy, where is it?"

"I have no document. I am not a rabbi. I am a Norman. Enemies have sold me as a slave. But I will—"

"Slave?" he jeered. "You are not worthy to be my slave. You will be brought to the Jews in Worms and Mainz as the bishop ordered you. You will collect the coffers of gold, but you will give them to Count Emich of Leinigen instead of to Peter the Hermit."

Appalled, Tancred did not speak.

Was there a real rabbi who had been told by the bishop to collect gold from the Jews to appease the marching Crusaders passing through their districts? If so, where was he now? Silenced permanently by Mosul, no doubt. Tancred noticed that the rabbi's tunic was too tight and was already tearing about his shoulders.

The Rhinelander kicked at the satchel, and Tancred, anxious to see if his belongings were intact, stooped to search. The Redwan falcon was gone. Was he misguided enough to think that a solid gold ornament would remain intact amid thieves? Yet he did not think the Rhinelanders possessed it, but Mosul.

Few of his possessions were left, only the pair of Moorish trousers and the lined woolen dress-cloak he had worn to see his grandfather the night he had escaped. At once Tancred realized an object had remained undetected by Mosul and the Rhinelanders. The relic that the old priest Odo had entrusted to him to return to Jerusalem had been overlooked. It was still wrapped in a white cloth and secured inside the pocket lining of the tunic.

He was about to put the cloak back when the Rhinelander's eyes glittered with greed. The cloak was yanked from Tancred's hand and exchanged for the smelly one the Rhinelander wore.

How long until the brute noticed the object?

In an instant the trousers were grabbed by another, and Tancred watched the last of his possessions disappear.

"You have learned a thing or two," said the Rhinelander maliciously. "But behave yourself, and you will live to see Mainz. Now get up. You will walk the journey."

Bruised and battered as he was, Tancred's wit began to revive. "I will ride in the cart," he challenged. "And I will eat. You need me alive, Rhinelander. I will do you no good dead or half-starved."

The veins in the big man's thick neck swelled, and he gestured to one of his men for his whip.

"I will have none of that," said Tancred, refusing to cower. "If that filthy thing touches me, I will die before I

collect the gold. Death is better than this. But if you un-
shackle me, I will get you even more gold."

"More gold?"

Tancred said nothing, hoping the knight would not
call his bluff.

"He is a strong lad and big," said one of them to the
Rhinelander. "He might turn on us."

"Without a weapon?" Tancred mocked. "Did you not
say I was a rabbi? Where would I have learned to fight
and overcome strong warriors such as yourselves? Are you
not all mighty men of valor?"

They exchanged glances, pleased, but the Rhinelander
watched him with small, shrewd eyes.

"How can you get us more gold from the Jews? Tell
me."

"No. Not unless I receive better treatment for my co-
operation."

The man scanned him with a hateful look. "Loose one
hand," he ordered. "Then bring him something to eat. If
that does not loosen his tongue, we will sever it for good."

Tancred knew he must be cautious. He had baited the
appetite of a hungry jackal. Now he must convince him
that he could deliver. He would not survive long unless
the big Rhinelander believed that he could not do without
Tancred.

For days they journeyed inland from Le Puy toward
the Rhine River and the town of Worms between Man-
neheim and Mainz. By overhearing snatches of conversation between the brigand-knights, Tancred learned they
were to join up with a contingent of Crusaders under a
certain nobleman called Count Emich.

Peter the Hermit and his group were expected to arrive at Cologne in April, but it appeared Emich intended
to make his own way to Constantinople, persecuting the

Jews and robbing them as he went. To kill a Jew in Europe, before even arriving in the Saracen East, was apparently seen by the Rhinelanders as vindicating "the slights to the honor of Christ and His mother."

Tancred was convinced a distorted knowledge of Scripture was a breeding ground for satanic delusions. Fired up by the zealous call to arms against the infidels, many could not distinguish the difference between those whom they came to fight and the people of the Book to which the Promised Land was given by the very God they claimed to be serving.

"Jew!" The Rhinelander spat at Tancred. "It was you who crucified Christ."

"I thought it was the Roman soldiers," quipped Tancred. "Is it not claimed that the lance that pierced His side has been found?"

"It has," he snarled.

"And who did it belong to?" Tancred inquired. "A Jew?"

The man's face mottled with rage, for he knew it had belonged to the Roman soldier.

"His mother," said Tancred, "whom you worship, from whose earthly lineage did she come? Was it not from King David, a Jew? And Christ, the very son of God who was born in the flesh by the Virgin, His blood and sweat which dripped from His crown of thorns and from His pierced hands and feet, what kind of blood was it, Rhinelander? German or Jewish?"

The Rhinelander's boot smashed into Tancred's stomach. He doubled, spitting blood, but refused to make a sound.

"There, more Jewish blood has touched the ground. That will teach you to mock me!"

He walked away, shouting orders to his men to mount.

A rider neared Tancred, tossing a skin of water to him. Tancred looked up, wondering. The man bore a scar across the entire side of his face. He had noticed him before as someone who kept to himself, saying little.

As he rode by, he leaned toward Tancred, his voice coming in a hoarse whisper. "You must not provoke him. He is Count Emich's captain, Wolfric, a bloodthirsty man who takes no pity on the weak."

"Then why do you ride with his lot?" Tancred challenged.

"Emich claims to be a count in Speyer, but he is naught else than a robber-baron, notorious in the area for a life of pillage."

"Help me escape, and you too can be free."

His eyes met Tancred's evenly. "He has my wife and daughter. If I should fail, they would be left to his mercy. And so I wait my hour."

Tancred pitied him. His situation was not so unusual, however. Serfs and their families were left to the good will of their vassal lords, and pity the man who had a surly master but a beautiful wife or daughter.

"Do you ride to join Peter the Hermit?"

"The monk is at Cologne. We may join up with him farther down the Danube, but for now Emich is content to raid the Jews along the Rhine. He has slain many in Speyer already. A pilgrimage is the last thing on his mind; it is plunder he wishes, and this is but an excuse to vent his hatred."

"Not all are in your position. They could turn against him."

"Emich is a worthless fellow, but his fiery speech provokes the crowds."

"And the blind follow him, paying heed to words that are fed by the hounds of hell."

"Not all who follow him like him."

"Yet they follow on and remain mute."

From the rider's expression, Tancred knew that he agreed but concern for his family stilled his tongue.

A shout from Wolfric for Tancred to get to his feet ended their discourse.

"They call me Leupold," the rider said.

As Tancred was ordered into the cart, he knew he could expect little if any help from Leupold.

From the regions of Speyer, they crossed the river Rhine and arrived near the German town of Worms on a hot summer's morning.

Count Emich and his followers had arrived not many days before and were camped in the forest. One look at the size of the camp, and Tancred felt a dart of despair and anger. He marveled that the man could gain a following of ten thousand. Armed with pikes and staves, his army thought nothing of hurling his troops against "God's enemies."

Tancred soon discovered that Emich exercised a fascination over his followers' minds.

"I am ordained of God to become emperor over Jerusalem," he preached to the crowd.

There was a great shout, and Emich looked about the sea of faces, smiling his pleasure over their devoted trust. When they were silent, he continued.

"On hearing of the expedition to destroy the infidels, I awoke the next morning, and behold, God's call was on me, Emich of Leinigen, and I received from heaven the blessed stigmata. I bear the very cross, not on my garment as you, but miraculously imprinted upon my flesh!"

A thousand voices hushed into a reverential sigh. The eyes of German peasants and soldiers fixed on him. The bawdy knight, dressed in a fur-lined cloak with a great sword in hand and a dirty goose at his feet, was accepted as a saint.

"A miracle happened," the people proclaimed to each other. "Did you hear? He bears the cross in his flesh! An angel must have been sent from heaven to bless him on his bed."

Emich held up the goose while he stood with feet apart, his eyes lifted toward the sky. The voices ebbed into silence as they breathlessly wondered what would happen next.

"This goose is our heavenly guide. Indwelt by the Spirit of God, she will bring us to the very spot where God wills us to draw sword."

Tancred glanced about him. The common people believed Emich. It was astounding. How could they believe that the same God who created the sun, moon, and stars, would appoint this man and a goose to be their guide?

Yet they did, and Tancred realized that while the peasants were religious, carrying crosses, mouthing the name of Christ in one breath and the holy mother in the next, they knew little if anything about what the Scriptures actually said. They were depending on others to feed them, looking to men to be their leaders instead of asking questions and seeking the truth as individuals. Like sheep without the true Shepherd, they were following a false shepherd to disaster.

But if he thought that Emich and his ten thousand were only a leaderless collection of peasants apt to go on a mindless rampage against the Jews, a look in the direction of the men about him swiftly put an end to that idea. Tancred also saw experienced knights and captains, nobles from France, England, Swabia, and the Low Countries, men who knew better than to follow a mindless goose or a man who claimed a stigmata. Men who should have known better than to vent their rage on the people of the Book, but whose hatred for them found in Emich a rallying point.

Wolfric moved his way to the front where Emich and his captains were gathered, and having said something, Emich turned a riveting stare on Tancred.

He obviously believed him to be the rabbi who bore a letter to the Jews of Worms, telling them to give this fool their gold coins.

Words were quickly exchanged, then Emich turned back to his followers.

"We will camp here for several days, until the goose decides to lead us whithersoever she is wont to take us. Go now; eat, drink, and be merry!"

A short time later, Wolfric strode up. "Be ready. At dawn you will take the letter to the chief rabbi and arrange for the gold to be brought to Count Emich. I will go with you to make sure you get much gold."

"I must go alone."

Wolfric smirked. "Do you take us for fools?"

"After listening to your robber-baron enthrall us with his miraculous stigmata and the goose story, how could I ever take you for fools?"

Wolfric was about to strike him a blow, when one of the other soldiers walked up. "The Count asks for you. I am to take the rabbi to the river to wash for the meeting tomorrow."

Tancred glanced hungrily at the cool blue waters of the Rhine.

Wolfric cast him a hateful look. "The day comes when we no longer need you. Then I make it my joy to cut your throat." He turned and strode away.

Tancred watched him go, thinking not of his threat but of the other soldier's words about washing in the river.

The soldier gave him a little shove in the direction of the Rhine. "Move, swine!"

Tancred stumbled forward, the chains about his ankles and wrists making it difficult to walk.

Only one guard . . . Could he lure him toward the shrubs where they would not as easily be seen by the others? Could he get him into the water, and if he could . . .

"I cannot wash with chains."

"Silence!"

"At least remove those on my hands."

"I said be silent!"

Tancred moved in the direction of the river and lowered himself to one knee. He exaggerated his condition, trying to bring handfuls of water to his face. "It is impossible to wash."

"The Jew is right," came a third voice. "Better loose him. I will stand guard with you."

That rasping voice; he knew it. Tancred turned his head to look and saw Leupold standing by the tree. There was a look in his eyes that caused Tancred's heart to beat faster.

CHAPTER 10

The Jewish Section of Worms

✤ Leupold gestured to the soldier with his pike. "Go ahead. I shall stand watch."

The soldier looked from Leupold to Tancred. Tancred turned back to the water, afraid his expression would give him away. For a moment there was silence, and he began to think the soldier would refuse.

Then he walked up to Tancred, stooped, and unshackled first his hands, then his feet. He was turning away when Tancred lunged, his forearm going around the soldier's throat. Leupold hurled his dagger.

A minute later, the Rhinelander's body was dragged into the bushes, and Leupold rasped, "Go now! Quickly!"

"What of you?" Tancred whispered. "Did anyone see you come here?"

"No one. Go, while the moment is yours."

Tancred hesitated only a second, then gripping Leupold's arm, he turned and fled down the bank, keeping close to the trees and shrubs. His first thought was to make his way back to Le Puy and Nicholas, but he could not dismiss the plot against the Jews.

Would it not be easier and safer to strike out on his own and forget the entire ugly incident? But the matter of justice pricked his conscience. Honor, too, demanded action. He found he could not simply cast these issues aside and pursue his own cause.

The Jewish leadership must be warned of what Emich and his followers intended to do. If there was time, they might hide the women and children, even their possessions, and if there were able-bodied men, they could fight. And too, he must warn the bishop and the governor of the sort of rabble gathered outside their walls. Surely the bishop would not stand by and condone bloodshed in the name of the cross.

It was late afternoon, but the sun was still hot when he entered Worms. With utmost care, he ventured into the Jewish section of the town. Small mercantile shops were closing early, for the next day was the Sabbath. The narrow stone streets were busy with children playing and women doing last-minute shopping. Wearing black coats, hose, and hats, the young men walked hurriedly along, discussing the Torah. Amulets, conveying Scripture verses, were wound about their arms and across their foreheads. Large brown eyes turned toward him, somewhat curiously, and Tancred realized he must look worse than a grimy peasant.

Quizzical glances soon turned to amusement as they noticed that his garb was far too short. The younger boys smothered their laughter, and others looked away. Did they speak Greek or Latin?

Tancred stopped and said, "Shalom, shalom."

Trying to hide their smiles, they repeated the greeting.

"Your chief rabbi, I must speak with him. Is he at the synagogue? Can you take me there?"

The word *rabbi* they understood but frowned and shook their heads at his other words. Tancred gestured toward the late sun. "It will be dark soon. I would speak with your rabbi."

They looked at the sun, then nodded they understood that the Sabbath was coming. "Rabbi," they repeated, and turning, pointed down the narrow street.

"Do you have swords?" he asked.

They stared at him.

"Swords," he repeated. "You must protect yourselves. You will be attacked!"

They looked at each other, then back at Tancred, and shook their heads showing they did not understand his language. He left them and several minutes later found himself standing before a low rambling stone wall enclosing a private orchard of olive and fig trees near the synagogue. Pigeons cooed as they roosted, and a small well offered the enticement of a drink of water, for the summer sun was hot.

He entered and refreshed himself, and when he looked up, he noticed an old rabbi seated on a bench in the shade, a worn manuscript beside him.

"Shalom," the rabbi said.

"I could wish peace for us both, but it is the ill news of destruction I bring you."

"Ah, and who is this that brings tidings of death?"

"You speak with a man who has tasted what it is like to be a Jew among those who claim to speak for Christianity but are liars."

The rabbi raised a white brow and scanned him.

"In truth, my mother was a Moslem. She is now dead. My father is dedicated to the Christian shrines. You may say I was taught the best and the worst of both religions. As a child I dreamed of both devils and angels chasing me. So far I have not been caught by either."

The old man chuckled, and his eyes glimmered with irony. "And were these devils Moslem or Christian? But perhaps we should not debate that. Maybe I should call you Jacob. He too dreamed of angels. But it was his brother Esau whom he feared was chasing him, and with good cause."

"I do not know this Jacob, but if he has felt as I have, the breath of a hunting pack upon his heels, he has my sympathy."

"Come, sit, and refresh yourself."

"There is little time. You must arm your community. Brigands wearing the cross will come demanding payment to aid their journey to Constantinople, but it is their own greedy appetites they intend to fill. The robber-baron is named Emich, and he has ten thousand followers. Not all will attack you, but those who do not will do nothing to stop those who will. You must arm yourselves and put your possessions in a safe hiding place until they move on."

"And how do you know all of this?"

"I was with them. Held against my will until a friend helped me to escape. Emich had expected me to come here with an official letter informing you to give generously to the Jerusalem expedition. It is a ruse, of course. The request is nothing more than a disguised threat. You must appease the peasant horde passing through or expect them to turn on you as infidels. But Emich will turn on you regardless."

The rabbi's eyes saddened. "Where are they now, my son? Are they very near?"

"Camped by the Rhine, near the woods. You have only a short time. You must appeal to the governor and the bishop."

"I know the bishop. He will have no part in a massacre."

"Good. Then you must act quickly to warn your people."

"I will act at once. And you, what is your name?"

"Tancred Redwan from Sicily."

"Rest awhile, and I shall return."

"I need a weapon, rabbi. They have stolen mine. And as you can see, I need clothing better suited to my calling."

"I will do what I can. I will call David. You will need food and a place to bathe."

The old rabbi hurried away, and Tancred saw that he had left the hand-bound book on the bench. While he waited, he picked it up. It was written in Hebrew.

Tancred was aware that a small boy stood staring at him. The boy smiled and pointed to the book. "I read Hebrew, Greek, and Latin."

Tancred smiled, aware of how exhausted and hungry he was. "If I had a year to sit and hear your doves cooing, I would ask you to teach me Hebrew."

"You read Greek and Latin?"

"Yes. I am a student physician and a soldier. Is the rabbi your grandfather?"

David smiled. "He is. And I am told to bring you to a fountain to wash. But you must hurry. The sun will set soon, and the Sabbath rest begins."

"I fear this night will not bring rest, David, but war."

"War?" he whispered. He looked to be all eyes. "Here in Worms?"

"When brigands roam in the guise of religious garb, there is great danger. But first I will take you and your grandfather to a place of safety."

"Are we not safe here next to the synagogue?"

"This is the last place you will be safe. Show me the fountain. We must hurry."

The rabbi returned with a group of armed Jews and a bundle of clothing. On top of the tunic lay a sword.

"It is the best we could do," said an angular man with coal black eyes and a beard. "I am Nathan. Our rabbi has informed us of your warnings."

Tancred grasped the hilt and tried the balance. It was not the sword that Mosul had stolen from him, but it was a good blade. "Have you sent word to the governor and bishop?"

"Word has been sent. They have promised to protect us."

"I do not question their word. But put not your faith in men's promises. You must also arm yourselves to protect your homes and shops."

"We wish no trouble . . ."

"It is not what you may wish for, friend, but what you must do to survive. You have enemies who would destroy you. If you look the other way and pretend such a thing cannot happen here in Worms, you will surely be killed."

The men looked at each other. "How do we know for certain you speak the truth?"

"If you had time, which you do not, you could send a delegation to Speyer. Emich and many of his followers come from there. Before they left they attacked the Jews. Many are dead."

"We will take no chances," said the rabbi. "The women and children—" he stopped.

From the street came the beating of horses' hooves and angry shouts: "Enemies of God!"

Tancred knew it was too late.

"Quick," he said. "Is there a back way?"

"Yes," said Nathan, "but—"

"Take the boy and the rabbi and seek refuge in the cathedral. I will try to gain you time."

The old rabbi turned to run in the direction of the synagogue.

"Stop him!" ordered Tancred. "They will cut him down if he goes there."

"Rabbi Efraim, come back!"

"Grandfather!" sobbed the boy, running after him, grabbing the hem of his long black coat. "Do not go, Grandfather! Do not leave me!"

"I cannot leave the parchments. There is the Torah and the Books. They will burn them!" Tears welled in his eyes as he looked down at David.

More shouts came from the street, then a scream. Nathan and the men with him looked toward the front door. "They are coming!"

"Find weapons," ordered Tancred. "Use anything!"

They scrambled to arm themselves, and Tancred grabbed the rabbi and the boy. "The cathedral, where is it?"

"Not far," the rabbi gasped. "The bishop's castle adjoins it."

"Go now!" Seeing the rabbi look longingly in the direction of the synagogue, he said harshly, "Would you see the boy thrust through the heart with a pike?"

The rabbi's eyes turned to him, horrified and angry.

"They will kill him as easily as they would you or me," warned Tancred.

"I will go," he breathed, grasping David. "Come, my

son, come! We must hurry. And may the God of scattered Israel defend us this night!"

The handful of Jews with him had managed to find weapons, such as they were. Grim and determined, they had gathered clubs, heavy rocks from the garden, and sharp pieces of broken pottery.

"Let us defend the synagogue," Nathan told the others, but Tancred laid a steady hand on his shoulder.

"It is useless. Save your lives if you can. A synagogue can be rebuilt."

"But not our Torah!"

"You can send for another from Mainz or Cologne."

They seemed resigned to accept his order and took protective positions as the wood door cracked under an ax, then caved in. Emich's followers stood there with pikes and staves, their eyes wild.

"Now!" Tancred ordered, and the men hurled the heavy rocks. Some of the soldiers fell, but others trampled over them and surged forward. In a moment they were surrounded. Tancred's blade thrust and thrust again. Nathan was rammed through with a pike, but not until two men lay sprawled at his feet. The Jews grimly fought on, snatching up the better weapons as Emich's murderers fell. They held their own against the attackers. A fire sprang up from the next room, and smoke filled the house.

"Break for the bishop's castle," Tancred shouted.

They fought their way out, and he slammed the door shut on the men inside, leaving them in darkness and smoke.

As evening fell and the Sabbath began, the street was filled with the ugly noise of pillage and death, while the smell of smoke hung in the air. The Jews were ahead of him, leading the way toward the cathedral. Tancred saw many others running in the same direction. He caught sight of the round towers and pointed domes of St. Peter and St. Paul. Would sanctuary await them, or would the doors be shut against their cry?

CHAPTER 11

In the Synagogue

✤ In the panic and confusion, Jews from all over, especially children and women, some carrying infants, ran toward the sanctuary of the cathedral. The old tried to keep up, aided by young boys. Young Jewish men and fathers armed with makeshift weapons held off Emich's followers. Although determined, the Jewish men were being cut down by the fifties and hundreds.

Looking back toward the rabbi's house, Tancred saw fire and smoke. Farther down the street, storming through the city gate, Emich rode into town surrounded by hundreds of followers brandishing pikes and staves. Leading Emich was a group of men and women prodding the goose forward.

The Rhinelanders, urged on by the nobles and captains, were looting shops, breaking into houses, and dragging the Jews through the streets.

Tancred's hand tightened about his sword hilt, and his blue-gray eyes narrowed. *If I had but fifty Norman warriors, I could teach those Rhinelanders a bloody lesson.*

But he was one man with a sword, a fact quickly brought back to him by a man who rushed at him with a spiked club. As he swung for Tancred's head, Tancred went down on one knee and thrust upward, his point taking his attacker through the throat.

Withdrawing his sword, Tancred moved into a grove of trees to catch his breath.

The bishop, along with the lords of the town and Christian neighbors, had come out to protest vehemently to Emich. Others in Worms were hiding the Jews and their valuables.

Despite the townspeoples' support, Emich's followers surged toward the cathedral, a haven for the persecuted. As the Jews fled inside, the heavy door slammed shut and was bolted from within.

The mob surrounded the castle shouting, "Send out the Jews!" Emich rode to the door, bearing his sword.

This was his moment of escape, Tancred told himself. He could do no more here.

He looked about. A way was clear, if he could circle back to what was left of the rabbi's house and then to the street. But he would not make it far wearing the tattered robe of a rabbi. For a short period he had tasted the bitter cup of being Jewish in a Gentile world, and it was not an identity he wished to continue.

He removed the dead Rhinelander's clothes and grimaced at the odor. If he were careful, he might find a lazy Rhinelander noble sitting astride a horse, and enjoy taking both his clothes and his horse. Villains that they were, they deserved worse, Tancred told himself.

He darted through the trees in the direction of the street, wishing to avoid further combat. Coming out of the glade, he emerged near the synagogue.

Emich's goose was nowhere to be seen, and Tancred

imagined that it had sought its own escape from its crazed master. But he did see a horse tied nearby. A fine horse, and although undernourished, able to take him to Constantinople. For he decided he would not return to Le Puy to find Nicholas but wait for him in the East. Nicholas would surely arrive in the company of one the feudal lords and his army.

As he neared the horse, he stopped, recognizing its owner, who appeared suddenly from one of the houses. The big Rhinelander Wolfric had a Jewish girl in his grasp, one who fought against him wildly.

He cursed and dropped her, and she fled into the synagogue. With a shout, Wolfric ran after her.

With sword in hand, Tancred went after him.

Inside, the candles were lit, and as yet, the place was untorched. The mob was too busy looting and killing.

Wolfric had hold of the girl, but Tancred flung the Rhinelander's arm aside. The big man whirled to confront him, and seeing who it was, his eyes hardened into blue granite.

"You," he grunted. He reached for his blade.

"Yes. I told you the truth, Wolfric. I am not one of these people; I am Tancred Redwan, a Norman from Sicily. But it is with honor that I take their cause to myself. It is in the name of one of their greatest Hebrew soldiers that I now take your head. Come, Rhinelander, and I will give your flesh to the fowls of heaven this day because you have lifted your hand against the seed of Christ their King."

Wolfric went white to the lips. How those words must have rankled him. He drew his sword and came at Tancred, but Tancred countered his blow and slapped the side of his blade against the big man's head.

He pressed Wolfric even harder by using all the Moorish sword skills that he knew, stepping backward, feinting, then attacking. He could see that his style confused the big man.

The Rhinelander was a poor swordsman, having only his size in his favor, but even that was turning against him. He was breathing heavily from exertion and sweating.

Tancred deliberately, coolly, kept up the attack, dragging it out. "You should apologize to this girl, Wolfric. You have behaved very badly. Tell her you are repentant. If you grovel before her on your knees, I may let you die easily."

Wolfric's eyes flashed with hatred. He lunged, but again Tancred warded him off. Then, tiring of the game, Tancred ran him through.

Their eyes locked; Tancred drew back his sword.

He turned to the girl. She was slumped across a table where the Old Testament scrolls were laid. For a moment he thought she had fainted.

He went to her, gently lowering her to the floor.

"Mademoiselle?" he said softly.

She did not stir. He looked into a lovely face drained white. The soft brown eyes were very still. Only then did he notice the spot above her heart where the Rhinelander's dagger protruded.

Her hand clutched something, and Tancred eased open her fingers and removed a small handwritten booklet, its edges worn thin from use. He was surprised to see that it was written not in Hebrew but in Latin.

He scanned the handwritten words, recognizing Scripture, some of it so worn from touch that the ink was blotched.

"To Rachel," was written on the first page. The rest of the words were from the New Testament, although he did not know from which of the books. He stared at it, turning it over in his hand.

"Let not your heart be troubled: You believe in God, believe also in me. In my Father's house are many mansions: if it were not so I would have told you. I go to prepare a place for you, and if I go and prepare a place for you, I will come again, and receive you to myself; that where I am, there you may be also."

Words from the New Testament written in Latin . . . A Christian Jew?

He looked down at her. Despite her ordeal, her expression showed no terror; in fact, the more he stared at her, the more he understood that she had died unafraid. The idea deeply moved him.

He gently picked her up and carried her to the back of the synagogue. A small door led out into a garden of olive trees, where despite the evil going on in the town, doves cooed in the trees, and bees hummed about a cascade of purple flowers.

He laid her under a tree and covered her with her cloak.

"Rachel, Rachel, if only we had met in another time, another place."

He slipped the booklet inside his tunic. "Shalom."

Inside the synagogue, he stooped beside Wolfric, who wore the Moorish cloak he had stolen from Tancred. It was dirty now, and he did not want it. But he quickly ran his hand along the inside lining. The small relic had not been detected. Taking the dagger, he slit open the lining, removed it, and placed it inside his tunic with the Scripture booklet.

The sound of running feet and voices reached him from outside. If he were to escape to Constantinople, it must be now.

CHAPTER 12

Constantinople, The Hippodrome
Summer

✤ Word of Western barbarians' arrival reached the emperor at the Sacred Palace. A Frank knight named Walter Sans-Avoir had arrived at Nish, a Byzantine garrison town on the frontier with Hungary. Emissaries had been sent to escort him to Constantinople.

Hearing this, Helena of the Nobility had sent her eunuch slave Bardas to Nish to discover Nicholas's whereabouts. On his return, Bardas brought good news.

"Although Master Nicholas is not with the Frank knight, he has assured me your uncle is among the peasant-army now nearing Nish. They are led by a monk, Peter the Hermit. The knight boasts of some thirty thousand journeying with the Hermit."

"Then I shall go to Nish with Philip the Noble!"

"Mistress, you cannot do anything so scandalous!"

"And why not? I shall bring my own entourage, and I shall be entirely safe traveling in Byzantine territory."

"Lady Irene will never permit it, mistress."

"Perhaps not, but since she is occupied elsewhere with

the bishop, no one will stop me from riding to meet Nicholas."

"But—"

"Come, Bardas, the way is open before us. We must go. News arrived only yesterday that my mother may be in Tabriz. I care not at all what these Western barbarians may be about. But Nicholas I must find. And when I do, he and I can leave at once for Tabriz."

Bardas frowned. "I fear it will not be so simple. First we must locate your uncle among the throng. Then you must convince him your informers are reliable."

"You grumble too much. Bring the chariot. Philip is at the Hippodrome, and I must see him before he rides out. He cannot leave without us."

Helena had been infatuated with Philip the Noble, son of Irene and reportedly the son of the great Greek general, as far back as she could remember. Now he was in military service to the emperor. Today he would be at the Hippodrome, the amphitheater that seated some sixty thousand and was fashioned after the one in ancient Rome.

Helena sat in the chariot with Bardas, not far from the main gate. The Hippodrome, meaning "horse course," had been built by Emperor Constantine when he had moved his seat of authority from Rome to Constantinople, forming the Eastern empire.

The Byzantines were already in the stands, anxious for the opening season games to begin. Soon now the emperor would arrive, and the Imperial Calvary would escort him around the stadium to the deafening shouts of "Hail to the emperor!"

Besides chariot races, there would be gladiators fighting wild beasts, political farces, clown acts, and the solemn pageants with luxuriant costumes, all to be performed at various times throughout the spring and summer season.

Helena recalled that as a child she had gone with her mother, Lady Adrianna, to the Hippodrome to view the parade honoring a general, who was returning victorious from battle. He had been paraded through Constantinople to the amphitheater in Roman fashion, followed by the rich booty of military conquest. The parade of booty and slaves had lasted well into the next day.

Some of the slaves were set free, celebrating grace; others were executed. But even these executions had not satisfied the Byzantine lust for cruelty and blood.

The circus had long ago replaced the intellectual forum of ancient Greece and was the focus of life in Constantinople. Here, in the Hippodrome, the ordinary Byzantine expressed his feelings, his inordinate impulsive nature, his love of the unscrupulous, and above all, his weak character. It was not beyond a rebellious populace to dethrone and torture a rejected emperor amid the applause of the mob.

"The Hippodrome is as much a part of Byzantine life as the Sacred Palace," her mother had once told her. "The temperament of the Byzantine would find life joyless without the possibility of exercising his rebellious and factious temper."

Helena peered anxiously through the crowd for a glimpse of Philip, while trying to keep the intense golden sun in the azure sky from beating down on her.

"I do not like this, mistress," Bardas repeated his favorite grumble. "This is no place for you. Oh that we had stayed in Athens! And what if Lady Irene discovers you have involved the Noble in your schemes to go to Nish?"

"Do cease your grumbling. She will not find out," Helena insisted.

Irene boasted of lofty plans for Philip's future, promising the position of minister of war, something that Helena knew Philip coveted. It was never clear to Helena just why her aunt insisted she stay away from Philip when they both felt strongly about each other.

One day I shall marry Philip, thought Helena. *Irene will not be able to stop me.*

"Philip knows about Nicholas's coming, and he has promised to aid me," she insisted with more confidence than she felt.

Bardas scowled. "Yea, mistress, but not by escorting you to Nish."

Helena knew the journey would be long and dangerous, but she refused to show her concerns. "I do not see why not. Irene travels across Byzantine territory, why should not I?"

Bardas seemed to set the matter aside and was instead scowling toward the amphitheater. "Today there will be chariot races, followed by the wild beasts. There are slaves from Cathay who will die."

The thought sickened her. "Hush, Bardas. Look, the cavalry is coming now. Stand, so Philip will see you."

Disgruntled, Bardas reluctantly did so. His scarlet trousers, edged in gold, caught the sunlight. A scowl dressed his broad face.

The Imperial Cavalry pranced forward amid cheers from the Byzantines. The emperor was approaching on his own royal horse, elegant in rich purple and golden splendor. The haunting call of the trumpets sounded; the hooves echoed like a drumbeat from the procession of royal horses.

Helena's eyes searched the elite cavalry for Philip. The very sight of the man she had loved since girlhood caused her heart to pound. She insisted she loved everything about him, from the somewhat haughty lift of his dark head to the lean smile on his ascetic face—however mystifying that smile appeared at times. She loved too his elegant dress and his growing authority in the Sacred Palace, even though his move toward power came by the schemes of Irene and the bishop.

She saw the flash of silver and black uniform and the commanding prance of fine-blooded horses and heard the clink of metal. Philip rode in the forefront of the cavalry as the newly elevated commander. He had seen her too, noticing the crimson trousers of Bardas, and he rode through the crowd toward her chariot. A flash of impatience stole across his face.

"Helena, this is no place to be now. Bardas, take her back to the palace at once."

Helena offered a sweet, placating smile, her dimples showing. She swished her peacock fan. "Now, Philip, am I but an unweaned child, unable to make any decisions of my own?"

His dark eyes flickered with affection that soon vanished. "Does Irene know you are here?"

Mention of Irene brought unrest between them. Helena felt the immediate prickle to her nerves but set it aside. She intended to go to Nish and that meant not locking horns with Philip over Irene.

"As usual, Irene is busy elsewhere in the kingdom sowing the seeds of your fame and fortune."

He smiled. "Let us hope they are not seeds of rebellion but success. What benefits my future will also secure yours, Helena. I will see to that."

She reached a hand to him; he clasped it, bent down, and brought it to his lips. For a moment their eyes clung together.

"What brings you here? Surely not to see blood," he stated.

"I hear you will be going to Nish."

"I wish it were not so. How better to serve the emperor's nephew in the western part of the empire? I have no choice but to lead troops to bolster the governor's garrison. We will also take food supplies."

"Then the Frank knight was right. A great throng is not far behind him following Peter the Hermit."

At the mention of the peasants, Philip frowned. "They are like a plague of locusts covering the land. The governor of Nish has sent word of plunder and looting in the kingdom of Hungary."

She laughed at the disdain in his voice. "Surely they are not that bad. I think you are only in a dour mood because you were called away from the side of the emperor's nephew."

Through Irene's contacts in the emperor's court, Philip had previously been sent into the western section of the Byzantine Empire to serve with the emperor's nephew, John Comnenus. The large military force was to guard against a Norman effort to recapture Dyrrachium on the expedition to Jerusalem. It had not been forgotten in the Sacred Palace that the Normans, under Robert Guiscard and his son, Bohemond, had previously fought there, intending to move militarily against Constantinople.

"I would think that you would be happy that so many 'locusts' come to pester the Seljuk Turks," she said.

"If those at Nish are supposed to defeat the Moslems, the emperor had best buy mercenaries elsewhere," said Philip with scorn. "A more miserable looking flock of peasants have yet to be seen. It is reported by Governor

Nicetas that most did not have horses or suitable armor. They will quickly become an army of corpses."

The thought of death sobered her. "But surely they are not all peasants? What of those dreaded Normans I have heard so much talk of? Are they a myth?"

At the mention of the Normans, his eyes darkened. "No, they are not myth. But if the word drifting to us out of King Coloman's Hungary is true, those who come are not the manner of knights the emperor had in mind when he appealed to the Latin West. The Frank knight who waits at Nish says a large peasant throng comes behind him following a monk named Peter. But under whose gonfalon Peter marches, we do not know, nor does the governor. Whoever they are, they breed discord and rancor wherever they trod."

Would Nicholas be in such a group? she wondered. And yet, had not the knight assured Bardas that he had heard of him?

"New messengers from Governor Nicetas arrived today," said Philip. "The barbarians complain to him of the lack of food supplies along the route. Those with the monk have resorted to plundering the Hungarian towns and farms, killing any who resist their murderous ways."

Helena frowned. Such a horde of warmongers did not seem a fair company for her uncle, but perhaps living for so many years in the West had caused him to grow accustomed to their barbaric ways.

She forgot the peasants under Peter the Hermit and instead tried to imagine what the knights under the Western princes might look like. Did they eat raw swine's flesh? Some said they never washed their bodies or changed their clothing. What were the Normans like? Were they giants with long blond hair reaching to their broad, naked shoulders?

Helena shuddered. She knew little about the men that her Greek culture had classified as "arrogant Celts and monstrous barbarians."

Nor did she understand the difference between the peasants and the so-called knights of the Western barons. She had heard Philip mention names like Lord Bohemond, who ruled the Normans in southern Italy; Raymond of Saint-Gilles from the land of the Franks; and Robert, Duke of Normandy, son of dread William the Conqueror.

But the thought of the peasants going without adequate food in their trek across Europe aroused her sympathies. "I thought you and the emperor's nephew had carried out the government's plans? Were there not to be stores of provisions at the larger towns on the route so that the barbarians could buy themselves food?"

Philip looked impatient. "We did not expect them to use the northern route through Hungary, and the official date set for their departure was August. Is it our fault if the fools arrived before we expected them? It was their folly to journey north, instead of west by sea and the Roman road. Peasants used to doing the work of farmers in Europe should have known this was not the time of harvest."

Helena had heard that the imperial government had sent officials along the western route who would be provided with interpreters familiar with Latin to make contact with the Crusaders. Even the captains of Byzantine ships, whose task it usually was to watch for pirates in the Adriatic, were instructed to bring word back to Constantinople of approaching Crusader ships so the officials could be on hand to greet them and take them to Constantinople. Military forces on the land route were stationed at key locations to serve as escorts and discreetly to put the Crusaders back on the road to Constantinople if they began to forage out of bounds. But the great throng under Peter the Hermit had bypassed all this by journeying through Hungary.

"All is not ill news, Philip. Bardas has discovered from the Frank knight that Nicholas will be among them."

He appeared troubled at the mention of her uncle's name, and Helena thought she knew why. Bishop Constantine had turned the patriarch against Nicholas and arranged his excommunication. Since Constantine worked closely with Irene in securing Philip's successful career at the Sacred Palace, Philip would wish to avoid a conflict between his own interests and Helena's concern for her uncle. As yet, she had not told Philip about the letter Bardas had delivered to Nicholas at Piacenza.

"If Nicholas is with the monk Peter, then I shall go to Nish to meet him."

As expected, he looked at her as though she were beside herself, but Helena lifted her chin a little to show her determination. "I shall be no trouble, Philip. And I shall hire my own guards. Bardas has a number of men."

"Can you not wait for his arrival here at Constantinople?"

"No. What I shall say to him is better said away from the city."

He was alert, his dark eyes searching hers. Helena decided that if she expected Philip to help her reach Nish, she must confide in him. Sharing her information with him involved some risk, for he was bound both by honor and by obligation to Irene and the bishop. But Helena solaced herself with the thought that Philip had vowed his love to her.

"My mother yet lives but as a slave, perhaps in Tabriz. I have written Nicholas. I expect him to help me find her and free her. But neither Irene nor Bishop Constantine must know."

Stunned, Philip stared down at her, working to hold the restless stallion in place. "Lady Adrianna, alive? Are you certain?"

"As certain as the trustworthiness of my informers. Oh, Philip, I must find her!"

For a moment he said nothing, and his expression was muted. "Why did you not tell me sooner?"

She was reluctant to explain that she suspected his duty to Irene would risk the safety of her informers. "You were away in the Adriatic," she said simply. "It was not safe to write it in a letter."

She was about to add the more important reason for her silence, that Irene was not above confiscating her correspondence to see what she had written, but she did not wish to make tension between them.

Philip appeared satisfied with her answer although he looked troubled. "You were wise not to write such information. If your mother is alive, her enemies will not want you to find her. You are certain you told no one else of this?"

"Only Nicholas and Bardas, of course."

"Good. Say nothing to anyone until we speak with Nicholas."

"We will find this Peter the Hermit along the Danube. The barbarian knight told Bardas they would pass through Wieselburg and Vienna."

"It is a dangerous trek. You would do well to wait at Nish. But Helena," he said more gently, "informers can be wrong. Your mother was placed in the monastery at Corinth. Her death by cholera was sworn to by the abbess."

"She was wrong! Or perhaps Irene warned her not to speak on punishment of death."

"Helena!" Philip's jaw tensed.

She could see he was angry and he did not believe her. He still thought of her suspicions as those of an emotional child tormented by nightmares. She wanted to tell him what she thought of Irene and the bishop, but silenced her tongue. Words spoken against Irene only hardened his position in his mother's favor.

Helena drew in a small breath and said simply, "Will you take me to Nish with you?"

He scanned her. "I shall take you, but as for your mother, I only wish for you not to be hurt by false hopes. Some informers will say anything if you pay them in gold."

She wondered at his seeming impatience with her informers and the idea that her mother might live, but it was enough for now that he would take her to the Byzantine frontier.

"Can you be ready in the morning?"

"I shall be ready."

He turned his horse to ride back toward the gate. His dark eyes flashed. "Be certain Bishop Constantine will hold me accountable for this reckless venture. If I were not devoted to what pleases you, I would not risk it."

He rode off, and Helena watched him, her heart thudding in her chest. Devoted, was he? But he did not believe her. He was only humoring her.

But Nicholas would listen. Surely he would take her to Tabriz to find her mother. And when she was free again, she would bear witness to the treachery that Irene and the bishop had worked against her. Then Philip would see that Irene could not be trusted, that she would do anything to attain her ambitions—and Philip's.

CHAPTER 13
The Road to Wieselburg

✣ Tancred found it difficult to put Worms and its dark
memories behind him. Had the attack been an isolated
event, or the beginning of a plan to plunder every Jewish
colony along the Rhineland?

Jewish colonies had been established for centuries
along the trade routes of Western Europe. Their ancestors
were Sephardic Jews who had come from the ancient land
of Israel and the Mediterranean basin. After the destruction of Jerusalem and the Temple by the Romans in 70
A.D., the Jewish dispersion brought many to the Rhineland, Prague, and Budapest.

They were able to keep connections with their brethren in the land of Israel, as well as with those who had
migrated throughout the Byzantine Empire and the Arab
lands. Being neither Moslem nor Christian, the Jews built
an international trading bridge between the Christian and
Moslem lands. Their technical skill and biblical heritage
had also made them preeminent in the practice of medicine. They were allowed no civic rights, but the ecclesiasti-

cal authorities offered some weak protection because of their usefulness to the community.

But jealousy over their financial success, mingled with satanic hatred for the race of people who had brought Christ and the Scriptures into the world, made the Jews easy targets for attacks. Most assaults were hidden behind the guise of religion, which made it all the more troubling. For it was a religion far removed from biblical Christianity.

Tancred crossed the Rhine and came at evening to the town of Regensburg along the Danube River. Peter the Hermit had recently passed through, and talk of him was everywhere.

Searching through Wolfric's bag, Tancred found two gold coins. He could be thankful to the big lout for that, whatever else he thought of him.

The coins proved ample to buy clothing and boots and a night spent at an inn along the river where he relished a heated bath and a succulent leg of roast mutton.

But it did not take long for ugly news to surface. Worms was not the only location where the Jews had been attacked. There was talk of a campaign that would march through the Jewish colonies all along the Rhine, in cities like Cologne, Mainz, Trier, Rudesheim, Neuss, Wevelinghofen, Eller, Xanten, and Prague. Here in Regensburg, Tancred heard of certain men from Peter's followers who had also attacked the Jewish community before departing. While Peter had not endorsed the attack, he had added fuel to the ongoing fire by expecting the Jews to fund his expedition. Giving would assure them that the Crusaders would march on peacefully. But Peter's guarantees proved worthless.

Already, thought Tancred, his leadership over the mob was dwindling. The criminal element whom he had accepted as a part of his following was taking the upper hand. The Jews had given liberally of their resources, yet the attacks came.

Peter's tactics, as far as Tancred could see, bordered on extortion. To what advantage was the liberation of Jerusalem to the Jews? Why should Peter expect them to support the expedition? The rescue of the shrines from the infidel was a cause borne by the Latin church.

Tancred doubted that the Council at Clermont would have endorsed the biblical right of the Jews to their ancient homeland anymore than the Seljuk Turks' right.

There was talk of a chest full of gold coins, rumbling along on a wagon in the Hermit's army, most of it donated by the threatened Jews.

The talk darkened even more. Ten thousand Jews had been slain in Cologne. And a German priest named Gottschalk, who had first ridden with Peter from Cologne, decided to stay behind to raise a German army. He was successful, and his army of thousands traveled the main road that Peter had followed alongside the Rhine. News from those fleeing the massacre told of how Gottschalk's march through Bavaria had brought him into the kingdom of Hungary on his way east.

From what Tancred had already heard about the stalwart Hungarian king, Coloman, the Rhinelanders would not find sympathy. Any trouble in his kingdom would be harshly dealt with.

It was reported that another Rhineland leader called Volkmar had led his rabble army into Prague, also killing the Jews. He too was reported to have entered the kingdom of Hungary.

Tancred rose early the next morning, anxious to be out of the Rhineland and closer to his destination, Constantinople. Coming to the Danube, he followed its eastern bank toward Vienna and Wieselburg.

King Coloman had made contact with the Crusaders. Tancred saw patrols of fierce soldiers, most of them mercenaries of other races, Petchenegs and Bulgars, riding guard along the river, hoping to thwart trouble before it began.

The land along the Danube held ancient forests with bountiful game. Tancred had seen deer and several bear. The river was also the northern route to the East, so it did not surprise him that he came on a large formation of tracks, all pointing in one direction.

Whose army was it? Peter would be advancing along the Hungarian frontier. By afternoon, Tancred caught up with them. He recognized the gonfalon as Emich's.

His army had gathered many horses, and that meant a large number of mounted knights, not simple footmen. The smell of wood smoke hung in the air. Topping a rise, he was confronted by a camp spread along the river.

Emich's army had indeed grown in size. How many, more than ten thousand? From their tents and armor, he had no doubt they were the Rhinelanders.

He rode well out of sight and stopped, keeping back in the trees. The bulk of the army was spread out along the river, but guards were set up to watch the road. Not more than a hundred yards away a dozen Rhinelander knights were gathered about a fire, all of them well armed and wearing chain mesh. They looked like a rugged and dangerous lot.

Wishing no contact, Tancred skirted the camp, keeping to the trees and turning toward the main road only when he would not be seen. This was no hour for unsuspecting travelers to be in the open.

Not far ahead was the garrison fortress of Wieselburg, which was under Hungarian control. If he rode without stopping, he might arrive in time to let its governor know of the plundering army making toward its bridge.

He had ridden on the road only a few minutes when he heard the clatter of horses' hooves coming toward him from the direction of Wieselburg.

Tancred rode into the trees and waited. The sound of their approach was careless. He saw them now, two riders alone on fine-blooded horses, some of the best and fattest he had seen since leaving Sicily.

At first Tancred thought he was seeing a mirage. Astride the horses was a Byzantine bodyguard and a damsel, both ornately dressed and boasting wealth and pomp. The damsel, on a black stallion, wore shimmering silk beneath a deep blue hooded riding cloak trimmed with white fur. He could see luxuriant dark hair framing a sweetly alluring face. Her expression also displayed determination.

Whatever she was so set on, thought Tancred, it had brought her into danger of the worst kind.

From her exquisite appearance, he judged her to be of Greek nobility. Next to her rode the huge bodyguard.

Tancred suspected that the guard would, of Byzantine necessity, be a eunuch. His large head was shaven, his broad face with marble-black eyes was set in a grimace, as though he were displeased. He wore crimson trousers, a black tunic, a gold chain across his broad chest, and a jeweled scabbard housing a sword. There were also rings and bracelets of gold and silver about his arms. Tancred guessed he was a favorite of his young mistress.

No doubt she was spoiled and accustomed to having her own way, which would explain the folly of her "afternoon ride," if that were what it was. Tancred felt a sudden rise of impatience.

Any woman was at risk riding abroad at such an hour.

But a woman who was beautiful and dressed in silk and jewels? Yet she rode boldly down the road.

His blue-gray eyes narrowed. His gaze shifted back to the bodyguard.

What manner of fool was this eunuch to permit such a tempting spectacle? Tancred thought of the huge camp of Rhinelanders a few miles behind him. He doubted if more than a handful of men in the whole lot would let them pass without attacking.

Tancred rode into the center of the road and stopped, his hand on his sword hilt. The bodyguard scowled and unsheathed his blade. The damsel drew up somewhat nervously, scanning him.

Tancred bowed his head in her direction.

The bodyguard stood up in his stirrups with a threatening frown. "Step aside, vagabond!"

Tancred smiled slightly. At least she had an angry bear sworn to her protection. He looked from the girl to the menacing gaze of the big Greek, and said calmly, "If I were you, Byzantine, I would sheath that blade. Waving it about will get you into more trouble than you can handle."

The eunuch puffed up like a bullfrog and was about to sally forth when Tancred whipped his blade from his scabbard. "I suggest you call off your riled bear, damsel, unless you wish to lose him. I come in peace."

She watched Tancred with a curious but cautious gaze, then rested her horsewhip on the bodyguard's muscled arm. "Wait, Bardas."

Again she scanned Tancred, holding her nervous mount steady, showing good horsemanship. "Who are you, and what do you want?"

He did not care to explain. "This territory is swarming with Rhinelanders."

"So?"

He guessed she had not heard of Rhinelanders. "They have been terrorizing the towns along the Rhine."

He gathered his reins. "Damsel, you best get back to your Byzantine caravan, wherever it is, and tell the commander to ride back to Constantinople."

She raised her chin a little. "Why should I do that? I am here to make contact with an army of bar—I mean," she hastened to amend her word choice, "of Western knights riding to swear their loyalty to the emperor."

He knew what she had intended to call them, and his mouth curved a little. The Byzantines considered all Westerners barbarians. He casually gestured back to the rich green forests toward Vienna.

"You will find plenty of barbarians not far from here. And they will surely live up to their reputation. Camped nearby is a brigand-baron named Emich. He has come from the towns along the Rhine where his followers killed and looted. They will soon move east on this road toward Wieselburg. When they do," he warned, "not a man, woman, or child will be safe in their path."

He saw her expression of alarm, but she swiftly covered it and said with cool nerves that surprised him, "Philip the Noble is well able to handle a skirmish with peasants if it comes to that."

He smiled. "Brigand knights from the Rhineland are not an army of peasants. These are knights, with armor and horses. They will not be impressed with Byzantine splendor. And if your Philip the Noble thinks so, he is a fool."

Her lashes narrowed, and she scanned him again, this time coolly. "I would advise you, barbarian, not to say that to him."

Tancred refused to be pricked by her choice of words. He smiled again. "The name is Tancred."

Her gaze was cool. "Whatever it is, you are in our way."

Tancred held her gaze, refusing to ride to the side of the road.

The big Greek moved his horse forward. "Out of the way, vagabond, or I shall cut you down in the road here and now."

"I would not try it. Western knights do not wave swords about unless they intend to use them. I suggest you save it for the army behind us. You will need it."

At the word *army*, the eunuch and the damsel exchanged glances. She looked dubious now. "I seek a good man, a monk by the name of Peter the Hermit. Surely you do not speak of his army?"

Tancred wondered how she would know of Peter.

"We left Nish two weeks ago, and I was told he was in Vienna."

Nish, a Byzantine garrison town on the border with Hungary, was several weeks' ride away.

"Then you crossed purposes. By now he is nearing Semlin along the Sava River. Why do you seek him?"

She started to speak but seemed to think better of it. "That is no concern of yours. Why should we trust you?"

Tancred said, "If you ride on, heedless to the danger, your bodyguard will not be alive by morning. I cannot say the same for you."

Her eyes widened a little, but she quickly settled her features into a determined composure. She was not a woman easily threatened. His curiosity was baited. Why would a Byzantine damsel of nobility be riding the rugged eastern frontier asking about a simple monk like the Hermit? From her determination he judged the reason to be of some importance.

The eunuch bodyguard became agitated, gripping his hilt and glowering at Tancred as though he were to blame.

"You are certain they are brigands?" she asked, frowning.

"As certain as I care to be. And while there may be a few good knights among them, the majority are a bloodthirsty lot." He gestured, "Your stallion will make a worthy prize; they will take him. I know not from where you are, but I suggest you turn back and ride as swiftly as your horse can take you."

The woman glanced ahead, and for the first time her eyes showed reluctance. "We are camped not far from here. Philip the Noble does not know I am gone. I rode out hoping to meet some peasants who might know of Peter."

Tancred's gaze swerved to the bodyguard who shifted uneasily in his saddle. They were obviously here at her insistence.

"I search for a friend traveling with Peter."

"How many soldiers does the Noble have with him?"

She turned and looked at her bodyguard as though wondering if she should speak.

"Thirty," he grumbled.

"He brought you here with a mere thirty men?"

Her expression showed her dedication to the man named Philip. Her tone became cool. "I beg your pardon, sir knight. But you do not understand who Philip the Noble is. He is the son of the great but deceased General Lysander."

Lysander he had heard of. His uncle Rolf Redwan had served at his side as a mercenary soldier until the general's death.

"Philip too is a soldier," she told him.

He was silent.

She flipped her reins against her gloved palm. "One day he will stand next to the emperor," she stated with emphasis.

Tancred lifted a brow. The boast of military prowess by the Byzantines amused him; they were far better at hiring mercenaries to fight their battles for them. "I doubt if the Rhinelanders will be impressed."

Irritated by his smooth contempt, she made no reply.

"There is a campfire not far behind me," he explained. "I saw a dozen men, all heavily armored. By now they have seen us and are making plans. If you are lucky, they went first to tell their brigand-count. If not, they could attack at any moment. We have wasted time talking. Where is your camp? The Noble needs to be warned."

She appeared concerned now and turned her horse to ride, gesturing abruptly, "We are east of here, not far from Wieselburg."

She galloped ahead, and the bodyguard rode after her. Tancred glanced into the forest, then followed. If Philip the Noble had any sense, he would not stay the night in the woods but would ride swiftly to the safety of the Wieselburg fortress.

CHAPTER 14

The Byzantine Campfire

✠ Tancred was uneasy. He had spotted new tracks a half-mile back. Could the Byzantine camp have already been spotted by the Rhinelanders?

"Keep an eye on the trees," he told the bodyguard named Bardas. "And stay to the left of your mistress."

She heard them talking and said over her shoulder, "Do you truly think we are in danger?"

"I am certain of it," said Tancred.

The camp was less than a quarter of a mile ahead. He could hear the din of chopping wood and an occasional shouting voice, and he could smell wood smoke. He was certain Emich's marauding army was aware of the three of them and their vulnerability.

"Stay close," Tancred told her and galloped his horse forward. The woman was quick to keep pace, with her bodyguard on her left, glancing toward the shadowed trees.

They raced toward camp. Tancred's horse ran proudly, as though determined not to be outrun by the finer, stronger Byzantine stallions. They swept into the confine, scattering pine needles. Several men hurried toward them, and Tancred's eyes scanned the camp's defenses.

A man in uniform with a circular purple cloak tossed about his shoulders walked up.

Philip the Noble, Tancred thought.

His manner was immaculate, and he wore purple leggings bound with leather straps that matched his cloak. Although there was a lithe movement to his body that indicated trained muscles, Tancred suspected his military leadership was pure boast and ritual. The young Greek was handsome, and his Byzantine expression was imperialistic as his dark eyes raked Tancred.

"You are Peter the Hermit?" came his commanding question.

Tancred gave him a measured look. The young man was proud and would not take suggestions with grace.

"Rhinelanders picked up your trail. If you stay till morning, you will all be dead or slaves."

The cool dark eyes measured Tancred. "I am Philip the Noble, the official Byzantine representative of the Emperor Alexius Comnenus, and in command of—"

"You have little time to mount and ride to Wieselburg," came Tancred's easy voice.

Philip turned sharply toward the woman. "Helena, where did you find this Hungarian?"

Tancred looked at her. She sat rigid, obviously irritated by his approach to the Noble.

"I do not know who he is. He rode up warning of brigands."

She did not mention her ride along the road. As Tancred met her gaze, she turned her head away.

"I am Tancred Redwan from Sicily. And if you want to

live to enjoy Constantinople again, let us forget the formalities and ride for Wieselburg. If we leave now, we may make it safely to the bridge before dark."

Philip ignored his suggestion. "If you wish to eat and drink before you commence your journey, one of my men will take you to the cook."

He walked to the side of Helena's horse to assist her down, ending the conversation.

Tancred flipped the reins against his glove and studied Philip. Whatever the Noble wished to do with his head was his business, but Tancred did not like the way he was exposing the woman to danger.

"Where have you been, Helena? You must not wander from the camp," Philip was saying, taking her arm to walk toward the campfire.

"I did not go far, Philip, and—"

"There is no time for food," Tancred interrupted, still seated in the saddle and refusing to be dismissed. "Risk your life and your men's, but what of her?"

Philip stopped and turned abruptly, his lips hard, but before he could speak, another masculine voice interrupted from the soldiers who stood nearby.

"Pay him no heed, Lord Philip. This Hungarian coward does not realize who we are. We do not run from a pack of barbarian peasants with sticks and stones."

Turning his horse, Tancred confronted the Greek soldier. Tancred's expression was half-hidden beneath his helmet, but his voice was deadly calm.

"I was once accused of being a rabbi. That, I do not mind, Byzantine. Nor do I mind being called a Hungarian. But a coward? I am a Norman. And if challenged, I will fight to the death with honor."

At the word *Norman*, the soldier backed off and walked away. Tancred turned a steady gaze on Philip. "An army of Rhinelanders is out there, which carries more than sticks and stones. You are far outnumbered."

"An army? How do you know?"

He ignored the hint of accusation in Philip's voice, as though Tancred himself were in league with them. He said easily, "I was in Worms when Emich turned on the Jews. The streets were littered with nearly a thousand dead. And I saw his camp a few miles back. He has even more men now. Say, twenty thousand."

Philip looked doubtful. "We are expecting a noble monk by the name of Peter. These thousands you speak of may be his followers. The governor of Nish was informed that a large company was coming."

Tancred might have smirked at the description of the Hermit as "noble." But instead he replied, "The Rhinelanders do not follow the monk although it was his rhetoric that stirred them up in Cologne."

"I know the peasants under the Frank knight who arrived at Nish have pillaged and looted the villages here in Hungary. It is the reason the emperor sent me ahead to meet this man named Peter. We have food supplies at Nish, and a number of guides to escort him and his followers to Constantinople. But I know nothing of murderous Rhinelanders." He scanned Tancred again, warily. "You say you are from the Norman kingdom of Sicily?"

So he understood Norman rule. "Yes. Palermo."

"You travel alone?"

"Alone. I seek Constantinople, but not as a vassal to your emperor. It is personal business that takes me there," he said, thinking of Mosul.

Philip's wariness increased at the mention of Sicily. Only ten years earlier the Normans under Robert Guiscard had fought the Byzantines for control of Dyrrachium on the coast of the Adriactic. "If you do not swear fealty to the emperor, how can I trust you?"

"My father was Count Dreux Redwan. And I have an uncle," he explained of his adoptive father, "who serves your emperor."

At the word *count*, the woman turned to look at him, shielding her surprise. He felt her eyes flitter over him, but he did not look at her. Although her physical beauty was memorable, she was haughty and proud.

"Your uncle, what is his name?" asked Philip.

"Rolf Redwan."

Philip recognized the name and he appeared to ponder the information as if wondering what to do next.

Tancred was not surprised that he would know of his uncle. Rolf Redwan was a strong man with a sword, and having fought with the Byzantine general Lysander, his uncle's reputation was known.

"He is the seignior at the Castle of Hohms near Antioch," said Philip.

"Yes."

At the mention of the Castle of Hohms, the woman stepped from the shadows toward Tancred's horse. She looked up at him.

"Seigneur Rolf Redwan is your uncle?"

"And my adoptive father. You know him, Lady?"

Her chin lifted, and in the glow coming from the fire, her loveliness was undisputed. "I am heiress of the castle," she stated. "Soon, he will serve me."

She was spoiled but possessed a strength of purpose in her behavior that he guessed was not easily controlled by Philip or anyone else.

"Truly?" he said. "Then he will serve you well, and you are honored to have him."

She lifted a brow, showing that his reply was not quite the response she had expected.

Evidently, thought Tancred, amused, she had expected him to be the one honored that his uncle was permitted to serve her.

"I ride there to meet him, Lady. I will be certain to express your pleasure to him at the use of his sword to guard your castle from brigands."

She watched him with a cautious but curious look, as though not knowing how to accept his boldness.

"I have not met your uncle." She touched the rim of her fur-lined, hooded cloak. "I have only heard of him. He serves my legal guardians, who have jurisdiction over the castle until my marriage."

"The Castle of Hohms is a worthy dowry. I am sure your guardians have an army of strong seigniors from which to choose your husband. Many warriors would battle for such a prize."

She dismissed him with a mere turn of her head. As his eyes found Philip, the Noble was watching him in a cool, speculative way.

"If you visit Seigneur Rolf Redwan, you will also find that Seljuk Turks have their eyes on the castle."

"I know of them. But we waste time talking. At the moment the Rhinelanders threaten all our heads, not the Turks. I suggest we ride to Wieselburg."

The Noble's expression hardened. For reasons of his own he refused to agree. "I thank you for your warning. Stay if you wish. Eat and sleep, but come morning I will ride on toward Vienna."

"By morning, you will be surrounded. I ride on tonight." He turned toward Helena, who stood with her back toward him. "Lady, I will take you with me to Wieselburg if you wish."

155

A small gasp escaped her lips as she turned to him, and her eyes widened a little over his boldness. Bardas took a step forward, about to unsheathe his sword.

"Enough, Bardas," said Philip. "The Norman was only trying to be gallant."

Tancred was not certain if Philip believed his own words. Philip's gaze was cold and even. "However, Norman, Helena of the Nobility is under my jurisdiction. You need not concern yourself."

Tancred recognized that glint in his eyes. The man would have no one near the damsel but himself.

"If you are wise, Lady, you will reconsider."

She turned and walked toward the fire, keeping her back toward him. Tancred felt a rise of irritation.

Did she think he would rob her of her jewels? Perhaps steal her away to some mangy hovel of barbarian design?

Tancred's mouth turned; he glanced at Philip who stared at him with icy dignity.

"As you wish." He looked over at her and said, "Au revoir, Lady.

Turning away from them, he rode his horse to the river to drink.

Tancred would ride to warn the Hungarian governor of Wieselburg, which he believed Emich's brigand army intended to attack. Stripping his horse of the saddle for a few minutes of rest, he rubbed him down with a handful of dry grass. The ride would be long and hard if he were to stay ahead of the Rhinelanders. His horse was in poor condition. He thought longingly of Alzira.

"You will have to make good time," he told the horse, who snorted its complaint.

As he rubbed down his horse, Tancred looked around Philip's camp. Most of the soldiers were mercenaries of other races, Petchenegs, Bulgars, Hungarians . . . less than half were Byzantine.

But Philip the Noble appeared to not know what he was doing. The supplies were scattered and without adequate guards, while Philip and those close to his command loitered easily about the fire drinking from goblets.

Easy targets for arrows, thought Tancred.

Nor was Philip intent on doing anything to prepare for an attack. He stood by the fire in his Byzantine finery. As he raised his goblet to drink, it glimmered in the firelight.

Tancred felt his annoyance growing. It was one thing to kill himself through his blunder; it was quite another to take so many soldiers with him and the woman.

She too stood by the fire, and when he looked at her, she turned away.

So she is the heiress of the Castle of Hohms. That placed her at risk even if she survived the night.

Helena, still wearing her hooded cloak, sipped the hot brew brought from Cathay and kept her back toward the Norman mercenary. *What if terrible brigands are waiting out there in the wooded darkness? But surely Philip would know if there was peril. He would not unnecessarily risk our lives. The Norman is arrogant.*

Despite herself, her curiosity over him grew. No doubt he ate raw meat and was a savage. She turned her head only a little and glanced in his direction.

Surely he lied. He was not the son of a count. And the Norman seignior guarding the Castle of Hohms, was he truly an uncle to this man? If he were telling the truth about the castle, perhaps he could also be trusted about the Rhinelanders.

Another glance, and she was surprised to see him

speaking in low tones to Bardas. Bardas listened with reluctance, then walked away.

The Norman had finished rubbing down his horse and was inspecting its hind legs. She knew about horses; they were bred on the family villa in Athens for racing at the Hippodrome. It was at Athens that Bardas had secretly taught her to ride well, despite his displeasure over the matter.

She guessed what the Norman warrior was thinking as he went about inspecting his horse. Casting a glance about her, she noted that Philip had taken Bardas aside to rebuke him for the afternoon's incident on the road. Normally she would have intervened, reminding Philip that her slave did not belong to him. But the distraction gave her a moment to slip away.

Dare she speak to the Norman barbarian? Would he think her too friendly? No matter. She must.

She stepped back from the firelight into the darkness. Then she made her way unobtrusively through the camp to where the Norman was stooped on the bank of the Danube, inspecting the horse's front hoof.

Helena was certain he had heard her come up, for he seemed attune to the slightest noise about him. She stood there, her heart thudding. Unexpectedly, although she had tried to fight against it, she feared what may lurk in the darkness of the trees about their camp. Silence surrounded them, broken by the wood in the fire that popped and sizzled, sending up sparks.

A slight breeze touched her face, and she shivered, but not from cold.

"You are wrong about Philip the Noble. He is not irresponsible."

"Why should it matter what I think?"

"It matters not at all."

"Then why did you come to tell me?"

"I will not have you think we Byzantines are fools."

"By morning it will not matter what I think."

"Are you always this rude?"

"I am but a barbarian. Do you expect chivalry?"

She drew in a little breath, her hands forming fists at her sides. She was about to whirl and flounce back to the fire, but something held her there. She said nothing, and neither did he.

Calmly he went on checking the skinny horse. She wanted to smirk, to denounce him and the horse as pathetic creatures.

"I shall ignore your manners, barbarian. Tell me, are you certain they will attack us?"

He did not look up. "I am certain. And either Philip knows little about the reality of battle, or he is mad with pride." He straightened and stood, looking down at her. "And his Byzantine superiority will not deliver you from the robber-baron."

Helena looked into stormy blue-gray eyes that were too intense beneath dark lashes. "You make up your mind quickly, Norman."

"Experience is a wise teacher, Lady. I was a prisoner of the Rhinelanders for a short time before I escaped. It is not something I would see others taste." He gestured his head in the direction of Philip. "Not even him."

Helena was curious about his being a prisoner, but he said no more and turned to saddle the horse. With his back toward her for a moment, she scanned him.

He was young yet possessed a sureness about himself that bordered on arrogance. Powerfully built, he was a warrior to be reckoned with. His rugged tunic, worn over chain mesh, was black, as was his riding cloak. He wore a belted scabbard and a helmet of some nondescript origin.

As though attune to her thoughts, he walked to the edge of the Danube and removed his helmet, quickly splashing his face and head. She could see that his hair was not long like those arrogant Celts she had noticed with the Frank knight, Walter Sans-Avoir. It was cut short to the nape of his neck, and when wet, it curled just a little. The color was dark brown, tinged with blond.

"I am ready to ride to Wieselburg. Are you coming?"

She managed a little laugh. "You are the most arrogant man I have yet to meet. Do you truly think I would ride off with you?"

Her words evidently did not disturb him, for a look of cynical amusement showed about his mouth. "You too make up your mind quickly," he said. "If I bother to take you to Wieselburg, Lady, it is out of knightly duty; not because I have designs on your favors." He folded his arms across his chest. "And I have no intention of involving myself with a woman, no matter how lovely."

She let out a breath. Of all the audacity . . .

"And if I judge your Philip to be a fool," he was saying, "then I estimate you to be spoiled and headstrong. You think your nobility will guarantee your safety here in the West? The brigands will mock your superiority. They will be looking at that gold pendant about your throat and the pearls in your hair."

Her hand flew to her hood. She had been careful to keep it up from the moment they had met on the road.

"How did you know there were pearls? I have been careful to—" she stopped.

"Careful to keep them hidden? What else would a Byzantine woman of nobility adorn her hair with?"

She whirled to go back to the fire, when his voice halted her.

"It is not me you should fear. I have yet to rob beautiful women of their tinkling ornaments. Besides," he said carelessly, "in Sicily I am heir to castle, lands, and galleons. Why I should care for a handful of baubles?"

Challenged, she whirled back to him, her cheeks warm. "I do not fear you, barbarian."

"No?"

"I am not afraid," she repeated, but even as she said it, she knew it was not quite true. Something about him hinted of danger, but she would not analyze it now.

"I said you were headstrong. I think you are also too wise to make the error of trusting Philip's military judgment."

The insult to Philip nettled her. It was true she wondered if Philip might not be a trifle lax when this stranger was so certain of brigands. But not trust him?

"I trust Philip with my life," she stated.

"An error. By morning you may hate him."

Helena knew a real dart of fear. Her fingers tightened about the folds of her ankle-length cloak. "You are trying to frighten me, to frighten all of us."

"With good reason."

"Perhaps you are working with those brigands," she accused, not believing so, but she could think of little else to say to defend herself against his words.

"I shall allow you ten minutes to get your horse," he said casually.

The audacity of such an ultimatum caused her cheeks to burn. "So you truly expect me to ride off with you?"

"To save your life? Why not? Besides, do you not have your menacing bodyguard in the red trousers to protect you from me?"

She could not see his expression, but she heard the goading amusement in his voice and guessed that, despite the dilemma they were all in, he was enjoying her indignation.

"I would not think of riding off and leaving Philip."

"He should not have brought you here. He is ignorant of the land and its people."

She thought of how easily she and Bardas had been able to slip away unnoticed. But it was unfair to blame Philip.

"He did not know I rode off," she argued.

"He should have. Is he not in command? He should have guarded you with ten soldiers. Even now you are alone with me, yet he does not make it a point to know. I could easily ride off with you, and who would stop me?"

She stood without moving, hearing the wind through the pine branches, not daring to breathe. Had she underestimated him? Perhaps he was not to be trusted after all. But no sooner did she think this than he moved his head, and in the starlight she could see the smile.

Helena's strength rallied, and she gave a little laugh. "On that pathetic horse? It would fall down dead between here and the fortress!"

"Yes, he is to be pitied, is he not?" He sighed.

"Such a horse, sir knight!" she mocked lightly, tossing her head. "If you intend to steal any woman of worth, you had best come up with some of the rich bounty you say belongs to your father, the count in Italy."

"Sicily."

She waved her hand with disdain. "Italy, Sicily, it matters not to me. I am certain the streets of both reek with smelly barbarians and arrogant knights."

"And monks. Do not forget them. That reminds me, why would a woman of spoiled nobility be seeking Peter the Hermit?"

She was still provoked. "It is none of your affair, but an uncle of mine journeys with him."

He gave a laugh. "An uncle of yours? With the little monk riding a donkey? Now this is perplexing."

"Not baffling at all. It so happens my uncle was a bishop at the Byzantine seaport of Bari on the southern coast of Italy. You see?" she mocked. "I do know something of your barbaric land."

He folded his arms and smiled. "I marvel that your cultured mind has room for anything outside Constantinople. Then let me enlighten you a trifle more, for Bari is no longer a Byzantine seaport but is under the control of my barbarian kin, the Normans."

"So it is. But it does not take superiority to scatter sheep," she quipped. "Hungry wolves are always a menace."

He laughed softly. "This uncle of yours who is a bishop, he is with the monk Peter?"

Helena hesitated, wondering if she should go on. She owed this man no explanation.

"Yes. The Frank knight who first arrived at Nish said Peter was not far behind him with a large following. He was certain that a bishop named Nicholas was with the monk. It is imperative I find my uncle, so I have come seeking him, for reasons I do not care to share with you."

He made no immediate comment. As the silence grew, she realized his expression had changed, and he was staring at her.

"Nicholas?" he repeated softly.

"Yes, Nicholas."

"From Bari?"

Helena stirred uneasily. Why was he so intent? "Yes, from Bari. But he left there some years ago."

A breath escaped his lips. "Ah."

Helena scanned him, for it sounded as though he knew Nicholas, and of course that was impossible.

He said, "I dimly recall Nicholas mentioning a niece in Constantinople, but I had no idea."

Her lips curved into a mocking smile. "And, of course, barbarian, you know my uncle?"

"I know your uncle, yes. If we speak of the same Nicholas, he is my godfather."

She could not restrain a laugh. "You are not only arrogant but can be quite amusing."

"The Nicholas I speak of is a bishop at Monte Casino in southern Italy. He left the Greek church over matters of doctrine. Am I correct?"

It was her turn to stare. It could not be . . .

"Yes," she breathed. "But how—"

"A long story of how I first met Nicholas. One that must wait. Well, well . . ." He offered a deep bow at the waist. "And now that I know you are his niece—"

"Ah, but I do not know that you are truly his godchild," she interrupted too sweetly.

He ignored her remark. "So I must insist you come with me to Wieselburg. How could I ever face Nicholas again, knowing I had left his spoiled, willful niece to a pack of Rhinelanders?"

"Oh, do spare me your chivalry, sir knight," she mocked lightly. "On seeing my uncle, I shall explain your riding away was a necessity ordered by the Noble, but one I wholeheartedly agreed with."

But beneath her light banter, she wondered, *Could he be speaking the truth? Was it a ruse? But how could he have known about Nicholas's reasons for going to Monte Casino?*

He smiled too politely. "Nay, Lady. I cannot. You see, despite your irksome behavior, I owe as much to Nicholas. Do get your horse, or shall I get it for you?"

There was a movement behind her, and Philip stepped forward surrounded with several soldiers. His eyes were fixed angrily on Tancred.

Helena whirled. Seeing his expression, her heart sank. Now there would be trouble for certain.

In alarm, she rushed toward Philip. "No, wait! It is not as you think."

But he pulled her behind him. "Bardas, take your mistress away."

"He is a friend of Nicholas!" said Helena, not certain she believed it herself but wishing no trouble. "Count Redwan is, um, his godchild."

"Godchild!"

Philip threw back his head and laughed, but his eyes were cold. "Ah, Norman, now I have heard everything."

"Yes, a godchild. Does that not make me related in some way to Lady Helena?" Tancred asked dryly.

Helena stood without moving. Not only did she not trust Philip's temper, but also a quick glance at the Norman showed a cool and deadly stare, despite his irony.

"This barbarian is a humorous liar," stated Philip. "And if he does not climb on his horse and ride out now, I shall see to it he does not speak his lies to another woman, ever."

Helena's breath stopped. She knew what to expect, and she was right. She heard the unmistakable whisper of the Norman's blade slipping from its sheath. Starlight fell in a faint gleam along the metal. Her heart pounded, taking her breath away. The soldiers about Philip drew their swords.

"Suppose you make good your threat, Byzantine," said Tancred.

Helena broke free from Bardas and rushed between them. "Stop it. Stop it!"

She looked at Philip and saw the cold, hard expression. "He did not insult me. And I will have none of this!"

Philip was unrelenting. "Take her away, Bardas."

"Then you intend to fight me?" came the Norman's calm voice.

Helena whirled toward him, her eyes on his sword. But she need not have feared, for Philip said with disdain, "My life and plans are too important to me to waste on a duel. But if you do not get on your horse and ride out now, I shall have you arrested."

"Mistress—" came Bardas's whisper, his hand on her arm. But again she shook free and boldly walked up to the Norman.

"Please go. I cannot ride out with you, nor would I if I could."

His eyes met hers. Despite being outnumbered, she saw no fear in his handsome features.

"Bardas," she ordered, "bring one of my horses for the Norman. This one will die before he reaches the fortress."

Philip jerked toward her. "Helena—"

But she confronted him, composed. "He knows Nicholas. It is the least I can do for him."

She gestured to Bardas, who stood gaping, his bulging eyes on the Norman.

"You heard me," she commanded.

The Norman's voice interrupted from behind her, "It is not necessary, Lady."

"It is." She turned and looked up at him, uncertain of his expression, for it was concealed. "I do not like cruelty to horses," she stated indifferently. "This one, why, it will die if you ride him hard."

"You owe me nothing."

"Nevertheless I shall loan you one of mine."

She looked to see if Bardas had gone to fulfill her command. He had. She refused to look at Philip and imagined he was furious.

"I shall lend him to you," she said to Tancred airily. "I will take him back at the fortress of Wieselburg."

She said *fortress* with deliberation to show him she intended to survive, despite his warnings of brigands. Anything to avert trouble now between him and Philip.

For a moment Tancred did not reply, and she could not guess what he was thinking.

"Then I am in your debt. I will take care of your horse."

Helena turned and walked back to Philip. His dark eyes were like ice as they fixed on her. She took his arm. "He is leaving. Shall we go back to the fire?"

Tancred stood in the darkness, watching as they walked across the camp. She sat down, scooping up a silver cup. Philip said something to her that she did not answer. A moment later he strode away angrily.

Tancred turned as Bardas came up leading a sleek, well-muscled black stallion. Mute, the eunuch's broad face was sullen.

Tancred surveyed the stallion. He was handsome indeed. Strong limbs and feisty, he was bred for speed and endurance.

"Tell your mistress I am grateful. And that I will not forget her generosity."

Bardas gave a sniff of contempt and dropped the reins into Tancred's hand. "His name is Apollo." He turned on his heel.

When Tancred reached for the horse, it put its velvety nose into his hand. He spoke, giving it a few pats. "Alzira would be impressed."

He threw his saddle on the horse, and it took the load eagerly, as if wishing to be off. He took his time, almost reluctant to leave now that the way was open before him. He stepped into the stirrup and mounted, turning to ride. He glanced toward the campfire. The damsel did not look in his direction.

Tancred walked the stallion along the bank of the Danube into the darkness and drew up to listen, shutting out the din of the camp to hear only the sound of the forest.

He rode forward, hearing the water from the river lapping the bank. The starlight fell on his path.

For several minutes Tancred sensed that something lay to the east that the stallion did not like. Tancred let him pull away, trusting the horse had caught the scent of a brigand.

And then he heard the scuffle of horses walking. A group of riders was coming from the forest toward the river bank. He rode into the trees. The night was warm and quiet; the sounds came closer. He kept his hand on his sword hilt, ready.

CHAPTER 15

Under the Pine Branches

✤ Tancred saw the approaching riders coming single file along the bank. For an instant each Rhinelander was starkly outlined against the sky, then disappeared into the darkness.

Scouts, he thought.

They were trying to discover how many soldiers Philip had. As soon as they learned that they outnumbered him, they would attack.

Tancred rode the stallion toward Wieselburg but could not go on. He turned from the road into the thick woods and rode back toward the camp. The late night sky glittered like a thousand jewels.

He dismounted, tied his horse to one of the bushes, and stretched out against a tree. There he waited; he knew what he would do. The last sound he heard before he fell asleep was the stallion's contented munching close beside him.

The attack came without warning, a rush of charging horses. Rhinelanders in armor and helmets, swinging axes, maces, and swords, came and came again, each time killing several more of Philip's soldiers.

Lying on his stomach in a corner of the camp, Philip the Noble, son of the renowned General Lysander, tasted the bitterness of defeat. Sweat trickled down his face into his eyes. From time to time he wiped his palms against his silk shirt. A pang of cold fear clutched at his belly.

On his right, a brigand lay dead in the dirt. This was the only enemy he had killed in the attack. Dead men littered the camp ground, most of them his own soldiers. The horses, as far as he knew, were stolen, so was the supply wagon.

He did not know where Helena was and feared to move from his position long enough to search. Had they taken her? He had heard no screams, but the cries of battle and the neighing of horses would have silenced her scream from reaching him.

He cursed bitterly in Greek and tasted the sweat on his upper lip. This was not the kind of battle he had expected to fight, nor had he thought to see so many barbarians swarming over the camp.

Like filthy insects they crept and crawled everywhere, killing, plundering, taking no pity. They were wild men, fierce, and determined.

How many of his own men did he have left, if any? He thought of the Norman and gritted his teeth.

Meanwhile Helena could hardly breathe beneath the heavy pile of pine brush that Bardas had covered her with. She had thought him mad when he had awakened her from sleep during the night and silently beckoned her to follow him. He had brought her some distance from the camp into the dark forest of tall pine where she saw several of their horses tied. He had pointed out a small hollow dug in the earth and, with an apologetic expression, implored her to lie down so he could cover her up with branches.

She knew Bardas too well to question the look of fear in his eyes. He had believed the Norman about the brigand Rhinelanders and was taking no chances.

As he piled the last branches on her, he whispered, "Make no sound, mistress. Stay here until I return for you, whenever and however long it may be. Do not come out, no matter what noise of battle you may hear. And if Christ be merciful to you and me, we shall meet again."

Helena had not been there long when she heard the crazed shouts of war, and the thundering of horses' hooves. How many? A hundred? Five hundred? She lay there without moving, terrified.

The noise came ever closer. She feared the horses would be discovered, and some brigand would find the blanket of pine branches too suspicious.

But no one came. Only the shouts of the dying reached her. It seemed to go on forever. How long would it last? Would they kill everyone? Philip! Her eyes stung with hot tears. And Bardas, would he return? And if not?

She had the horses, that was all. Could she manage to find her way back to Wieselburg? Her legs were cramped from lying in such an uncomfortable position, and terror tried to master her mind. The spicy scent of pine filled her nostrils, and her mouth tasted dirt.

Then she heard footsteps. Bardas was coming back. Her heart pounded.

The branches were lifted away, and debris fell on her

face. A glimmer of dawn greeted her, as she stared up at a Rhinelander in armor.

She wanted to scream, but no sound came from her dry throat. She stared. Those blue-gray eyes . . .

The Norman warrior looked down at her. He was rugged, handsome, and dreadful all at once in his Rhineland armor. The helmet was conical, the leather jerkin ringed with pieces of steel, and he now carried a bow and several other weapons he had taken from the brigands. A slight smile touched his mouth as he scanned her.

"I see you survived the night. You were not too uncomfortable I hope?"

She ignored that and sat up, brushing the leaves and dirt from her cloak. He reached a hand to help her as she scrambled to her feet, but she refused it.

Although trembling with relief, her voice was accusing. "You! Now that it is over, you come!"

His face revealed no emotion. "If Nicholas were not a friend, I would not have returned at all. He would never forgive me if I did not rescue his niece from brigands. I see Bardas brought the horses as I asked. Let us go."

She halted, stunned. *As he had asked?* She watched as he went for the horses.

In a moment he was back, seemingly undisturbed at the carnage that had taken place during the night. Helena pointed to the small shallow in the ground where she had lain buried.

"Was this your idea?"

"You are alive."

Helena refused to show her admiration. She turned away and started toward the clearing that had been their camp.

What of Philip? Was he alive? Was he wounded? And Bardas? She began to run when Tancred's hand caught her arm, turning her about face. His eyes narrowed as they met hers.

"Do not go there. I do not want a fainting woman on my hands."

"I do not faint."

"Few are alive," he said more quietly and watched to see her reaction.

For a moment she did want to faint. *Few were left alive.* Her eyes searched his, questioning, for she was afraid to ask.

"Fear not. Your courageous Noble, son of General Lysander, lives to fight another battle. But he is wounded."

"Wounded!"

"It is nothing. Only a surface scratch. Your eunuch is tending him now."

Her knees went weak with relief, and for a moment she felt herself going down.

He caught her about the waist, and Helena quickly stiffened, pulling away. "I am well, thank you, Norman."

"Good. We have a long distance to ride, and the Rhine-landers will be swiftly on our trail."

Her fear mounted again. "On our trail? But why? They have stolen everything; they think us all dead!"

"Because if my guess is right, they will try to take Wieselburg. If we get there first, the town may have a chance to survive the bloodshed and looting. Can you ride? You are all right?"

"Yes, but the others?"

"They will manage. As soon as I bandage your courageous Byzantine commander, we will go."

"You bandage him? I am surprised you would lift your hand to help him."

Her barbs did not appear to disturb him. His smile was disarming. "I am also a student physician."

Irritated by what she assumed to be a cynical remark, she made no reply. But despite her anger, she understood that had it not been for his instructions to Bardas, she would have been taken captive.

CHAPTER 16

On the Road to Wieselburg

✦ The fortress town of Wieselburg was on the Hungarian frontier not many miles past Vienna. Philip the Noble was stern and silent during the ride. Tancred knew Philip had not forgiven him for being the man to save Helena. The idea that Tancred had been right and that Philip had lost all but eight of his soldiers goaded his pride. Philip had not admitted his error but leaned emotionally on Helena for pity.

Tancred liked him less and less. It was wearisome to watch the damsel coddle his wounded spirits.

"When will you stop feeding his pride by making excuses for him?" Tancred asked her.

"Philip the Noble needs no excuses."

"Men are dead because of his vanity."

"And you are being boastful."

"Because I was right? Those men who died were good soldiers. They deserved to live."

"All men deserve to live," she said stiffly.

"Not all. But these were wasted on a battle to serve the vanity of a weak man."

He noticed her hands tighten on the horse's reins.

"You do not know how important Philip the Noble is in the Sacred Palace."

"Perhaps he should stay there in his silk finery, amid goblets and slaves who attest to his greatness. The real world of warriors would only mirror his lack of backbone."

"Ride ahead, barbarian. I do not wish for your company nor for your words of wisdom."

"He is a man ruled by ambition."

"Perhaps it is not ambition made of his volition but of others'."

"Always protecting him. What do you see in him?"

"I have known Philip since we were children. We were both placed under the guardianship of certain people in the Sacred Palace. I intend to marry him."

"Most obviously. Why else would you draw him under your wing?"

"Go away."

"A weak man driven to greatness, whether by his own or others' desires, is a risk to himself and those around him."

"A risk! Because of those despicable Rhinelanders? How was he to know there were so many? He was brave, determined to fulfill his mission to find Peter the Hermit. And he thought he could protect his men and me. He knew how much I wanted to find Nicholas—"

"Then ask Nicholas what he thinks of Philip."

"I need ask no one, not even Nicholas. Least of all you! Do you not know that there are those who would see him stand beside the emperor?"

"Then the Seljuk Turks may soon sit on your emperor's throne."

"While Philip the Noble stands beside the Emperor Alexius Comnenus, you, Norman barbarian, will bow."

"Nay, damsel, I have more respect for the honor of God than to bow to dogs in royal purple."

She jerked the horse's reins and galloped ahead of him.

Bardas left Philip's side to ride up to Helena. He cast Tancred a look of daggers.

Tancred understood Bardas' jealous care for his mistress and had nothing against the big Greek. He sensed that, while Bardas did not trust Tancred's Norman ancestry, he grudgingly respected his abilities and was grateful for the success of Tancred's plan.

They had ridden hard and long into the night, stopping only for a quick meal and to rest the horses. At dawn they neared Wieselburg.

As they rode single file along the bank of the Danube, white cranes spread their wings and took off from the tall grasses. Under a lavender daybreak, the Danube looked gray-blue. By noon they rode beneath a hot sun in the clear summer sky.

Tancred kept some distance from the others as he rode ahead, partly to scout and partly because he knew they resented his leadership, especially Philip. Tancred knew Philip's wound was superficial but that the role of sorely injured military commander proved useful to hide behind.

Philip claimed to the remaining soldiers that he had fought single-handedly long and hard, making himself into some gallant martyr who had been willing to die alone to protect his charge.

Yet when Tancred had entered the camp after the

Rhinelanders had ridden away, he had found Philip hiding under a burned wagon, far removed from the battle. Only one brigand lay nearby whom Philip had stopped with his sword, while the ground farther in the thick of things had been littered with dead.

Tancred was certain Philip had withdrawn shortly after the battle began and had abandoned his men. If it was as Helena said, that certain powerful Byzantines sought Philip's advancement, he would not lose his military position. Philip would be certain to boast of his heroic stand; none of his men would dare to disagree.

Riding toward a clearing where a number of trees had been axed, Tancred stopped behind some trees to search the area unobserved. Not more than a hundred yards away a pitched battle seemed to have taken place. Broken lances and pikes, clothing, and parts of human bodies were strewn about.

What group had fought here? Surely not Peter the Hermit's? Had the Wieselburg garrison fought here, and with whom?

Later, they came to the junction of the Leitha River and the Danube. Here the walled fortress of Wieselburg stood somber gray against the sky. The fortress, Tancred noticed, was flanked by swamps.

Near the branch of the Danube, they came upon a wooden bridge built to cross to the gate of the town. A group of mercenaries patrolled the bridge. They were alert and drew up in an offensive position as Tancred left the others to walk his horse toward them.

"I would seek an audience with your governor. I have ill news he must hear."

The thin, hawk-like face of the soldier in command showed no expression as he scanned Tancred, then the others farther back. His fierce black eyes took in Tancred's armor, recognizing it as belonging to the Rhineland.

Had that pitched battle then been with Rhinelanders? wondered Tancred.

"Who are you? Who do you represent?"

"I represent myself. I am Tancred Redwan from Sicily. These," he said gesturing behind him, "are my friends. We seek shelter, and I seek an audience with whoever is in command. Trouble comes behind us."

"We have already confronted brigands."

"You will battle even more of them. There is little time to talk. Let us through."

Before the soldier could question him further, Philip rode up, sitting straight in his saddle, his cape thrown back over his shoulder. His handsome expression was hard, his dark eyes flickering with muted disdain.

"I am Philip the Noble of Constantinople, representative of the emperor. I demand to be taken to the governor."

Philip had emerged from the cocoon he had huddled in for the last day and night. Once again he was the Greek commander in control, daring anyone to question his authority. Tancred cared not at all; if the man wished to strut, let him. But he would also see the governor and offer him his own report of the danger at hand.

Bardas galloped up, pointing behind him. "The barbarians are behind us, Master Philip. Look!"

One of the Wieselburg guards had already spotted the army and was shouting orders from the tower wall.

Tancred's gaze swept the clearing. Emerging from the forest along the ridge, a huge army moved forward toward the bridge and Wieselburg. Tancred's heart lay heavy. This was no horde on foot with pikes, but a well-equipped army of many thousands.

Behind them came creaking wagons pulled by strong oxen, and what Tancred saw convinced him that Wieselburg was in mortal danger. Siege-engines, those movable towers that a besieging army push up against a city's wall, filled with five stories of soldiers to storm the ramparts.

How many men did the Hungarian garrison have?

Philip saw the formidable engines and said quietly to Tancred, "Let us hope the governor is well-equipped. I would give anything now if I had Greek fire."

Although many in the West did not know about Greek fire, Tancred had heard of it from Nicholas. Its ingredients were secret, known only to the Byzantines, but it was said by some to be a mixture of quick lime, sulfur, and petroleum. The catapulted missiles exploded into a rain of fiery flames on the enemy.

Greek fire had been used successfully by Constantinople for centuries, defeating great armies outside her beleaguered walls. Greek ships used it to guard the waters surrounding the city, for the missiles even set the water on fire.

Helena rode up, the wind tugging at her hooded cloak. "Who are they? Are they the same men who attacked us?"

"They bear no gonfalon," said Philip, narrowing his gaze to scan the oncoming army.

"Is it possible they could be friendly?" she asked. "Perhaps it is Peter the Hermit."

"No," said Tancred, "it is not the monk. This is the same group that wrought havoc all along the Rhine. It is Count Emich. But he has gathered even more fighting men than he had before. Those siege-engines he did not have when he first arrived at Worms. Someone powerful has aided him. I can only think of one person who might have, Godfrey of Bouillon, although the feudal lord may not know he has aided a vicious destroyer."

"Maybe the siege-engines are to be used against the Seljuk Turks," she said.

Tancred exchanged glances with Philip.

"No, my dear Helena," said Philip, "they are meant for one purpose. The count and his followers intend to conquer Wieselburg for themselves. Come, ride quickly over the bridge. It may be that the governor has an army equal to the task confronting us."

Tancred doubted it.

CHAPTER 17

Wieselburg Fortress

✤ From every key position about the fortress, soldiers appeared, although there were not nearly enough to fight Emich. Could they hold out against him?

The ragtag group from the Byzantine camp rode across the wooden bridge to the sound of the hollow thud of horses' hooves, the Danube flowing beneath. As they approached the gate, it swung open, and soldiers stood armed with weapons, silent and suspicious.

Tancred and Philip led the others through. The captain in charge brought them up the steps of the square tower overlooking the wall. The governor waited, staring out at the army of Rhinelanders gathering across the river near the forest's edge.

The Hungarian official proved older than Tancred had expected. His hair was gray, but he was strong and carried himself with dignity, a riding cloak about his shoulders.

"Welcome back to Wieselburg, Lord Philip, Lady Helena. It is of concern you arrive at a dark time."

"We saw the ruins of another army," said Philip.

"Another Rhinelander. The cry for a Crusade against the Turks has also fed the appetites of jackals. I understand your Byzantine troops were also attacked, Excellency."

Philip paced, one hand on his wounded shoulder, as he outlined his stand against the Rhinelanders resulting in the death of his men. Tancred remained silent. Philip's courage was overstated.

His gaze moved to Helena. She walked to the other side of the keep, looking out.

"I have but eight soldiers left," Philip was saying. "How many soldiers have you, Governor?"

Tancred became alert. He looked from Philip's impatient face to the governor's worried frown. Surely the governor would be wise enough not to listen to Philip and his plan to attack the army.

"Throwing men at Emich will be a waste," said Tancred.

Philip's eyes were cold. "Do you expect us to hole up here like rats for weeks of siege? Or do you pretend to be a guide through the swamps?"

Tancred looked at the governor. "Even five hundred men cannot destroy Emich's army in an open attack."

The governor appeared to agree and measured Tancred. "Do you serve the Noble?"

"I travel alone. I came upon members of his contingent near Vienna. My presence here was to warn you of the Rhinelanders, but you have already made contact with one of their armies, we saw as we rode toward your town."

"Rabble! King Coloman sent orders to give them facilities and supplies. But the leader, a renegade priest named Gottschalk, led them in pillaging the countryside. Sheep, oxen, wine, corn. They killed some of our peasants, and a young boy was impaled. Coloman brought troops in to control them, and they resisted. They are dead now or scattered."

"Emich will also ask permission to pass through Hungary," warned Tancred.

"He has already sent a message. King Coloman has rejected his request. I now fear the rabble will attack us."

Philip paced. "Talk of peace and a bribe may convince him to withdraw."

A typical Byzantine tactic, thought Tancred.

"Emich cannot be bargained with," said Tancred so firmly that the governor noticed.

Helena too turned her head slightly. No doubt the governor wondered how Tancred would dare contradict the emperor's military emissary.

"I am inclined to agree," said the governor.

He looked at Philip, who stared coldly at Tancred.

"Word has arrived, Excellency," explained the governor, "that Jews have been massacred along the Rhine. Here also in our own kingdom, at Prague and Nitra. The bribe would have to be hefty to convince Emich to withdraw."

"Do not trust him," warned Tancred.

Philip's mouth was cynical. "Then you know this robber-baron so well?"

Tancred did not choose to explain about his ordeal as a captive. Philip was anxious to reach Nish on the Byzantine frontier, and there was little Tancred could say to convince him.

"Well, Governor?" pressed Philip.

"My orders from King Coloman are to deny the Rhinelanders entry. We doubt not what the scavengers will do if we let them cross the bridge."

Philip walked swiftly to the breach to look out. "Then

we will defend the bridge. The barbarians will soon tire and withdraw. Have you men enough?"

The governor favored Tancred with a look. "What think you?" Philip's head jerked in their direction.

"The bridge can be defended indefinitely," said Tancred. "Skirmishes cannot be made against Emich's men on the other side of the Danube. But know that by doing so, you will not turn him back. I think Emich has no intention of fighting the Seljuks. I think he has an appetite for Coloman's kingdom. He will try to build his own bridge farther down the Danube."

The governor's alarm was visible. "The kingdom of Coloman?" Philip impatiently turned from the breach to face them. "Fear not, Governor. Human nature does not change. The heart of man is greedy. This Rhinelander will surely withdraw for a bribe. It will save lives."

The governor wavered in Philip's favor. "You may be right about a gift."

"The heart of Emich is not only greedy but also deceitful," said Tancred. "Trust him if you insist, but I have seen what he has done to the Jews who sent him gold."

Helena turned to scan him.

Philip turned on him, his dark eyes angry. "Would you have us do nothing? You have seen his siege-engines. If he crosses the bridge, he will take the town!"

The governor looked out the ramparts at the formidable army camped across the Danube near the forest. Soldiers crawled about like ants.

"Wieselburg has little gold to offer him," said the governor. "In all the fortress I would be blessed to collect even a satchel, and that includes robbing the church coffers."

"There are jewels," said Philip evenly. "Byzantine jewels of worth and prominence. My rings, for example. And

I have others. Lady Helena also has gems of value. As emissary of the Eastern emperor, I will head a delegation to Emich."

"Do so," said Tancred, "and you throw jewels to swine. As it is written, 'They will turn again to rend you.' "

Philip, anxious to prove himself before Helena, was determined to confront Emich with a delegation. So far, Helena had stood in silence, her back toward them as she looked out.

Tancred walked to her, but she avoided his gaze although he could see she was tense. "Are you willing to send your jewels to the Rhinelander?"

She touched the gold Byzantine cross, encased with clear blue sapphires and rubies, that graced her throat. Her eyes swerved to Philip, who stood beside the governor. Philip's eyes were riveted not on Helena but on Tancred.

"Well?" said Tancred.

Her warm, brown eyes rushed to his and momentarily faltered beneath his steady gaze.

"Lady Helena?" came the governor's apologetic voice. "What say you?"

She briefly scanned Tancred then abruptly walked to Philip. "Your decision is a wise one. As you say, it will save lives."

"What of you, Norman?" challenged Philip. "Will you stand here contesting me or ride with us?"

Helena kept her back toward him as she faced Philip. Tancred would not risk his head nor his reputation on Philip's scheme.

"I have seen the countenance of Emich once too often. I wish not to look on it again. I will stay and rest," he said lazily. "I wish a hot bath, clean garments, and a hot meal."

Philip looked triumphant, as though he had proven

Tancred lacking. "Then do stay, Norman. I shall see to the matter of the barbarians myself."

"As you wish. If you will excuse me, governor, Lady Helena." Tancred left the keep, taking the steps down to the courtyard.

He was certain Philip's scheme would not work. And when it failed, he had his own. Only then would they listen.

While in town, Tancred purchased a fine, dark blue, woolen tunic that looked to have come from the merchants of the Eastern empire. He bought a lighter undertunic with full sleeves and, at last, boots. Fine leather boots that pulled over woolen hose and came just above the calf. He also replenished his lost daggers although his purchases were not as fine as the Damascus daggers taken by Mosul.

Mosul. Where was he now? Constantinople? Baghdad?

Tancred removed the ring from his small leather pouch and again placed it on his hand. The ring of his grandfather, al-Kareem, would buy important information.

Like Philip, he was anxious to ride toward Nish and the Byzantine Empire. If it were not for Nicholas's niece, he would leave alone in the morning by a postern gate, traveling by way of the swamps.

But he could not bring himself to ride out alone, and he knew she would not desert the Noble. Again he wondered what dilemma had brought her here to find Nicholas in the face of such uncertainty. One thing was clear, she did not trust him enough to tell him.

In her chamber supplied by the governor, Helena removed the pearls from her hair, then gathered her other jewels, a gold pendant studded with emeralds, rings, gold bracelets, and earbobs, and placed them inside a small brocaded bag.

"You are sure, mistress?" Bardas looked displeased as he saw her draw the cord closed. She had her doubts but refused to entertain them. She told herself that Philip knew what he was doing.

"If it will save our lives? What is gold? Yes, I have seen enough bloodshed. Where is Philip now?"

"In the keep. He will ride out at dawn with a dozen men."

"Take me to him." Helena donned a crimson cloak woven with silver thread. Then she walked with Bardas through the shadowed courtyard toward the keep, a square tower, crenelated at the wall and pierced with arrow loops to serve as the garrison's ultimate refuge.

She had not seen Tancred Redwan since that afternoon. He refused to ride with Philip. Surely it was not because he was afraid. He had already proved himself a warrior. Was it because he disliked Philip so, or because he was certain that a gift to the brigand leader would fail?

She frowned. Whatever the reason, he was difficult to please. He seemed to go out of his way to prove Philip wrong.

The keep was similar to ones she had seen at the Castle of Hohms near Antioch.

"Wait for me. I wish to see Philip alone."

At each level of the huge, square tower, a door led off into other parts of the tower. She took the chiseled steps, lifting her skirts as she climbed, feeling the dampness penetrate. At the top, the square room faced outward over the Danube.

She did not see Philip. Had he stepped out with the governor?

She waited, keeping the small bag of jewels hidden under her cloak. The night was pleasant, with warm breezes coming through the openings. The stone floor was hard beneath her slippers as she crossed to the other side.

Who would guess that so lovely a scene hid a menacing army with siege-engines? A white moon, ancient with secrets, displayed its brightness above the dark forest. Below, ripples of silver danced across the Danube.

She lowered her hood to feel the breeze touch her hair and drew in a breath, more a sigh. She told herself she had been a fool to leave Constantinople, until she remembered her mother.

What must she have gone through when sold as a slave! How had she survived?

Helena found consolation in remembering that her mother's faith in Christ was strong. Where she was now, could she possibly be looking at the same moon, and perhaps praying for her daughter who had been told she was dead? Did she know moments of happiness or at least peace?

Helena thought of Nicholas, and her hopes mounted. The governor had said Peter the Hermit had passed peaceably through the Hungarian frontier and was now nearing the Sava River. Nicholas would be with Peter. Nicholas, whose strong arms would enfold her and relieve some of her burden.

But what if the brigand army could not be bribed to pull back? What if they lay siege to the fortress? Far worse, what if they sought to scale the walls with their armaments? She remembered the swamps and shuddered.

She reached a hand to the cross about her throat, the only piece of jewelry that she had kept. Her mother had given it to her in Athens on her twelfth birthday.

Would God hear her prayers for deliverance, not only for herself now but also for her mother?

A footfall on the stone floor caused her to whirl around. She dropped the small bag of jewels. It landed on the floor in a shaft of moonlight, and the gold threads in the small bag shone.

She was relieved to see not some strange soldier but Tancred. He appeared less harsh without the garb of the despised Rhinelander, and she tried not to notice how striking his looks were.

He stooped and picked up the bag, his eyes coming to hers. "You waste these on an evil man. It will only sharpen Emich's appetite. He will wonder how much more may await him inside the fortress."

She remembered that Tancred had been a prisoner of the Rhinelanders. "Is he the man who held you captive?"

"No. One of his captains. A miserable clout named Wolfric. He is dead now."

She tried to hold back her growing curiosity about Tancred. "How did you become his prisoner? Did you serve him long?"

He hesitated, as though debating how much to explain about his past. "No, not long. I have a cousin to thank that I served him at all."

"A cousin!"

"An enemy. I search for him."

Her eyes drifted to his scabbard, barely visible beneath a dark cloak. "You killed the Rhinelander named Wolfric?"

"If I am alive, it is only because I do not intend to die so easily. He tried to kill me. And a girl. She is dead."

Helena folded her arms, for she felt cold. She remembered what he had said about the merciless attacks on the Jews. "A Jewess?"

"Yes."

"You knew her well?"

His eyes came to hers. She turned away to look out.

He must not think I am curious about him.

"No."

"What will happen do you think?"

He walked up to her. He weighed the small bag on his palm. "You are certain you wish to part with them?"

She refused to answer, pretending she did not hear.

"You are generous to throw away your jewels to defend Philip's tactic. But your show of confidence will not bring him success."

She stiffened a little. He understood her motive in backing Philip. That was somewhat unnerving, seeing that they had only recently met. So much of what she did escaped Philip's understanding. "You did not answer my question."

"Emich will receive Philip in peace. He will take the bribe." He held up the bag. "And he will swear that he will withdraw, then change his mind."

She drew in a small breath. "You might be wrong."

"At Mainz, the chief rabbi sent a delegation with gold asking that Emich not attack. He took the gold, then attacked the Jews the next day."

"How wretched."

Silence closed them in. She started to walk away.

"You have yet to tell me what desperation drove you to risk this journey to locate Nicholas. You will not find him in the following of the Hermit. I left him in Le Puy. He will come, but not with the hordes of unruly peasants. He is too much the warrior-priest for that. He will no doubt arrive in Constantinople in one of the disciplined armies of the feudal princes."

She whirled. "But the Frank knight who first arrived at Nish was so certain!"

"He was misguided. Perhaps he wished only to please

you. Then again, he may have known of a priest named Nicholas and assumed it was your uncle.

"You may not believe this, but there is a great difference between the rabble Crusaders you have come across and the real Western armies that will arrive at Constantinople. The main fighting force has not even left Europe yet."

If the feudal princes and their knights were anything like this man, she thought, she could understand the difference. The possibility that Nicholas had not even departed yet pierced her with a dart of despair.

Suppose she must return to Constantinople without him? How would she explain her rash actions to her aunt and the bishop? Philip would defend her, and yet she understood that uncertainty over his security in the emperor's service would make him cautious.

"You think Nicholas is yet at Le Puy?"

"I am certain he is. The barons will not leave until August." He watched her with subdued interest, as though curious about her behavior.

Helena remembered the official starting date set by the Latin pope and the Eastern emperor. "I was so certain," she breathed. "I would not have come had I thought—"

She stopped, wishing to say no more. "And now this!" She gestured about with dismay. For a moment all courage seemed to flee like shadows in the morning light.

Tancred leaned against the wall, simply watching her, his face in the shadows. "You might tell me why you seek Nicholas. It must be important to goad you into taking this kind of risk. I thought so when I saw you and Bardas on the road."

Should she tell him about her mother? But what did she truly know of this warrior?

She changed the subject back to their dilemma. "What

if you are right? What if the Rhinelanders do not pull back
but lay siege to the fortress? Suppose they scale the walls?"

"Then we will fight them."

"But you are far outnumbered. Why do you stay?" *You
once mentioned leaving undetected by the postern gate.*

"If they take the town, I will see that you get out of
here."

Her eyes darted to his, searching, but his expression
was inscrutable. He added, "Like I said, I cannot allow
anything to happen to Nicholas's niece."

"Does Nicholas mean so much to you?" she asked with
a hint of cynicism. His answer took her off guard.

"Yes. He saved my life when I was a boy. For a time he
even raised me at the monastery. All that I know of Christ,
Nicholas taught me from his own copy of the Greek New
Testament."

She was moved but found herself saying, "I do not
wish to be your responsibility."

He was undaunted. "Nevertheless, your wishes come
second to what Nicholas would expect of me."

"I have Philip to see to my care."

His smile provoked her to add, "And Bardas. I bid you
a good evening, sir knight."

She swept past him and out the door.

Tancred stood with the governor in the tower, watching Emich's soldiers try to fight their way to the bridge. An
arrow struck a brigand, and he fell from his horse; a Hungarian soldier was speared, followed by Emich's retreat.
The skirmishes had been going on for days.

"We must hold the bridge at all costs," said the governor. Philip stood tense and angry. His plan had not
worked. The gift had been taken to Emich, and Philip had
received fair promises, only to have a skirmish fought the

next morning at the bridge. While the skirmishes went on, Emich was pillaging on the other side of the Danube.

Emich's soldiers were building their own bridge. If they could move the siege-engines across the river, it was only a matter of time before they took the town.

"There is a small chance to defeat him," said Tancred.

Both men looked at him and were willing to listen now, for all other hopes were fast dying.

"What do you suggest?" the governor asked.

"In Sicily, the Normans were once held up in a castle surrounded by enemies. They knew they could not outlast the siege nor were they strong enough in numbers to confront the enemy openly.

"But my father knew that the Norman reputation for savage fighting was held in respect and fear. He began a rumor that the Great Count Roger was coming.

"The less hardy of the enemy army decided they would soon be outnumbered and would lose their heads. It sent a panic among them, and they fell back to their camp.

"That enabled my father to lead a sortie from the castle. After a short battle, they were routed.

"We might send a rumor that King Coloman will arrive soon with his army.

"Who knows? Emich might bolt and run. Beneath all his cruelty, I believe he is a coward. Most robber-barons are, when they stand alone."

Philip's enthusiasm surprised Tancred. He had expected Philip to make light of the idea.

"Bravo, Norman! Your skills may yet save the day. What say you, governor? Shall we play his military tactic?"

"What choice have we? Let us try it."

"It may be that your knowledge of the ways of your fathers can benefit us," said Philip. "Win this battle, open the route for us to return to the Byzantine garrison, and I will see you enjoy a worthy reward in Constantinople."

His change worried Tancred. What sudden alteration of mood would motivate Philip to no longer oppose him? Did he now think that Tancred could somehow be of benefit to the realization of his ambitions?

Philip cast him a lean smile and offered him a make-believe toast from a goblet. "To the military glories of the Normans! May your shadow never grow less, as long as it walks tall next to mine."

CHAPTER 18

The Enemy's Camp

❖ The seeds of rumor that dread King Coloman was coming with a large army were sown by men dressed as peasants and sent to the other side of the bridge.

Within hours, the fearsome gossip had spread. Who among Emich's army had not heard how Coloman had utterly defeated their fellow Rhinelander, Gottschalk? His followers had been slain in the massacre as Coloman showed no mercy. The few survivors were now in Emich's army.

The fearsome cry went out. "King Coloman is coming! He has an army of twenty thousand. Not a man, woman, or child will be left alive!"

By afternoon, spies reported to Philip and Tancred that the Rhinelanders had ceased building their own bridge and were back at their main camp some distance from Wieselburg.

Philip was more pleased at the success than even Tancred. "It worked, Friend Tancred. We shall rout them. Word will reach Nish of my victory!"

Obviously Philip was thinking that a victory over so large an army would cast a shadow over his previous defeat at the camp. It could then be said that he had come back strong against his enemy to strike a blow of justice.

Tancred was astride Apollo, and Philip beside him on his own horse, ready to make a sortie. The soldiers from the fortress numbered perhaps two hundred.

Tancred saw a bishop had arrived to bless them. When he came to Tancred, he obligingly lowered his helmet, placing his sword forward to receive the blessing. The heat of the summer sun pounded on him.

"In the sign of the cross, conquer."

A little disturbed, Tancred repeated the words, unsure of his motive, unsure of many things, but determined to win. Flashes from the past paraded across his mind: the quiet days as a student physician, now his gauntlet gripped a sword-hilt; his grandfather and the Koran; Nicholas and the Greek New Testament; Mosul and his betrayal; the beautiful Jewish girl at Worms and her handwritten Scripture booklet, which was now next to his heart. He had memorized most of it in the quiet late evenings by the campfire.

Tancred lifted his head and saw Helena, the wind softly catching her cloak. In a moment she reached Philip, and he bent to her, taking her hand. In spite of those about them, they saw only each other.

Tancred heard him say, "I will live. And we will return to Constantinople."

Her eyes clung to Philip's, and then he rode ahead. Tancred walked Apollo up beside her and paused, but she did not turn to recognize him or even show that she knew he was there. He waited.

At last she turned, her eyes warm but reluctant. Tancred bent toward her, extending his gloved hand. Her eyes widened, and she stepped back. The glimmer of embroidered gold on the small jewel bag resting on his palm caught the sunlight.

Then she understood he had not been seeking her favors on him as a knight but was offering her something. She flushed, and her eyes rushed back to his, confused.

Tancred bowed his head. "Your jewels."

She took them, hesitantly, but before she could reply, he rode on to the head of the column.

Soon they could see the camp ahead through the trees. Tancred wanted to get the robber-baron Emich in memory of the thousands of Jews from Cologne to Mainz. And yet he knew well enough the danger of a personal vendetta.

How often had Nicholas lectured him at Monte Casino. "Remember, vengeance is mine says the Lord. If you battle, battle for justice, for honor, for the widow, for the orphan, for the church, for the cross."

The sprawling campground loomed sullenly against the shadows of the sunset. Tancred watched the small guard in service to the baron take up positions around his tent.

Tancred and a Petcheneg soldier had ridden ahead to scout, leaving Philip and the two hundred men out of sight some distance away in the forest.

"Ride back and inform Philip the Noble."

"And you?"

"I will circle in for a closer look."

When the soldier had left, Tancred rode a short distance through the trees until he could again see the center of the camp, Emich's gonfalon, and his chief knights. All appeared quiet and unsuspecting in the settling darkness.

It was dusk when Tancred rode back to where Philip anxiously waited. Philip stood up, his handsome face showing his excitement. His boots crunched the dirt as he walked toward Tancred. Philip's knee-length cloak of exquisite black brocade fluttered in the breeze. His dark eyes flashed with triumph. "We have taken prisoners."

Tancred dismounted and followed him to the small campfire. He found two prisoners tied and seated on the ground. Their bearded faces showed no fear, but their brows were wet with sweat. One of them smirked his disdain for Philip.

"Greeks," he said with a snort. "Babes! You do not frighten us. We know you hide your swords in your pretty scabbards. We bathe our swords in the blood of your hired warriors!"

"Where did you find them?" Tancred asked Philip.

"By the bridge. They swear that Emich is not in their camp. He has gone back to Regensburg, and his knights have ridden with him."

They were lying of course. Tancred eyed the two prisoners. They were not as certain of him as they had been of Philip, and they measured him.

Tancred deliberately drew a dagger from his sleeve. "Normans do not waste their swords on murderers of women and children. We reserve them for strong opponents. We use daggers on cowardly pigs. I saw you in Worms, near the Jewish synagogue."

The Rhinelanders were afraid now, for they could see that he was not a weak Greek.

"What do we know of Jews? Nothing," grumbled one.

"I think you lie."

The man squirmed. "It was not me but him," indicating the other man.

"Shut up, Hemlef," growled the other.

"You tell him what you think of Jews, yes?"

"Hemlef!"

"Your leader, Emich," said Tancred. "Where is he?"

"We know nothing about the count."

Philip stepped up and gestured abruptly to one of the Petcheneg soldiers. "We are wasting time on barbarian fools. At the Hippodrome in Constantinople, we have hung disfavored emperors by their big toes over hot coals. Death takes several days, but it comes eventually."

Tancred showed nothing. He guessed it was a ruse by Philip to frighten them. That he would do so, surprised Tancred. "Normans cut out the tongue and pluck the eyes next."

"Wait! We talk, yes? Yes?"

"Yes," said Tancred. "And one of you will lead us to Emich. You," he said to Hemlef. "And if you fail, your friend here will be a feast of fat things for the ravens, understand?"

Hemlef nodded.

Philip wasted no time. At a signal the two hundred men mounted to ride. Tancred had the Rhinelander lead the way, with his hands bound. They rode swiftly through the night and in a short time reached the edge of the forest that faced into the camp.

Emich's brigands were directly ahead, a fire near his camp shed light on the gonfalon. Around the camp perimeter, few men were on guard duty, and there was no evidence that they suspected an attack. Apparently they thought they were safe for the night and intended to withdraw in the morning before King Coloman arrived.

Philip spoke to the prisoner. "You, barbarian, will lead Redwan to the brigand's tent."

"He is not there. The count knows he is hated, even by his men. The gonfalon is a lie. The count is in a humble tent near his horse, so he can run like lightening."

Tancred turned to Philip. "Give me a dozen men. I will get Emich."

But Philip seemed to have second thoughts. "This barbarian made a fool of me and slew twenty good men. I will take this prisoner and bring Emich back alive."

Tancred did not like the sound of it, but Philip had already turned to the soldiers. "The rest of you will follow Redwan."

They slipped through the darkness, moving silently toward the camp. The tents were scattered throughout the camp; horses were staked nearby. Philip and the dozen men with him moved off into the darkness, the prisoner showing the way.

The small group of less than two hundred men with Tancred were either fools, mad with vanity, or they would prove sufficient for the survival of Wieselburg. They all had armor and horses, and Tancred arranged a thunderous, Norman-style charge.

"Charge full speed ahead through the very heart of the camp," he told them. "Your horses and armor are your first weapon. Shout as one man, 'Glorious King Coloman!' "

He looked from one end of the line to the other, adding, "After that, you are on your own. May your swords strike in the name of justice."

They charged, the horses gaining speed. Their hooves thundered, ripping open the turf. The wall of riders crashed into the center of the camp, riding down tents and soldiers, and scattering their horses and mules, sending panic.

"Glorious King Coloman!"

The Petcheneg mercenaries, fierce fighters from the Steppes, gave an eerie yell that pierced the night. Their horses looked riderless as they swooped through the

camp, the warriors clinging to their sides. Arrows whis-
tled, metal struck metal. They set fire to the standing
tents. Many fell where they were. Others fled into the
night.

As swiftly as it began, the sortie was over; the camp was
ablaze with fire and drifting smoke.

Tancred felt the heat blast his face. He rode Apollo a
distance away.

Where was Philip?

A man sprang toward Tancred from the darkness,
whirling a treacherous spiked morning star above his
head. Tancred's lance rested on his saddle. Grabbing it, he
hurled it into the man's chest.

Philip rode up, grim and terrible, sweat dotting his
soiled face.

Tancred guessed the outcome before being told.
"Where is Emich?"

Philip sat rigid on his horse, the glow of the flames
reflected on his face. "He had such a horse. I have yet to
see the like of it for speed."

"You let him escape?" Tancred asked through gritted
teeth.

"Do you speak thus to me?"

Tancred swung his horse and rode toward the western
side of the camp.

The men and prisoner who had ridden with Philip
rode up. "It is no good, seigneur. We chased him into the
forest, he and the Frank knights with him. We trailed on
for some distance, but they lost us."

The terrified prisoner was wet with his sweat, looking
at Tancred and the sword in his hand.

Emich had escaped. Where would he go now? Back to
his home in Leinigen?

With a gesture that showed resignation, Tancred lowered his blade.

Perhaps the collapse of Emich's so-called Crusade, following so soon after the fall of Gottschalk's, would impress the Rhinelanders that they were in error. Punishment had been meted out to those who had persecuted the Jews. And for himself and others who believed the entire Crusade movement to be unharmonious with the Scriptures, nothing had yet occurred to justify the cry: "God wills it!"

CHAPTER 19

Nish on the Byzantine Frontier

❖ After they arrived at Nish, a dinner was given in Philip's honor by the Byzantine official, Nicetas, who was pleased to hear Philip's report of a sweeping victory over the marauding Rhinelanders. The official spoke of new trouble, this time from the peasant-Crusaders traveling with Peter the Hermit, and of displeasure coming out of the Sacred Palace at Constantinople.

"But all that can wait until the entourage sent by the emperor arrives at dinner."

Nicetas's home was a paradise for Helena. Worn from the hazardous journey and disappointed over the failure to find Nicholas, she solaced herself in a warm, scented bath.

I will not think of the trouble awaiting me.

She once again had a bed of feathers, satin covers, and soft fur rugs beneath her feet. Accustomed to the ease of the Sacred Palace, she shuddered as she remembered the journey into the barbarian west. And it had been for naught.

She groaned. Nicholas would not even leave Le Puy with the feudal princes until next month.

Assuaging her disappointment and the fears of returning to Constantinople to confront the wrath of Lady Irene, she concentrated on looking forward to the grand dinner to honor Philip.

And there was so much to enjoy where she was. The home had marble baths, rich brocades of gold and purple hangings, and a banquet hall surrounded by gardens and running fountains. To enjoy such luxury at Nish was surprising, seeing that it was only a garrison town. But Constantinople was not many miles away, and perhaps Nicetas could afford such Byzantine pleasures.

Helena took pains to look her best for the affair honoring Philip. Her gown was white silk, with purple threads interwoven with gold, forming small delicate crosses throughout. A purple sash, evidence of her position in the royal house, graced her waist. Her hair was adorned with intricately woven threads of gold and combs embedded with pearls. She remembered that the pearls would now be in the hands of the Rhinelander had it not been for Tancred Redwan.

As she left her chamber and went below, the stairs, gardens, and towers blazed with torches. Greek officials wore rich costumes of Byzantine brocade, and the high-crowned, turban-like hats with upturned brims glittered with gems.

Bardas delivered her to the marble hall, then waited in the garden. As her eyes scanned the room, she looked for Philip, but he was not there yet, nor was Nicetas.

She hesitated. From another room, a slave approached her and bowed, extending a silver tray with a letter.

"For you, Lady Helena. It arrived an hour ago by horseman."

Helena tensed. She stared at the letter marked with the royal seal. It was from her aunt, Lady Irene.

She had known, of course, that the day of reckoning would come when her aunt would learn of her absence from Constantinople and that she would need to explain her journey with Philip to Nish. But she had counted on Nicholas's arrival to offset the difficulty certain to await her.

The moment of confrontation with Irene had not seemed so fearful to Helena when she left Constantinople. She had not even anticipated returning there but had imagined herself leaving Nish with Nicholas for the long journey to Tabriz to free her mother.

But now, what could she offer as a palatable reason to her aunt for going off with Philip? Far worse, what would she do if Irene discovered she had gone on to Wieselburg? And that she would have been abducted by brigands had it not been for Tancred Redwan?

She stirred uneasily. Lady Irene must not meet Tancred. For that matter, it was best that Governor Nicetas not speak with him. She knew it was a half-truth that the victory at Wieselburg was Philip's success. There was little question that the Norman was both clever and a courageous warrior. Their safe arrival at Nish had as much to do with Tancred as it did with Philip, but the warrior's abilities must not be permitted to overshadow Philip's.

Fortunately Tancred would not be in Nish long, she told herself. As far as she knew, he may have already ridden out. He had his own quest; what was it? Something about finding an enemy cousin and his uncle serving at the Castle of Hohms?

Her thoughts turned again to Philip. Neither was it advantageous for him to disclose to Irene and the bishop what had happened at the camp. The Norman from Sicily must fade into oblivion, friend of Nicholas or not.

Yet she felt a prick to her conscience. She was grateful for surviving the brigands on that horrid night at camp and for the return of her jewels.

Cautiously Helena opened the letter from Lady Irene.

Helena,

I cannot adequately express my alarm upon returning to Constantinople to discover your reckless behavior! You have always been headstrong, a young woman destined as it were to destroy her political opportunities in the palace. Alas, I have labored endlessly to protect you from yourself. I now fear that foolishness is bound within your heart. Bishop Constantine and I must henceforth reconsider your future and what is best for all concerned.

Helena stopped reading. What could her aunt be insinuating? Gripping the letter, she read on.

Do not forget you come of age this spring. Your debut can no longer be delayed, however strongly you wish to oppose it. It is enough that you risk your own future in Constantinople, but is it a light thing for you to risk Philip's? Your unwise behavior in goading him to take you to Nish has not only tarnished your reputation but has also brought Philip's wisdom into question at the Sacred Palace. He is being called back to Constantinople at once to report to the minister of war. As for you, my niece and legal ward, I have given strict orders to Nicetas to restrain you there at Nish until I come myself to bring you back. I do hope you understand the harm you have brought upon Philip. Lady Irene

No, thought Helena, *it cannot be. Irene is lying. The situation cannot be as serious as she makes it out to be. How like her to sow fear in Philip's heart. She knows how desperately he wishes to please and honor the emperor. She will use it to her own advantage. But exactly what was that?*

Voices and laughter caused Helena to look up. She was unable to move, her eyes riveted on the small assembly that walked through the banqueting hall. For Irene was part of the group.

She entered in a stunning costume of purple, a woman who appeared much younger than her years. Helena knew that Irene was several years the senior of her mother, Adrianna, but exactly how many, Irene had carefully kept a secret. Her hair was flaxen, woven into a tiered crown, her eyes a dove gray. Her skin was the envy of younger women in the palace, seemingly ageless.

Beside her walked Governor Nicetas. Philip was at her left hand, his brocaded cloak about his shoulders. He wore a broad-rimmed black hat sparkling with gems, and he did not look pleased.

Had Irene already told him that he had been called back to Constantinople?

Helena gripped the letter hard against the side of her skirt. Did he blame her? No doubt Irene had made her appear as a rash fool.

Helena's cheeks grew hot as her eyes fixed on the older woman. Then she noticed the man who entered just behind Philip. Tancred. What was he doing in their company?

Her unease mounted when she briefly took in his appearance. His semi-circular cloak was black with gold trim. The fine tunic beneath was of handsome Byzantine design, small brocaded squares of black and gold. It was disturbing that his commanding presence could overshadow Philip's.

Tancred was watching her, but his expression showed nothing of what went on in his mind.

She tore her eyes away. Her own troubled thoughts darted back to her aunt. Drawing in a small breath, she forced herself to walk across the marble floor. She paused to wait for the group to come to her. She could feel Irene's unflinching anger, yet in the company of the others, it was masked.

"Helena, how well you look after so dubious a journey. Philip has told me all about it. But I must hear it from you as well."

What had he told Irene? Had he mentioned Nicholas? But he would not mention the information gathered from informers about her mother.

Helena tried to hide her alarm as she received a dutiful kiss on the forehead. "My aunt," she said breathlessly, "what a pleasant surprise. I only now received your letter. When did you arrive?"

Irene smiled. "Yesterday. I thought it best to send the letter anyway. I cannot have you running off again on some unscrupulous adventure. Your unexpected disappearance from Constantinople brought fear to the bishop and me. And Philip! What a predicament you placed him in."

She turned to Philip. "Is that not so, Philip?"

"You must not blame Helena," he said stiffly. "I will take full responsibility for her actions and mine. I should have sent a message ahead inquiring if the monk Peter had arrived and if Nicholas was with him."

So he had told Irene the reason for her journey to Nish.

"It was not Philip's mistake but mine," Helena hastened to say.

"No matter," Irene said. "Whatever the reason for your journey, it is forgotten."

Was it? Helena wondered. She did not trust her aunt.

"Philip is to return to the Sacred Palace," said Irene. "The minister of war is ailing."

At the mention of the minister of war's health, Philip looked at his mother, and Helena thought she imagined a glint of feverish pleasure in his eyes. He said nothing in response to this news, however, and Irene turned toward her.

"Your unwise venture, Helena, has turned out well for Philip after all, despite the dreadful news that Nicholas is on his way to Constantinople."

Helena expected her aunt to look on the arrival of Nicholas with displeasure, but why had the journey suddenly benefited Philip? What of the scathing letter Helena had just received?

Irene's expression was triumphant as she turned to the Byzantine official. "Nicetas, here, has told me of Philip's victory over the yapping mongrels from the Rhineland."

Philip's victory? thought Helena. She hesitated to glance at Tancred.

Nicetas showed pleasure as he smiled at Philip. "Let it never be said that you showed yourself anything other than the son of the great General Lysander."

Helena knew what Tancred must be thinking, but he masked his feelings with a polished poise. Would he say anything to the contrary? She ventured a glance in his direction. A hint of amusement showed about his mouth. Helena fanned herself too briskly.

"As a Norman, you have no doubt heard of General Lysander?" Nicetas was asking Tancred, a subdued look of ironic humor in his own smile.

"A Byzantine to be respected," said Tancred. "My father fought in the Norman army with Guiscard against him at Dyrrachium."

The light retort passed with a chuckle from Nicetas, and even Philip showed humor.

"It is to our benefit, Nicetas, that Tancred has agreed to aid us on the frontier with the peasants following Peter. I can attest that he is a good man with the sword. When this ordeal is over, I may steal him into my service at Constantinople."

Helena swished her fan. Had she heard correctly? She noticed the change in Philip. He no longer appeared to resent Tancred's presence as he had before the victory at Wieselburg. The change in both men made her cautious.

"Philip is right, Seigneur Redwan," said Irene. "You must come to the Sacred Palace. He has told me of your uncle's service at the Castle of Hohms. There are dangerous days ahead for Philip, for all of us. Loyal men are not easily found."

Tancred gave a casual bow. "I am honored, Lady Irene, but I have a personal quest to fulfill."

Whether he was truly honored was debatable, thought Helena, and she wondered at his manners. This was not the barbarian she had thought him to be. Was he indeed the son of a count?

"My service here at Nish will be brief, as Philip will explain to you," said Tancred. "I have another matter awaiting me in Constantinople, and from there, it will take me to my uncle at Hohms."

"Philip or I may be of benefit to this mission of yours. When in Constantinople you must be our guest, if only for a short time."

Again he bowed. "I shall remember your generosity."

Helena felt a breath of unease. Irene had power in the palace. Her aunt was involved in astrology and counseled many in high places.

Helena was certain Irene was in love with Bishop Constantine, who was not a bishop at all, and that together they planned her demise, even as they had her mother's. Helena supposed she was an expendable pawn, who was being used to enable Irene to acquire the Castle of Hohms through Helena's marriage to Philip. Who knew what other coveted prize Irene might have in mind and figured out a way to get by using Helena?

"Come, let us dine," said Nicetas.

As they moved toward the banqueting hall, Helena hesitated, falling behind. She wished to escape, to be alone, and cast a glance toward the garden where she had left Bardas.

She picked up her skirt and turned to make her escape but found Tancred standing there. She hesitated, then began to brush past, but he intercepted her.

"How disappointing. The governor loses the light of his banquet."

She brushed aside the faint pleasure she felt from his compliment. "I expected you to be gone from Nish by now."

"To see you again, I had no choice."

"And if I do not wish to see you?" she asked somewhat flippantly, for his presence was disturbing.

"Then I would not trouble you. But since you are Nicholas's niece, what either of us may wish does not matter so much."

"I see you are as impertinent as ever."

"And you are as haughty." He folded his arms. "I would think you might show me some gratitude."

"I already thanked you for returning my jewels."

His smile was disarming. "I speak of Philip's victory at Wieselburg. It appears to have saved him from Lady Irene's displeasure."

She could say nothing to that, but refused to acknowledge the truth of what he said.

"I remained silent for you, not him. The victory seems to have gotten you both back into her favors. I noticed you were tense when she spoke of her displeasure at your disappearance. She also mentioned the concern of a bishop. Who is he?"

She hesitated. "Constantine. But he is not a true bishop. He is an enemy of Nicholas."

"And yours also, I gather. I must learn about Constantine when I see Nicholas. Your aunt is a beautiful and clever woman."

She felt rankled. "You were quick to notice."

"That she was clever? Tell me, is she as politically ambitious and dangerous as she appears?"

"If you do not wish to be burned, avoid the dragon's lair," she quipped.

He smiled a little. "I am an expert at that. She is dangerous?"

Helena wondered why he pressed for an answer. Was he curious about her aunt, or about the wariness she showed in Irene's presence?

"You might ask Nicholas, if you truly do know him. And you might ask my mother," she said in a moment of bitterness. "But she is not here to explain."

His smile vanished. He scanned her. "Your mother is no longer alive?"

Helena was about to say that she was a slave but caught herself. Why should she trust him? Especially if Irene had plans to hire him into Philip's service. Yet somehow she could not see him submitting to her aunt.

"You must excuse me. I have no pleasure in the banquet."

He did not step aside. "Shall I escort you back to your chambers?"

It was the last thing she wanted. "I have no need for a mercenary soldier. I have Bardas."

"Tancred, my friend!"

They turned toward the grand dining hall. It was Philip. He walked toward them.

"Join us, Tancred. My aunt wishes your company at her table."

Tancred bowed toward Helena and left.

Helena turned away to walk toward the garden to find Bardas, but Philip took hold of her arm. "You cannot go now, Helena."

"The evening is ruined by her arrival. She plots against me. Can you not see?"

"Helena . . ."

"Oh, Philip, can you not see how she traps you with promises of advancement in service to the emperor?"

"My dear, you do yourself ill by such accusations. The news of my service to the minister of war is reason for us both to celebrate her arrival. She is my mother, Helena."

"But of course she would celebrate the news of his illness. Is he not in her way? She has so many plans for you, all of them tainted."

His lips tightened. "What is that supposed to mean?"

She did not explain. She dare not. "I am surprised you would ask the Norman to serve you in Constantinople."

"Does it bother you? He is useful, despite his conceit," he said airily. "I may need a man like that."

"You cannot always use people, Philip. He cannot be controlled as easily as you control lesser mercenaries. Send him away. Speak to your mother. She will listen if you say you do not like him."

He gave a short laugh. "Should I fear him? Has he not proven himself skilled?"

"And his skills flatter you."

His expression hardened. "Irene has heard that the emperor is not pleased that Lord Bohemond and the Normans are coming to Constantinople. We made light of the battles fought in the past, but it may not be so innocent. Tancred knows the Norman lords. He is related to William the Conqueror. He will be of benefit to me to gain the emperor's approval."

The emperor, the emperor, could he think of nothing else?

"I am weary after the long journey. Make my excuses to Nicetas and to Irene. Good night, Philip."

"I love you, Helena," he whispered suddenly, desperately.

She felt her heart catch and looked into his dark eyes. The warmth and the sympathy crumbled her defenses, and her voice caught as she lay a hand on his arm. "And I love you."

He smiled, his hand squeezing hers. "I will see you tomorrow. We will prepare for the journey home."

She nodded and left, walking into the garden as he looked after her.

Outside, a breath of wind stirred the fragrant trees, and a fountain splashed.

Bardas was waiting and stood. Another slave appeared from the shadows, approached Bardas, said something, then passed on.

Bardas came to her, taking her through the courtyard to her chambers. As he did, he slipped something into her hand.

Once in her chambers she glanced at the note. *April 1. The Street of the Spices.*

The words were written in the hand of an informant she knew well. Did he have more news of her mother?

She must think of how to outwit Irene. Irene knew nothing of the search to find her mother. The months spent and the wealth invested to buy news from informants was a well-kept secret. Only Bardas knew. And now Philip.

She felt restless. Could Bishop Constantine have discovered what she was doing?

She studied the words a second time. If caught, it would mean the end of her search, even the death of her informant. And her mother?

Yet what choice did she have? What if the informant had news that her mother was alive?

Once back in Constantinople, she would keep her appointment on the Street of Spices and wait for Nicholas's arrival.

CHAPTER 20

The Marketplace Outside Nish

❖ Nicetas was alarmed at the approach of Peter the Hermit's throng, and Tancred did not blame him. The news arriving from the town of Semlin and the route along the Sava River spoke of riots, plunder, and death. Nearly four thousand Hungarians were said to have died.

As soon as Tancred had arrived at Nish, Philip had brought him to the Byzantine official. Now that Philip believed Tancred was valuable to his own success, he hoped to hire Tancred into his service. He had recommended Tancred to Nicetas to see to the problem of peasant-Crusaders under Peter.

Tancred wanted nothing to do with the matter until discovering Lady Irene had arrived from Constantinople and would be returning Helena by the route the peasants would take.

Because Tancred was fluent in Latin, he had been asked by Nicetas to meet the peasant-Crusaders who were camped near Nish and to set up markets for them to buy.

After Tancred left Helena and Philip, he entered the

banquet hall where Nicetas awaited him. The governor arose and gestured to the seat next to him.

"Ah, Tancred, you are the man I wish to see."

When Tancred seated himself, Nicetas said, "I have a large garrison here, and with the fresh troops that came with Lady Irene from Constantinople, we can handle any trouble from the peasants, if it comes to that."

Tancred knew he also had strengthened his Byzantine forces by hiring local Petcheneg, Bulgarian, Kuman, and Hungarian mercenaries.

"You understand the risk of allowing so great a multitude as follows Peter to linger long at Nish," Tancred warned. "The mob grows restless, as the town of Semlin can tell you. It only takes a few rabble to provoke a riot."

"Yes, I fear Peter has lost control. I will allow them no longer than three days near Nish to replenish their food supplies."

"Another suggestion. While they obtain food, I would hold hostages to keep them under control. Only when we can escort them away from Nish would I release them."

"You may have as many men as you need from the garrison to ride with you. The sooner this business is taken care of, the better I shall sleep. I wish no trouble on the inhabitants of the empire."

So this is Peter the Hermit, Tancred thought. This is the man whose preaching kindled a fire in the emotions of some fifty thousand peasants to follow him blindly on a thousand-mile journey to where? Supposedly Jerusalem the golden, to certain victory over the unbeliever because God willed it.

Was it not reported that the religious leaders had signs, wonders, and miracles to back up their cry for the Crusade? Did not such claims prove that God was urging them forward? Did not angels go before them, cheering them on? Naught else was needed but faith.

Faith, mused Tancred. *What if one's faith, however strong, however sincere, was placed in a lie? Would the falsehood become truth?*

Sincerity of motive. Was it enough? And if one drank from a goblet that held poison yet sincerely believed its contents to be pure, would it be harmless?

Perhaps Peter was a humble man; perhaps the pope had truly believed that his call for the Crusade was God's will. Did a holy God wink at this error in the use of His name?

As Tancred sat astride his horse in the military escort sent by Nicetas, he heard the quiet laughter of the men who were with him. He too might smile at the sight, but he dared not. It was too tragic for laughter.

Peter the Hermit was coming toward him with his peasant-Crusaders, who were too many to be numbered. Peter rode ahead in the vanguard. As he neared, Tancred saw he was a little man, very thin.

He wore a soiled woolen shirt with a hood, and over this a cloak without sleeves extended to his ankles. His feet were bare. His angular face, darkened by the sun, peered out from beneath his cowl, framed by unkempt hair. His expression appeared to be as morose as the weary face of his scrawny donkey.

Behind Peter rode a sizable number of lesser nobles and their knights from the land of the Franks and the Rhineland. Each knight had six footmen equipped with weapons.

Tancred's eyes fell on a wooden cart drawn by oxen. He caught sight of the money chest he had heard about, money taken from the Jews for the glorious Crusade to free the holy sepulcher from Turks. The cart rumbled along beside Peter's entourage.

Behind the money chest, Tancred saw an unending procession of Europe's peasants plodding forward. Most of them were on foot, but scrawny donkeys, oxen, and some horses were interspersed among them, along with farm animals—most of them stolen from fellow peasants in Belgrade, Semlin, and the countryside of Hungary.

Old men and women, maidens and children, thieves, prostitutes, the honest, the noble of heart—all trudged forward toward Constantinople, toward Jerusalem. Even the infirm hobbled along, believing a miracle of physical healing awaited them if only they could pray at or touch the sepulcher.

The men carried weapons, most of which were farming implements. If there were a miracle to be reported in the peasant Crusade, Tancred thought dryly, it was that they had survived the journey this far.

But he was convinced those folk who had been robbed of their goods by these peasants would not consider their survival a miracle but a curse on the land.

Tancred found the scene angered him. What manner of testimony were these Christians, who killed, looted, and behaved foolishly in the name of Christ?

Words from the Scriptures he had found written in the booklet belonging to the Jewish girl flashed across his mind. "You who make your boast in the law, do you dishonor God through breaking the law? For 'the name of God is blasphemed among the Gentiles because of you,' as it is written" (Romans 2:23–24).

But the sheep, he thought, *were not to blame for the desperate situation they found themselves in. They grazed on the grasses their shepherds led them to. They followed where the voice of the shepherd called. These poor sheep had believed the zealous cry that had echoed across Europe from Clermont, "This Crusade is God's will."*

As Tancred looked out on the pathetic scene, he thought he understood clearly for the first time how dangerous religious zeal can be without God's Word as judge and critic of the actions and the intents of the heart.

Heresy, decided Tancred, was born of man's zeal apart from a knowledge of the entire Bible.

These masses of peasants, he thought, *and even Peter the Hermit, were following the religious experiences of their leaders, with no foundation of truth to test the accuracy of what they were being told.*

Tancred could see nothing in the Hermit to warrant his following, despite all the fair words he had heard about the man. Tancred remembered the peasant Niles and the girl Modestine and decided that multitudes followed Peter the Hermit because he had promised a land flowing with milk and honey. In their desperation they had reached out to grasp the soiled hem of a little monk as blind as themselves. For if Peter were a prophet, he would not be leading them to a certain death by the scimitars of the Seljuk Turks.

Tancred rode alone to meet Peter, whose worried eyes sought news of open markets for his followers. Tancred halted his stallion and opened a legal document. He held up his gloved hand, and Peter's group became silent.

He read aloud in Latin from the imperial rescript: "To Peter the monk and noble and illustrious men, from Nicetas, Governor of Nish and from the Byzantine authorities sent by the emperor from Constantinople. Greetings. Serious charges of an unsavory nature have been brought against you by the authorities of Belgrade and Semlin along the Sava River. It is reported that you have stirred up quarrels and disturbances. Therefore, if you ever hope to find favor in the sight of our majesty, we enjoin upon you, by Byzantine authority, that you do not presume to remain in any of our cities for more than three days, and that you will lead your expedition as quickly as possible to Constantinople with steady and harmonious leadership. We will give you guides, and we will cause you to be furnished with the necessary food by opening markets along the way at a just price. To buy at the market at Nish, hostages are required to insure there is no trouble. They will be safely returned as soon as you move on in an orderly fashion. Farewell."

Expecting some grumbling, Tancred was touched with new sympathy for the little monk when Peter broke down and wept with gratitude. He assured Tancred he would surely abide by the laws of Nicetas and the Byzantine Empire. Once again Tancred was convinced that Peter had long ago lost control of his followers and that the quarreling knights and footman did as they wished. Peter looked weary, worn, and anxious to be on his way. Two leaders from among the knights rode forward, scanning Tancred with hard faces.

"Be it known, Greek, that we are honorable knights. We offer ourselves as hostages until the people buy food from your markets. I am Geoffrey Burel, and this my fellow is Walter of Bridewell."

Tancred said nothing. He gestured for them to be led back toward Nish while Peter looked on. The people were quiet, more anxious to reach the markets than they were over the care of the two knights.

Tancred rode guard with his large contingent of soldiers, as they led the peasants to the marketplace. The soldiers kept the peace while the peasants thronged the booths and the fruit and vegetable stands.

The day was hot and sultry. Along the high road came

an endless stream of people, carts, and animals. Fragrances of overripe melons, purple grapes, figs, thin-skinned cucumbers, leeks, and garlic filled the air. The grounds of the marketplace were scattered with fruit skins covered with ants and flies. Soldiers were everywhere, and Tancred rode in the saddle, wearied by the sun.

A group of soldiers rode past on patrol, their imperial saddle cloth and fringed reins bearing witness to their Byzantine loyalty. The thin-faced warriors wore pointed helmets of gray, with a circlet of white cloth around their brows. Tancred's eyes fell on the scimitars they carried, and he felt wry amusement. Little did Peter's group know that the soldiers keeping them under watchful eye were mercenary Seljuk Turks.

Ahead, voices lifted in argument; horse hooves rattled over the stones.

Another quarrel, thought Tancred wearily, and rode to see what it was about.

A peasant girl was arguing with a fruit stand owner over the price of a melon. In the heat of disagreement she dropped it, splattering juicy orange fruit and seeds on the ground.

"You will pay!" the shopkeeper demanded, flushed with anger and the day's summer temperature.

"Nay. I demand justice!"

"Justice! You sought to steal my melon. You deliberately dropped it!"

"It fell from my hand. I will not pay!"

"Thief. Mongrel barbarian. Go then! Be gone!"

But she stooped to gather up the broken pieces into a bag, brushing off the dirt from the yellow flesh.

"What? Nay," he shouted at her. "It was a trick. You dropped it to steal it by deceit—"

"It is sour. Not even sweet. It is full of ants."

Tancred squinted at her from beneath his helmet. That voice. He knew it. Modestine.

As the argument raged, Tancred drew a Byzantine besant from his tunic and tossed it to the shopkeeper. "It is paid for."

The shopkeeper snatched it up, looking curiously at Tancred. But satisfied, he cast a disgusted glance at her and turned to the other customers.

Seeing Tancred astride the horse, Modestine stared, shocked, then cried gleefully: "Monsieur priest, it is you! It is you!"

Holding the bag with the pieces of melon, she rushed into the street to the side of his horse, smiling up at him, her amber eyes gleaming like gems.

Her lot had not improved, he thought. If anything she looked more dirty, and her hair had grown another six inches. It trailed way below her back in snarled ringlets.

"Where is Niles?"

"He is here, monsieur. We are both with the good Peter. We could not stay at the abbey. Our hearts and souls wept for Jerusalem."

Tancred's brow arched. He gave her a searching look, and she blushed, clutching the bag.

"You could not be content at the abbey believing Jerusalem's streets were built not with stones but chunks of gold," he said.

"Oh, monsieur, everyone was taking the expedition! Even the abbot. And so we came with him."

"Where is he?"

She heaved a sigh, more exaggerated than genuine. "Oh, monsieur priest, he drowned in the Sava River. The Hungarians were shooting arrows at us as we fled on rafts that we built—"

"Built or stole?"

"Monsieur, you harm my heart. Built with our own hands."

"And the wood? You robbed the forests no doubt," he teased.

"Oh no, monsieur, we used the wood from their houses. The infidels fled into the mountain, so we took possession, and then used the wood."

Tancred stared at her. "You tore up their houses to make boats?"

"Not me, nor Niles, but the knights and the other men. They said we had to cross the river because King Coloman was coming with an army. After the fighting, with so many Hungarians dead, everyone feared."

"With good reason. And the peasants whose houses you tore up for boats were not infidels. They too were Christians."

Modestine gasped with unbelief. "Oh no, monsieur priest. The men, the knights under good Peter, would never do anything so wicked."

"No," he said dryly. "Of course not. And the abbot drowned trying to flee?"

"Many could not swim. Others were killed. Many were taken. They are now slaves. Friends of mine and their children have disappeared."

"I warned you not to come, mademoiselle, did I not?"

"Yes, and your words were wise, says Niles. He has said a hundred times we should not have come. But it is too late now."

"Where is he?"

She pointed down the road to a field. Tancred saw a small, makeshift tent with some horses. The horses of the brigands. The tent roof was made of sun-deteriorated cloth.

"We are there, with the horses. He guards them. You will come?"

Tancred rode up and dismounted, and the girl ran to lead Apollo into the shade.

"He is a beautiful stallion," she said.

"He is not mine. He is loaned to me."

Modestine shouted for Niles, and a moment later he appeared. His reddish hair was tinged golden by the months of direct sun, and his face was brown and hard. He wore a ragged tunic and a pair of boots that were too small. Where he had gotten them was anyone's guess.

Niles saw Tancred, recognized him with a sudden smile, then limped toward him. "Seigneur Redwan, by the saints, it is you!"

Tancred smiled and stepped under the cloth roof to escape the sun. He removed his helmet. "So you and Modestine are with Peter. No wonder there has been so much trouble along the way," he jested.

Niles had the grace to flush beneath his tan. "You have heard of the evil that litters our trail. I am ashamed, Seigneur. I did not know it would be this way, I had thought the priests could keep order and reverence among us, but alas, there are too many. I have seen Peter the Hermit but twice since we left! He rides far ahead in the vanguard, days ahead, while quarrels break out daily up and down the march."

"But it was not always this way," Modestine hastened to add.

"No," said Niles wearily. "When we left Amiens, and marched to Cologne, everyone was well behaved. Hymns and chants could be heard up and down the columns. The knights fasted, and the priests led in many prayers each morning and evening. And Peter would come riding along the column to speak words of courage and faith. But then in the Rhineland . . ." he stopped.

So he knew of the Jews, thought Tancred.

Niles quickly rushed on. "And in Hungary, King Coloman was friendly and his people gave us food. Some joined the expedition. Then certain Rhinelanders among us began to quarrel with the Hungarians over a matter I know naught of. They stole wine, and when well drunk, they turned on the Hungarian peasants with stealing and killing, burning down houses and storehouses of grain." He clasped his head between his hands. "Would God I had stayed in France!"

Modestine was at his side, her arms around his. "But we are soon home to Jerusalem, Niles. And our vines!"

He brightened and looked up at Tancred. "Yes, we have vines. Show them to Count Redwan."

She disappeared outside the flimsy shelter. Tancred saw that it consisted of several small rugs spread on the ground, two stools, and cooking utensils.

"What made you decide to come?" Tancred asked. "Why did you not stay?"

Niles shook his head almost numbly and could find no answer. He stared down at his too-tight boots.

"This is madness, Niles. And what happened at Semlin and Belgrade is only the beginning."

"I know that. But it is too late. I have heard the knights say we will cross the waters to the East as soon as we reach Constantinople."

"A worse mistake. Peter and his few knights cannot defeat the Seljuks."

"Walter Sans-Avoir is waiting for us with fifteen thousand."

"And most of them are only peasants like yourself. Do you have a weapon?"

Niles hesitated. "A sword belonging to the brigand. The rest we sold for food at Cologne."

"A sword," repeated Tancred. "That is more than most have. The Seljuk Turks own fast horses, and every man is armed with scimitars and bows."

"I believe you speak the truth."

"Then stay here. If you go with the others across the Bosphorous into Asia Minor, you walk to your death. Wait for the feudal princes to arrive with their armies."

Modestine came in carrying a wooden box. Niles opened the lid, and Tancred looked inside. Fresh cuttings from grapevines rested in damp soil.

"It is a long way yet to Jerusalem," said Tancred.

"We will keep the cuttings wet," said Niles quietly, as though he spoke from habit and not from conviction.

Modestine grinned. "In Jerusalem, monsieur priest, we will plant a vineyard. We will have fig trees and olive trees."

She stood and smiled proudly. "And God will give us many children to work our land."

For the first time, Tancred noticed that she was expecting a child. He took a handful of the damp soil and pressed it into Nile's hand. "Plant them here. Nicetas thinks well of me. I will try to get you a piece of land. Small now, but you can increase it. How much better to find rest here, near a strong garrison. Your baby will be safe. The weather is good for farming. You have seen the excellent produce at the fruit and vegetable stands."

At the mention of the marketplace, Modestine brought out her broken melon, offering Tancred the fattest piece. He accepted a smaller section and flipped off a crawling ant.

"We have come this far," said Niles. "We must go on.

We would live in the holy land. Besides, I have taken the vow."

He turned his sleeve toward Tancred to show the cross. The once bright piece of cloth was faded, the sleeve torn.

"Then I wish you God's protection." Tancred stood, and Niles faced him.

Tancred took the last of his gold besants and gave them to him.

"Count Redwan, we could not—"

"For the coming child. And perhaps you will think again of staying, of planting your cuttings here at Nish. Adieu, my friends."

That night, Tancred returned to his quarters to find Philip waiting. "Well, friend Tancred, except for a group of Rhinelanders quarreling with a townsman, we have avoided trouble. Nicetas is pleased. Once again you have proven yourself invaluable to us."

"You flatter me. I did no more than any of your mercenary soldiers. Did Nicetas release the two hostages?"

"Yes. The peasants will start for Sophia first thing in the morning, as will we. Lady Irene is anxious to be back at the Sacred Palace with Helena, and so am I. I have long planned to aid the minister of war. This is my finest opportunity."

Tancred removed his armor. He wondered about the position Irene had gotten Philip. Exactly who was she?

"Are you related to Lady Irene?"

Philip's expression tightened. "She is my mother."

Tancred watched him leave. The position of aiding the minister of war meant much to Philip. How much authority did Irene have in the emperor's palace?

He remembered Helena and her dilemma. Was she as anxious to get back to Constantinople? There was much about her past and her present situation that she had not wished to explain to him.

The next morning, Tancred rode with the military escort flanking the Byzantine entourage that carried Lady Irene and Helena down the road toward Constantinople. The chariot was surrounded by Irene's personal guards and slaves as well as soldiers under Philip and Tancred. Irene traveled with the pomp of a queen.

Helena sat beneath a canopied top of crimson silk with a gold fringe. She refused to look at Tancred as he rode by, but occupied herself with fanning her face with peacock feathers.

They had not traveled far from Nish when trouble broke out. Philip rode up to Tancred, his expression angry.

"The Rhinelanders who quarreled last night have set fire to the mills by the river."

The fire was raging, the smoke darkening the sky above the river. Tancred hailed one of the peasants from the caravan. "You, what is your name?"

"Lambert, Seigneur."

"Find Peter. Tell him what has happened. Tell him to come with all speed on that donkey of his. Nicetas will hear of this attack and demand new hostages."

"Yes, Seigneur, yes."

The townspeople along the river were running wildly away from the spreading flames. The mills were burning fast, and black billows of smoke spiraled into the morning sky.

The senseless attack would bring Nicetas's wrath on the peasant-army, thought Tancred.

As he turned to ride toward the garrison, soldiers rode swiftly toward the retreating peasant-army, swords unsheathed.

CHAPTER 21

On to Constantinople

✣ Petchenegs with pointed helmets and small shields rode fiercely toward the Crusaders. The Rhinelanders had only a flash of warning before the soldiers were upon them.

Tancred heard the pounding hooves, the death cries of men struck down, and the clash of metal. In a short time punishment had been wrought by the increasingly impatient Nicetas. Many were dead, and prisoners were taken as hostages.

The donkey bringing Peter the Hermit came trotting. He looked dismayed, and Tancred ordered the soldiers to take him to see Nicetas. But while the monk conferred with the Byzantine governor, a riot broke out.

"You cannot trust these miserable Greeks. They are full of treachery," shouted someone in the crowd. "Innocent men sworn to the oath of the expedition are dead! And now Governor Nicetas has taken prisoners. Come, let us teach these Greeks a lesson!"

Tancred rode his horse into the gathering crowd,

drawing his sword. "Do not be fools. The governor will retaliate again if you attack. You have lost men; save your fighting for the Turks."

"You are one of them!"

"Some among you found it amusing to set fire to the houses and mills outside the walls."

"It is naught compared to what they will have now!" shouted a gaunt footman.

With teeth bared in anger, he heaved his pike toward Tancred. Another lunged at him.

Tancred wheeled his horse, trying to move out of the surging mob's path. Petchenegs rode into the fray to aid him, swiping with their scimitars. Confusion broke out.

Amid shouts and screams, the fighting exploded. Within minutes a battle raged. Thousands surged blindly forward, attacking the town's fortifications. The garrison troops drove them back, swinging scimitars and using arrows. Masses fell beneath the horses' hooves.

The order came from Nicetas even as Peter raced on his donkey to warn the mob to cease. Nicetas, his patience gone, ordered a full-scale assault on the rear guard. The peasant-Crusaders were scattered; many bodies littered the ground.

The Byzantines in town, furious at the burning of the mills, rushed to aid the garrison. Men, women, and children were taken prisoners.

"God's money chest," wailed Peter the Hermit. "It is gone!"

"They have stolen it," shouted the knights, "and the oxen!"

Tancred saw the remains of the broken cart and several slain knights on the ground. The chest, brought all the way from Cologne and containing the coins the Jews had surrendered, was lost or stolen.

As the fighting continued, Peter turned on his donkey and fled for the hills surrounding Nish, followed by some five hundred men on horses. The people ran in all directions, and Tancred caught sight of men, women, and children being led away into captivity by the citizens.

He rode ahead to the front of the peasants' column. Those in front knew little of what had happened, and the garrison soldiers urged the remaining peasants forward toward Constantinople, anxious to be rid of them.

But by morning, news of the massacre had spread. The people wept. Where was the good Peter? Was he too slain? What of their friends and family members? They were slaves. Would they ever be free again? And who would lead them to Jerusalem now?

Tancred searched for Niles and Modestine. They had wisely ridden toward the front when the fighting broke out.

Modestine was weeping, and Niles was grim.

"All is not lost," he said. "We have the horses."

But when she would not be comforted, he looked up at Tancred astride Apollo. "We lost the vine cuttings."

On the road to Sophia, many stragglers joined the remaining Crusaders, coming out of the forests and mountainsides where they had fled. At Sophia, Peter arrived on his donkey, a worn and troubled man, so dismayed at the turn of events that he threatened to give up the expedition. But when another seven thousand arrived, he took heart, counted his losses, and decided to go on. A fourth of the peasant-Crusaders had been lost in death or captivity during the battle.

Tancred was more anxious than ever to reach Constantinople and pursue his own quest. He had tasted too deeply of the bitter cup of the peasant-Crusade.

At Sophia, on the road to the Queen City, they were

met with a second envoy sent by the emperor to lead Peter to the walls of Constantinople, promising free food to the peasants along the route.

In a week they reached Philippopolis, a city founded by Philip of Macedon and built on three hills. Tancred found it a lovely city in a vast plain, full of Greek splendor, with high walls, domed Greek churches, and temples.

The Byzantines were so moved by Peter's tales of suffering that the citizens brought gifts of money, horses, and mules. The little monk was smiling again; a new surge of victory spread through the ragged army; and Niles and Modestine discovered fresh vine cuttings from a sympathetic grape grower. The peasant-Crusade lived on.

Two days outside Adrinanople, more envoys came to greet Philip and Lady Irene and to bestow on Peter a message from the emperor.

A Greek envoy in purple and black, astride a fine horse, read pompously to Peter and the throng: "The expedition will be forgiven for its crimes, as the people have already suffered."

Again the monk wept at the joyous favor being shown him by the emperor. By August they arrived outside the great walls of Constantinople, where Peter and his followers would camp until the arrival of the main army under the feudal princes.

PART THREE

CHAPTER 22

Constantinople

✤ Shafts of morning light filtered between puffs of clouds like gold dust sprinkling the Sea of Marmora. Bronzed slaves dipped their oars, slicing through the water without a ripple as the guard galleys passed the water gate and the broad marble steps of the Sacred Palace. The monotonous tone of their voices chanted in time with the oars' rhythm.

Tancred rode Apollo though the Golden Gate. A lean figure with a hawk-like countenance left the crowds and rode up silently beside him.

"The Queen City dazzles even her most cynical guests, does she not, master?"

That voice! Tancred turned his head. Zakeem, his Moorish friend and ally from Palermo, grinned at him.

"Zakeem," he exclaimed, "you are a welcome sight! But you are late, Father of Craftiness. Where were you when I was sold as a slave by Mosul to a pack of Rhinelanders?"

"Ah, master, I waited at Palermo until I grew ashamed of my slothfulness. I guessed you had caught Mosul's trail and followed him here to Constantinople. I was right. You have come."

"But I did not catch his trail as I would have wished. I came with the crusading peasants and by hired service to Philip the Noble, an unpleasant journey, I assure you."

"I saw the peasants." Zakeem sobered. "They will die if they cross the Bosphorous to confront the Seljuks."

"They are blind, believing they will conquer."

Zakeem's dark eyes were troubled. "And the Turks, they cry 'Allah' and believe he will save them."

"God is no respecter of persons, Zakeem. What matters is truth."

"Well said. At least you are safe. And Nicholas?"

"He is only now leaving with the armies of the feudal princes. We will wait here for him, but we will not be idle. The ring of al-Kareem and your crafty old eyes and ears will find news of Mosul in the bazaars."

Zakeem was right about the Queen City. Although Tancred had seen Cordoba in Spain, and Rome in Italy, the proud city of the Byzantines knew no equal. Like her sister Rome, she was built on seven hills and looked down on her awed visitors and guests with the indifferent superiority of a beautiful woman adored by too many suitors.

Tancred scanned the splendid ramparts. Who among the warring races had yet been able to conqueror this city? The double walls, thirty feet high and more than seventeen miles in circumference, boasted eleven gates guarding the landward side of Byzantium. The peninsula lay between the Sea of Marmora and the Golden Horn, with the Bosphorous separating the city from the purple hills of Asia.

Tancred had heard tales of the great battles with the invading Huns and Visigoths, who had besieged the city only to pack up and return from where they had come, leaving her intact. Always the ruling emperors managed to hire mercenaries to do their fighting. Just as the Emperor Alexius Comnenus had sent ambassadors to Pope Urban in the West to ask for Christian warriors to ferret out of the Byzantine kingdom the now invading Seljuk Turks.

As in the past, the warriors came. The peasants under Peter were not the fighting men the emperor wished; these would be good servants to the Western knights, water carriers, cooks, and washers. But the emperor placed his hopes in the great lords and the hundred thousand Ironmen.

The crenellated towers on the great walls that Tancred gazed on were enriched by the luxuriant growth of ivy, wild vine, and Judas trees in fragrant bloom. The towers arose before him like massive sentinels guarding the ancient civilization of Greece, with proud heads lifted to the sky.

Morning business had already begun at the Golden Gate with a babble of confusing dialects. Several large caravans of merchants, bringing their wares from Baghdad and Cairo, were passing into the city.

Tancred and Zakeem fell in beside the hustle of camels flowing into the city. The tall, brownish-gray beasts swayed past with their hump bales from the East loaded with prized goods for the bazaars: ambergris, spikenard, frankincense, leather goods, silk, dates, pomegranates, and olive oil. Barefoot slaves, using small whips to chase away beggars, trotted beside the camels.

In the room Tancred shared with Zakeem, he opened the window that looked directly onto the cloistered quarter of wealthy Venetian merchants.

Beyond the stone walls that were built along the seaward side of the quarter were wharves and quays, with the houses of seamen and dock workers crowded onto pilings over the water. The city within a city faced the Bosphorous Sea, and ships from all the known world's ports were seen moving from the open sea into the strait of the Golden Horn.

Tancred could look across the Bosphorous, dark under gathering clouds, to the low hills of Asia. From there, the ill news had reached Constantinople that the peasant-Crusade under Peter the Hermit had been destroyed by the Seljuk Turks. The Crusaders had ignored the emperor's call to wait for the feudal armies of the princes and had begun pillaging the areas outside the walls of Constantinople, robbing summer palaces and churches, and taking metal from the roofs, evidently to make weapons.

Tancred had heard that the emperor had sent them by boats into the territory of Anatolia, held by the Seljuk Turks, at the Crusaders' boastful request. The news at first was of minor success. The peasants made forays against the Turks but then turned on the Greek Christians in the villages, thinking they were infidels. They rounded up flocks and herds and tortured and massacred the Christian inhabitants, even roasting babies on spits.

When the news arrived in September that the peasants had come to an ignoble end, Tancred was not surprised. They had managed to take a castle, and the Turkish sultan sent a high military commander with a large force to recapture it. With the castle's water supply cut off, the Crusaders surrendered. All who refused to remove their crosses were slain; those who yielded were sent in captivity to Antioch, Aleppo, and far into Khorassam.

The rest of Peter's following, reported to be some twenty thousand, marched to a narrow, wooded valley to avenge their brethren. Near the road to Nicaea, the Seljuks were lying in ambush. Knights with their footmen, priests, women and children, the old and infirm were

239

slain. Only those young boys and girls whose appearance pleased the Seljuks were spared and taken into slavery.

A lone Greek who had been with the peasant-Crusaders had managed to find a boat and escape to Constantinople to inform the emperor. At once Emperor Alexius sent ships to rescue some three thousand, who were trapped at Civeot.

It was ironic, thought Tancred, that Peter the Hermit, the one man who had initiated the peasant expedition, had escaped. He had remained in the city of Constantinople and was now waiting for the feudal princes to arrive, the very thing that both the pope and the emperor from the beginning had urged him to do.

And Niles and Modestine? Tancred had not been able to locate them in the refugees saved from Civeot. He assumed they were dead.

The peasant-Crusade had come to an end.

Tancred gazed out across the waters, looking beyond the mountains and thinking of the great city of Antioch. But before Antioch, he would journey to the Castle of Hohms. There, in command of mercenary soldiers, was his uncle Rolf Redwan.

He wanted to be on his way riding to see him and to find Mosul. But the problem now facing him was immense. He must exercise patience and wait for word from his grandfather's informant. Zakeem too sought information in the bazaars.

For Tancred to locate Mosul in his own arena was to place himself in a position of weakness. Tancred must know for certain where Mosul was. Did he serve a sultan who would defend him against his infidel Norman cousin?

Tancred and Zakeem had turned up little information. Rumors abounded. But the informer who knew al-Kareem had not shown up. Had his grandfather been unable to contact him? But Zakeem assured him the messages had been sent.

"Patience, master, will reward our stay in the city."

They heard rumors that Mosul was in Egypt, Baghdad, even Tunis. Some swore he was in Constantinople. Each day Tancred and Zakeem took turns wandering the bazaars, waiting for the informer who knew al-Kareem to come from the black tents of Aleppo, near Antioch. Like a stallion biting at the bit in his desire to race, he tasted impatience.

Then one day a slave of Philip the Noble appeared on the wharves asking for Tancred. Zakeem brought him word, and he went to meet the slave in the shadows of sleeping ships' hulls and creaking quays. A written message was delivered, and Tancred returned to their small room.

Philip the Noble desired an audience with him at the Sacred Palace. "I promise, friend Tancred, my offer will be well worth your service."

"News, master?"

Tancred folded the message and placed it inside his tunic. He belted on his scabbard. "The courageous Noble has requested my presence at the Sacred Palace."

Zakeem tossed bits of raw meat to his falcon. "Can you trust this soft Greek? I do not like him."

"Nor I. But our purse is in need of gold coins, Zakeem. If we are to pay our keep here and fill our bellies, it is worth hearing what he has to say."

There was something else he did not tell Zakeem. Tancred wondered about Nicholas's niece. He had not seen Helena since he had left the Byzantine town of Sofia. And, as much as he liked the stallion, he would need to return Apollo to his mistress.

CHAPTER 23

The Street of Bazaars

✤ The din of creaking cart wheels mingled with the bray of a donkey and the complaint of a camel unwilling to rise from its knees under the load of spices. The sedan chair carrying Helena moved down the arcade where the forums and shops of the bazaar ran for two miles. She would walk alone among the hundreds of stalls, and somewhere among the exotic din, her informant would slip up beside her.

"I do not like what you are doing, mistress," Bardas kept repeating. "I have a feeling of ill omen."

"Your ill omens make for worse company than an aged hen." Between the squares of the Agustum and the Taurus, the bazaars set up under porticoes lined the street as far as Helena could see. People thronged the street, and the sedan chair slowed.

"Wait here." She descended from the chair and walked passed the goldsmiths' benches and the money-changers' booths. Merchants sold everything from salt fish to Byzantium silk and perfumes. The perfume sellers had their special stands in the square before the palace.

She paused. A Greek family of acrobats entertained the passersby. Helena counted six children. The small crowd applauded, and a few tossed coins to the ground.

She started to walk on when a dwarf at her elbow bowed before her. He grinned, his bright eyes darting across the street to the flower stand. He extended a single white blossom.

"It blushes in your presence, O fairest among women." As she handed him a coin he whispered, "The flower stall" and moved on.

She walked across the crowded street, careful not to soil her skirt. In the stall with its assortment of flowers, herbs, and oils, she pretended to be interested in buying. She showed no surprise when she heard a familiar voice that insisted she behold the most beautiful flower in all Constantinople. Her nameless informant was disguised as a merchant. Just where the true merchant was she could only guess.

She remained calmly disinterested as he sought to make his sale. Finally his voice lowered. "Your mother yet lives. She is ill."

Her heart raced. She blinked back the tears. Her mother was alive. "How ill?"

"Her life is in question."

"Where?"

"Jerusalem."

Jerusalem! Helena could not move. "I must go to her."

"Try the home of ibn-Haroun. She is a slave."

"A slave only? No worse?"

"No."

He lay a cascade of flowers across her arms. She left the

leather purse of jewels on the stand, partly hidden under a package of dried herbs.

Her heart beat faster, keeping time with her steps as she walked back to the chariot. Her mother was alive, and she would go to her. She wanted to run, to shout for joy! But she did not dare.

Did Irene or Constantine have spies following her? Deliberately she stopped at other booths and pretended interest. At last she was seated in the sedan chair. As they moved off, she said, her eyes sparkling with joy and hope, "She is alive, Bardas. My mother is in Jerusalem. A slave in the home of one ibn-Haroun. And I shall go to her."

Tancred's eyes were busy as he crossed the city on horseback. Zakeem rode beside him on his Arabian mare, with the falcon perched on his shoulder. Constantinople's population was large and diverse. From every country people came, either for business or pleasure, filling the streets with activity from morning until night.

Tancred recognized the turbaned merchants from Persia and Babylon who mingled with the Russians dressed in furs and sporting great mustaches. His eyes caught the glitter of citizens of more distinct background displaying their silks with gold embroidery as they sat on fine horses.

Zakeem looked about the throngs uneasily. "These Greeks, I do not trust them. Their minds are their swords."

Neither did the Western princes with their stalwart knights trust the Byzantines. They would have been insulted to know that the feeling was mutual. The suspicions between East and West bred not only misunderstanding but also dislike. Only the cry to liberate Jerusalem from the Turks and the greed of the young West for new wealth, land, and learning had enabled the two cultures to meet together under the guise of unity.

Tancred was under no illusion; the expedition to free Jerusalem was motivated by political advantage for the emperor. The lands of Byzantium were under Seljuk domination, and he needed the swords of the Western knights. News of the approach of the feudal princes circulated throughout Constantinople.

The Sacred Palace grew in its uneasiness. While the city was prepared to receive them in peace, what of the Norman prince, Bohemond? Was the son of the famed Robert Guiscard prepared to bow the knee to the emperor?

"The king of the Greeks did well to call for the bold knights of the West," said Zakeem. "And yet if I were one of the princes, I would be forewarned. The king lies awake at night hatching his schemes."

Tancred rode easily in the saddle, amused with Zakeem. "Alexius Comnenus would find your term *king* an insult. He views himself as the true Roman Emperor of the East and West."

Zakeem pulled a bright orange from his pouch and began to peel it. "He imagines too much, this Greek. Be proud, master. Few men such as yourself can boast of being related to William the Conqueror and to the House of the great al-Kareem."

Tancred's eyes glinted with irony. "I am certain the emperor will not be impressed with my Norman ancestry. Nor the Moors. He has not forgotten the Norman army that battled his men near the walls of Constantinople. Is it any wonder he looks on Bohemond with caution? The Noble too remembers."

Zakeem relished the sweet, juicy orange. "The Greek

Noble is tiresome and no skilled swordsman. He wishes you at his side for he grows tall in your shadow."

"Yet if we are to journey East to find Mosul, the Noble's wages in gold will make the time spent in his service worthwhile. And I think of Nicholas."

Zakeem had discovered by wandering the camp of the feudal lord Godfrey of Bouillon that Nicholas journeyed with Bohemond. The Normans would arrive by April.

"Speaking of mercenary soldiers, you will meet many fine ones at the Armory and many Normans," said Zakeem.

Soldiers gathered everywhere and came from every class and country. One could see the well-dressed adventurer, the mercenary with his sword or scimitar, and the corsair, all soldiers in their own right, whether in gaudy uniform or rugged dress. It was the one class in Constantinople where Tancred felt at home.

The great bazaar quarter ran the entire street of the Mese, an area of nearly two miles, with shops and forums located beneath ornate porticoes. Here, the world mingled, spreading its lavish goods for inspection, dazzling the eye and filling the nostrils with exotic goods.

With Zakeem now prowling ahead on foot, leading his horse, Tancred leisurely rode Apollo through the throngs of merchants and buyers. He passed the booths of money changers whose tables were covered with coins; workbenches where the smiths sold gold, silver, pearls, and precious stones; weavers of rugs displayed their prizes from Samarkland, some with the intricate design of the eternal pomegranate; and merchants offered tea and porcelain from as far east as Cathay and ivory and indigo from Hind.

Zakeem grabbed a bunch of bananas and tossed the

merchant a coin. He turned to Tancred as he peeled one with vigor. "Eat, master," he said.

Tancred's attention was cut short by a band of soldiers galloping down the street. They were part of the Imperial Guard. Not far behind the soldiers came a private sedan chair bearing nobility, carried by running foot slaves.

Unexpectedly a group of beggars gathered on the street and hindered the flow of traffic. Seeing Helena of the Nobility seated in the expensive lift, they converged on it.

"Alms, O goddess of beauty, alms? For the blessing of Allah!" cried one.

"For the blessing of the Virgin!" cried another falling to her knees.

"Alms, most merciful one!"

Tancred's attention was arrested by the sight of the familiar young woman seated next to Bardas. She wore blue saffron silk embroidered with tiny moline crosses of glimmering gold.

Bardas stood, whip in hand, scowling down on the beggars. "Away, rank dogs! Move!"

Bardas cracked his whip into the air and grumbled like an angry bear protecting its cub. "You dare block the path of nobility? Be gone, vermin!"

Tancred's attention left the grumbling eunuch to fix on Helena. She was glancing about impatiently, but something in her face suggested she was preoccupied and unaware of the beggars. Tancred flung coins onto the street. At once the beggars scattered to gather them, clearing the way.

Her surprised gaze darted to his, paused, then as he bowed in her direction, looked away in dismissal. "Ride on, Bardas."

Tancred smiled as he watched the sedan chair move

forward. She did not turn to favor him with another glance.

He suspected there was more to her haughty behavior than appeared on the surface. If he were conceited, he might think she wished to avoid him because she did not wish to risk her emotions. But she was undoubtedly enamored with the Noble. What she saw in the man was beyond Tancred's understanding.

At the Sacred Palace where he would meet Philip, Tancred left Zakeem. "See what you can discover of Mosul in the Armory," he suggested.

"I shall also visit the bazaars again. By morning I will be waiting at the palace steps."

Tancred was escorted to the Agustum, a magnificent square surrounded by colonnades and segregated on the south and west by the palace of the Senate and the Imperial Palace. The splendor was unrivaled; not even Baghdad compared to this.

From the slope cascading down to the Sea of Marmora, he gazed on the magnitude of terraced buildings forming what was called the Sacred Palace. Here, from the days of Emperor Constantine, each successor to the throne took care to add to the great residence. Palaces, reception halls with marble and gold mosaics, pavilions cloistered in fragrant greenery, barracks for the imperial soldiers, libraries, famous baths and churches—the Sacred Palace had all the pomp necessary for the ceremonial life and culture with which Byzantium dazzled her barbarian visitors.

A slave appeared from the garden and bowed. He was bare from the waist up, and his muscles glistened with oil.

"My master regrets he is not here to greet you. He will return late."

The slave gestured toward the winding garden steps made of marble. "If you will follow me this way to the Noble's chambers?"

"Your master is most generous."

CHAPTER 24

Helena's Chambers

✣ Winter was over, and the Greek nobles who wore the purple belt of royalty were arriving from all sections of the Byzantine Empire to take up their usual summer residence in the private palaces located in Constantinople's wealthy sections. For weeks the slaves had worked to prepare the luxurious living quarters for the arrival of their aristocratic masters.

While Philip was on business at the Castle of Hohms, Helena had arrived from her winter home in Athens with Bardas. But news had just come that Philip had returned to the Sacred Palace, and she was expecting him to escort her to the emperor's majestic banquet.

Tonight would begin the long season of exquisite dinners, games at the Hippodrome, theaters, carnivals, and other celebrations that were so much a part of Byzantine culture. Since Helena's family owned a silk shop on the Street of Bazaars, her luxurious gowns were specially designed in sumptuous colors—bright clear purples, indigos, crimsons—and each tunic was woven with delicate threads of gold.

Tomorrow a grand circus would be led by the emperor on his royal stallion, followed by games in the Hippodrome. Spring in Constantinople was going to be exciting, but if her plans went as expected, she would not be in the city long enough to enjoy it all.

The feudal princes of the West with their armies of knights were arriving, and soon now she would be on her way with Nicholas to locate her mother.

She leaned over the balustrade to peer into the courtyard below the portico. Had Irene once again stopped Philip from coming to see her? Or perhaps Philip had not yet returned from the Castle of Hohms.

She was too cautious to ask many questions from the slaves in the summer palace. Except for Bardas, the other eunuchs were loyal to her aunt. No doubt every question she asked concerning Philip would make its way to Irene.

She had not been permitted to see him alone since their return to Constantinople from Nish in August. Almost immediately Philip had been sent away on business for the ailing minister of war, this time to the regions of Antioch and the port of St. Symeon.

"Did the Noble's dromond return from St. Symeon as expected?" she casually inquired of a slave.

The slave showed no expression. "The dromond docked this morning at the Golden Horn."

Then Bardas would have delivered her message to Philip.

The slave walked on slippered feet to light the colored lanterns in the white-columned portico. Helena waited in the open, salon-like room facing the backdrop of the sea. Even as she strained to see down to the cobbled courtyard, she heard sandaled feet below.

Bardas ran toward the pavilion with a flaming torch in his great fist. His broad oiled face was agitated, and his shaved head glistened in the harsh light. He paused from his rush, seeing Helena above on the gallery leaning over the rail.

"You are late," she called.

"Lady Irene detained me. She has bidden me to see you safely to the Sacred Palace."

"What of Philip? He did arrive? Did you find him?"

"He arrived. But Master Philip was called to see the emperor before the banquet, and I could not relay your message."

The emperor! Helena was stunned to think he would have a private audience. What could it mean?

"That is not all," said Bardas darkly, looking up at her. She read the tone of caution in his voice. "Yes?"

He glanced over his shoulder into the courtyard to see if any slaves hovered in the shadows listening. "The bishop comes to speak with you."

For a moment she forgot Philip. The bishop. She felt a tremor of unease. She did not like the subtle change in plans. She would depart at once and perhaps escape the meeting. Did he know anything about her visit to the Street of Spices?

She leaned over the balustrade. "Hurry, Bardas. Prepare the caique to take me to the banquet. The emperor's procession will soon begin."

"The caique waits at the watergate, mistress."

"Then go now. Wait for me."

"Do not forget your cloak. The spring nights turn suddenly chill. This is not Athens."

"You sound like a mother hen," she said with a laugh. "I can take care of myself. Tonight, I come of age," she added, thinking of her birthday.

"I was afraid you would say as much and get yourself into woe," he said with a gloomy gesture.

He turned and left the garden, the light of his torch slowly disappearing.

Helena turned to snatch up her cloak when the click of the bishop's heels echoed among the marble pillars. She turned to confront him.

"Good evening, my dear Helena. How charming you look."

Constantine stood there, a dark form against the light of flickering torches on the pavilion wall. Tall and strongly built, he wore a handsome black and scarlet cloak, trimmed with silver fur. His dark hair was long and thick and pulled back according to religious custom. He held the usual wide-brimmed black hat belonging to his sect. His magnificent Greek eyes contrasted with his masquerade as a holy man of quiet ways.

Helena refused to show fear. "Do you come peaceably?"

Constantine arched a brow. "With blessings, if you do as I say."

She tensed. *Do as he says?*

"Is it your blessing or Lady Irene's?" she asked coolly.

"Your aunt did not send me."

"I find that difficult to believe."

He heaved a wearied sigh. "You are too much like your mother, suspicious. Matters may have turned out for the better had she been able to control her tongue. But alas. . . ."

"Sir, you would do better to wear the dress of a mercenary soldier."

"What? And lose my seat at the emperor's sumptuous table?" he mocked. "My role is satisfactory for what I have in mind."

"No doubt Irene agrees."

"I have come as a friend. Do hear what I have to say."

Helena might have laughed, but she dared not mock. Neither must she show fear. To survive palace intrigue, she would not allow herself to be backed into a dungeon.

Constantine walked across the polished marble floor and stood between two slim white pillars facing the Sea of Marmora. The setting sun left traces of violet and green against the distant hills of Asia Minor. The crimson edge of his cloak moved about his knees in a whisper of warm wind as he walked to gaze across the waters.

"For your sake, you would do well to cooperate with your aunt."

"Cooperate? And what could she possibly have in her mind?"

He looked at her gravely. "It is about Philip."

Immediately she tensed.

"Irene and I both understand that you and Philip have long had marriage in mind. Now that you have come of age, you would naturally be making plans."

With the arrival of spring and the season of Byzantine entertainment came Helena's birthday debut, which meant that she must marry within the year to gain possession of the castle, its lands, and the sizable tribute. Her fingers tightened about her cloak.

"Philip has written me from the castle," she stated. "We have often discussed marriage. We both assumed it would be this summer."

"Yes, until recently Irene accepted those plans. We both did. We are fond of you, as you know, despite the trouble your mother has brought to us all in the past. We never held you accountable."

Her heart thudded, and her fingers felt cold.

His black eyes met hers evenly. "You cannot marry Philip."

With determination she threw the ermine cape about her shoulders and remained outwardly calm. "I am sorry, but I will marry him. You may go back to Irene and tell her so. Neither you nor Irene will dictate our lives."

"You may persist in your determination, but Philip is too wise to contest."

Uneasiness crept into her outward confidence.

"The will of the emperor is law."

She searched his face. "Why would the emperor bother about me?"

"It was necessary to convince him of the expediency of your political marriage to the Seljuk prince, Kalid, son of the Emir of Antioch."

Helena stared at him, her confidence shattered. The news was preposterous.

"Arrangements are working out well. For your hand in marriage, the Seljuk is willing to discuss Byzantine control of Antioch. Something Emperor Alexius greatly desires."

Her stomach seemed to lurch. Impossible! Marriage to an emir? No, never!

The Syrian city of Antioch, until recently, had belonged to the Byzantine Empire. Now the Seljuk Turks swarmed over Asia Minor. From where the two of them stood on the portico, they could look across the Bosphorous Sea into the growing Seljuk empire.

"In several weeks you will be taken to the port of St. Symeon. There, a caravan from Antioch will take you by land to the city with the elegance afforded a daughter of the emperor himself."

"Nay! Marriage to a Seljuk Turk? I would rather be dead."

He gave her a cynical smile. "Dramatics do not become

you, Helena. The Seljuk prince is rich and powerful. And he is a handsome man. You could do far worse in these dangerous days."

This was Irene's vile scheme! Irene thought to be rid of her by sending her to Antioch. Never!

"You have no choice, my dear. With the death of your mother, Irene is your legal guardian."

She wanted to shout her triumph, that her mother was not dead. But she would be a fool to let him know. They would throw her into the dungeon until she confessed where her mother was.

"Irene betrayed my mother. Now she plots against me."

"Do not look so downcast. You are not the only woman to find herself in a marriage agreement with a man she does not love." He paused. "The memory of Philip will fade. The Seljuk is a strong man. Very clever. Your wedding gift will be the finest racing horses bred in Aleppo."

Infuriated, she grabbed a honey-colored agate vase, worth many gold besants, and hurled it viciously. It cleared Constantine but passed through the open window to the courtyard below. An imperial guard looked up, ready to sound an alarm, but Constantine motioned that all was well.

"I refuse to be sold like baggage. I will appeal to the emperor himself. I will tell him how you and Irene have beguiled him!"

"Seek audience with the emperor, and it will be to your harm. Have you forgotten your mother was arrested for treason?"

As if she could forget!

"I demand to see Philip."

He looked bored. "Philip will do nothing. Do you think he will risk his future in the Imperial Palace? Believe me, Helena, he will walk away from you before he surrenders his political ambitions. Only Irene can secure his success."

"You are wrong about Philip. What do you know of his honor and commitment to noble things? He will not walk away."

He laughed. "Noble? Philip? You will prove yourself a fool if you go running to him."

"I will risk it. He is in love with me."

"What man with Philip's appetites would not love a beautiful woman? Yet for a young noble like Philip, there are always beautiful women. But a growing future next to the emperor? Ah, that is another matter, my dear. One that is not easily attained."

Stung, she remained silent. Of course Philip was ambitious. And he desired to please the emperor. But he had vowed his love to her, and she did not fear that the strength of that love would weaken in the face of this scheme.

"If you love Philip, stay away from him," he said flatly. "He is entrusted with a task, that if successful, will bring him the emperor's acclaim. Do not mar his future by insisting he share it with you."

Not even the idea of Philip's success made an impression on her mind. She must see him at once! The bishop went on speaking, but his words were lost. She stood staring at the Asian hills splashed with gold and rose hues. Prince Kalid . . . Antioch . . . the Castle of Hohms . . .

"The feudal lords are even now arriving from the barbarian West," he was saying. "The expedition to capture Jerusalem from the Seljuk Turks will soon begin. The emperor needs these barbarians. Yet the gathering of massive armies beneath our walls makes for tension. Franks,

Italians, Rhinelanders," he stated with contempt. "All arrogant, untrustworthy! Now the Normans under Prince Bohemond are soon to arrive. Suppose they unite? The emperor is wise not to trust their temperament or their motives. Yet he needs their sworn loyalty. Philip must flatter their arrogant egos, dazzle them with the promise of riches. His task is difficult, and even more so where the arrogant Normans are concerned. He is now entertaining Hugh of Vermandois."

Helena knew little of the disposition of these feudal princes, except that Nicholas rode with Lord Bohemond and the Normans from Sicily. Bardas had discovered this from a bishop in the army of the feudal prince, Godfree of Bouillon.

Count Godfree with his army of seventy thousand knights and footmen from northern France and Germany had arrived in December, with his two brothers, Eustace, Count of Boulogne, and Baldwin, Duke of Lower Lorraine.

Bardas had already reported to her of the journey of Hugh of Vermandois, brother to the king of France, the first of the feudal princes to arrive. His ships, so it was reported, had perished in a dreadful storm on the Adriatic. Some went down with the swells, the rest were battered into the rocks on the Illyrian coast. Hugh had arrived, humiliated.

However, the emperor was cunning enough to entertain him as a great king and soothe his injured pride.

"The emperor gave him gifts of gold, silver, and expensive Byzantine clothing," said Constantine. "He has sworn his loyalty. But the Normans may not be won so easily. Bohemond is a wily and diabolic lord! The emperor has not forgotten his lineage to William the Conqueror."

Now numb, Helena stood there. Philip would not let her down, nor would Nicholas.

"You have no choice in this Antioch matter. If it pleases the emperor that you go to Antioch, you will go."

Bishop Constantine turned and walked toward the door. He paused and looked back. "Irene will be angry if you do not show yourself tonight. Gather your emotions together. I know you well enough to believe you will not faint in contemplation of your future. Like your mother before you, you have too much spirit for that."

He shut the door behind him.

Helena stood there. Slowly comprehension began to flow back into her mind, and her thoughts raced. She cared little about the barbarians from the West that Philip must humor. She had had her share of barbarians at Wieselburg and Nish. And she cared even less about the emperor's concerns for Antioch. She would not become the bride of a Moslem emir to secure the emperor's political intentions. It was enough that she and the Castle of Hohms were to be given as a prize to Prince Kalid. Absurd! Never. Her breath came rapidly, and tiny rivulets of perspiration ran down her ribs. Oh, when would Nicholas arrive?

She must not panic. Tomorrow she would go to the Church of St. Sophia to pray for Christ's intervention.

And Philip? She must see him alone to let him know of the treachery his mother had heaped on them both. Now was the time to think coolly. She would not sit idly by and be sent to Antioch.

Dare she go even now to the imperial section of the palace to find him?

They will not look for me in his chamber.

She picked up her skirt and ran across the terrace to the marble steps and down to the lighted courtyard.

There, between the pillars of the pavilion, the wide steps led down toward the seawall. A thousand stars winked in the ebony sky above the marble threshold of the St. Barbara Gate.

Bardas arrived at the steps in a sedan chair, and trotting slaves carried them down to the water-landing. The caïque that would take them to the Sacred Palace was docked, and guards waited with their flaming torches dancing in the light breeze.

Seated in the caïque with its colored lanterns sending lances of light on the water, Helena drew her cloak tightly about her. The tang in the air smelled salty, and the wind off the water ruffled the white fur about her face. Hearing the water lapping against the caïque soothed her troubled mind.

"Antioch . . . ," she murmured, again tasting the exotic name.

Bardas looked at her. "Mistress?"

She shook her head and refused to meet his eyes.

The muscled arms of the slaves sent the oars gliding powerfully through the shining dark swells. Helena stared across the water to the Sacred Palace where a myriad of lights blazed.

When they arrived, the Imperial Guards belonging to the emperor were on duty, wearing crimson cloaks and bronze helmets. Byzantine galleys were docked at the bank, and colorful pennants fluttered in the breeze.

At any other time her heart would have pounded with excitement, but tonight she felt dazed, even sickened. Philip was the only one she could turn to for help.

Slowly the painfulness of reality begin to flow back into her mind, and her thoughts raced. She shivered as the uncertainty of her future settled on her soul.

Moslem Antioch . . .

Farther in the distance, standing on the blunt barks, humble fishermen lowered their nets into the dark water hoping for nothing more than a profitable catch. Helena would catch far more than a fish! She stared at them, her plans forming in her mind. Instead of attending the banquet, she would go directly to Philip's private chambers within the palace and wait for him.

No, she could not do that. The guards watching his door would know who she was at once.

She must get past them, but how? An idea began to form. Helena watched the slaves go about their duties with stoic faces, blending into the scene.

She would dress as a slave girl. She would carry a tray of wine and food, and tell the guards that Philip the Noble expected the tray. Would it work? If she disguised herself well enough, it might.

It had to work, she told herself. Then, from Philip's chamber, they would escape on horseback to Athens.

She glanced sideways at Bardas. He would certainly put up a cantankerous fuss, but she could bully him into getting her the slave garments. Then once at the Sacred Palace, she would slip away and change in the darkness of the garden. Could she reach Philip's chambers without being stopped?

CHAPTER 25

The Sacred Palace

❖ Night deepened on the Sea of Marmora. At the Sacred Palace bright lights from a myriad of lanterns and torches blazed their kaleidoscopic colors through colored glass.

When Helena arrived at the palace with Bardas, the procession of guests was lining up the marble steps leading into the reception hall to form the welcoming party for the emperor. Lady Irene was not yet in sight, and Helena's heart thumped in her throat. This was her one opportunity. Could she slip unseen into Philip's private chambers?

From the portico, Helena could look down the avenue to the torch-light procession bringing the emperor to the banquet hall. Then came the echo of the prancing hooves of royal stallions, the roll of chariot wheels, and the cadence beat of drums. The roar grew nearer. Soon the trumpet tribute would pierce the night. Wherever Helena's eyes moved she saw the giant Scandinavian ax men, the imperial bodyguard of the emperor. They were brilliantly arrayed in scarlet cloaks with gold edges, their heads protected by plumed bronze helmets of the Immortals. They now moved to line the avenue for the emperor's arrival.

As every eye turned to look down the avenue, Helena inched backward as stealthily as a cat into the shadowed portico.

To the garden, she thought, as she sped down the steps, past the lighted rooms and spacious colonnades. She would be safe in the garden.

Bardas waited in the shadows. "This way, mistress." They ran together until they were cloistered amid the darkness of chinaberry trees and of shrubs on the opposite side of the avenue facing the banquet hall. Here she stopped, gasping, holding the pain in her side.

After a moment she whispered, "Did you bring my disguise?" "Yes," he hissed with disapproval, his broad face sullen. His brow arched. "Do you not know that Master Nicholas will surely have me thrown to the bears for this?"

"Did you bring the tray of food?"

He sniffed. "I did as you ordered. Know this, mistress, the disguise you don places you in many dangers."

"There is no time to talk now. Lady Irene will be arriving."

Bardas retrieved a bundle from behind the bushes and scowled. "It is good that your sweet and godly mother does not see you now."

Mention of her mother only strengthened Helena's resolve to proceed with her plan. She snatched the bundle from his arms. "Keep watch."

He did so, grumbling, "A dungeon beckons. I feel the dampness in my bones."

"The last thing I need is your glib tongue casting shadows on my path."

"You may silence me, but you will not silence your

aunt. Once she discovers you have plotted behind her back to marry Master Philip and escape to the Castle of Hohms, she will be wroth. She and the bishop weave a dark plot."

"All the more reason to act . . . Bardas, this is a monk's cowl—and for a generous build!"

His broad back stiffened. "My first duty is to protect you, mistress."

"In an oversized monk's robe?"

He inhaled with dignity. "A clever disguise. I am well pleased with my efforts."

"The guards will surely know I am not a slave in this! Where did you get it? Nay, do not explain, I can take no more. Oh! What shall I do? And there is no time to exchange it."

Bardas remained rigid.

"If this ruins my opportunity to see Philip," she warned, "'I shall throw you to the emperor's bears."

He snorted his disbelief.

"I shall trip over the hem."

Helena struggled until she managed to slip the heavy, drab garb over her silken splendor, undoing sections of her elaborate hairstyle as she did. The hem fell to the walk like a weight about her feet.

"What of my hair? What did you bring?"

He mutely handed her a woolen mantle, avoiding her glare. "It weighs more than I do!"

Could she get by with it? She was not quite the image of a true slave girl. Perhaps the guards would be too busy with thoughts of the emperor to notice.

A minute later she said nervously. "Well, Bardas, is Helena of the Nobility a slave, or is she a monk?"

Bardas turned slowly. He winced. "I tell you, mistress,

I shall not rest with a moment's peace until this wicked night dawns with the sun."

"Fear not, my croaking toad, once I sneak past the guards into Philip's chamber, I can hide there until he arrives. Now go. Wait for us at the royal stables. Philip and I will escape while Irene and the bishop are at the banquet."

"Do not underestimate them. Their will to thwart your cause is bound and twisted together as iron to iron. Does the Noble possess the strength of a Greek god to tear it asunder?" He leaned toward her. "The golden goddess Irene is queen of signs and potions. With them she woos those who seek the knowledge of the ancient idol-gods."

Helena knew that her aunt was involved in astrology and rare drugs, which she used on those who sought her advice. She suspected that even the wife of the emperor was somehow beholden to the teachings of Lady Irene, who imagined herself a medium for the stars.

She shivered beneath the warm robe. Philip too, from the days of childhood, was brought up under her teachings and held the stars in reverence. The knowledge of this disturbed her, yet she had said nothing to him. Likewise the bishop who claimed allegiance to the holy Scriptures and to Christ, felt no twinge of conscience in dabbling with the diabolical.

But, then, he is no true servant of the church, she thought. "You need not warn me of that, Bardas. We both know she will do anything to control those in power. I am sure now that my mother understood this. Now it is me she hopes to control. But I shall yet outwit her, not only about my mother but about Antioch. Wait and see if I do not. God is surely with me."

"I perceive a black cloud of gloom appearing on the

horizon. Plans that are hastily made too often become en-
tangled in Byzantine intrigue."

"You and your gloom," she scoffed. "I shall not be defeated. Go now. Enough said."

Ignoring his lowered brows, she hurried over the
lawn, dragging the monk's robe behind her, and disappeared among the plantain trees.

In the spacious garden court, Helena paused behind a
bubbling water fountain to catch her breath. The other
guests were arriving. These would not attend the royal
feast but the celebration that followed.

Her path wound toward the seaward side of the garden where a guard galley of the emperor slipped past the
steps of the palace. Behind the galley came the gilded
caïques of important guests, each small boat aglow with
bright-colored lanterns.

Helena cautiously made her way through the shadows
of fragrant shrubs. At any other time, she would have
paused with delight to drink in the heady sweetness. But
not tonight. Nothing mattered tonight but escaping with
Philip.

Through the shrubs, she glimpsed the stairs ahead,
with their side-gardens and towers blazing with yellow-red
torches. In the light came flashes of golds and purples, the
rustle of silks, and the masculine step of cordovan leather
on marble as the strolling guests passed by. The scent of
Judas tree blossoms hung heavily in the night air, and
laughter floated to her ears.

But it was broken by the echo of the Imperial Cavalry's
hooves coming up the avenue. At once the atmosphere
took on a somber note, and the guests scattered to hail the
majestic procession.

The emperor's entourage! thought Helena with excitement.

She was forced to wait in the shadows of the trees before crossing the avenue. Straining on tiptoe to get a clear
view down the street, her eyes riveted on the approaching
chariot. The majestic horses pranced to the steady drumbeat. Their thick, glossy manes and tails, which had been
brushed until they gleamed in the torchlight, were
adorned with gold and silver ornaments. The torchlight
procession had begun as a foot walk through the gates of
the emperor's residence, and now with pomp it ascended
the wide street beneath the white walls of the Sacred Palace. As the procession neared the banquet hall, the haunting tribute of the royal trumpets blared forth.

Helena stared, heart in throat. *How magnificent!*

When the entourage reached the square, the Byzantines greeted the processional with voices raised in loud
salute: "Hail to the Emperor Alexius, always fortunate and
victorious! Hail to the emperor!" Taut with excitement,
her brown eyes were large and sparkling as the royal chariot passed and she caught a glimpse of the emperor. He
stepped from the chariot, and Helena had a clear view.

Tradition fixed his costume, and she saw that he wore a
purple mantle over one shoulder with a rope of pearls.
Behind the emperor, muscled slaves carried a sedan chair,
and she glimpsed Lady Irene in white silk, her golden
hair gleaming with rubies. Beside her sat the empress.
Next followed a chair carrying Bishop Constantine, wearing his cloak of black and scarlet, his collar lined with
white marten fur. At his side sat a young man. His features
were well-defined, his pointed beard and mustache vainly
kept.

Helena's eyes narrowed. His gilded dress was some
sort of uniform, and his manner suggested ruthless intelligence. Could this be Prince Kalid?

She did not see Philip in the emperor's train. Did he

already know of the plan to send her to Antioch? If he did, he would be trying to locate her so they could escape.

The Imperial Guard moved forward to escort the emperor through the courtyard and the arched colonnades to the grand hall. Nothing was in view except their bronze helmets and scarlet cloaks.

The avenue began to clear, and Helena crossed the street precariously. She climbed the marble steps, carrying the tray of wine and sugared fruits.

Torches blazed on the walls of the massive hall. She glanced about, and seeing no one, sped down the corridor that led to Philip's chambers. As she neared, she slowed to a cautious walk, then suddenly stopped, hearing a clink of metal and the heavy tread of boots.

A guard stood nearby, his scarlet cloak fluttering in the evening breeze. His head, bearing a bronzed helmet, lifted, and empty eyes confronted her.

A tiny fear, like a kindled flame, sprang up in her heart. "God most merciful, most mighty," she whispered, nothing moving but her lips as she walked softly forward, keeping her face averted.

A moment later, she stopped in front of him, seeing nothing but the scabbard that held his sword in place. Her throat went dry.

"The Noble Philip has requested wine and food for his chamber this night."

She felt his cold eyes take in her garb.

"Who, and what, are you?"

Her tray began to shake, the goblets tinkling. "I am the only daughter of my mother, who lately has come to serve God in the monastery."

The moment of silence exploded with uncertainty. "Since when does a woman of vows serve wine in the Noble's quarters?"

"Um . . . since ordered thus by Bishop Constantine."

"But the Noble is not in his chambers."

"This I know, lord. He will return after the emperor's banquet tonight. It may be that the emir's son from Antioch will come with him."

"For his guest?" he said of the tray.

"Yes, for his guest."

"You may enter."

With a tingle down her spine, she walked past him, fearful that he would change his mind. The marble floor beneath the soles of her feet felt smooth and cold, and the hem of the robe swept along behind her. She imagined his heavy boot unexpectedly stepping on it to stop her progress.

One . . . two . . . three . . . she held her breath until she rounded the corner and was out of sight, then rushed as fast as the robe would allow her to the door of Philip's chamber. Once inside, she shut the door with its straps of iron and collapsed against it. She began to tremble, the tray clattering. Cautiously she set it on the agate table.

For a moment she shut her eyes, trying to gain a measure of self-control. Her heart slammed in spite of the effort.

There was no sign of Philip, but the lanterns were bright, as if he were momentarily expected. Through the wide open terrace past the white Corinthian columns, a scented garden stretched down to the seawall. In the distance, the slaves who guarded their masters' caïques until the banquet was over appeared as figurines. She watched the colored glass of the lanterns wink blue and gold as the boats bobbed up and down with the rhythm of the swells.

Beyond the sea, the hills of Asia stood like hunched

camels against the skyline. She shivered. Beyond those hills lay Antioch.

Muffled steps in the next room arrested her thoughts. Her eyes averted to the brocade drape leading into another of Philip's chambers.

Philip was here. He must have returned unnoticed by way of the open colonnade and the garden.

She removed the monk's robe and threw it aside. With cold fingers she rearranged her tresses, making sure the pearls were in place.

She must look as white as the snow on Mt. Athos, she thought, and gave a pinch to both cheeks, then inhaled deeply. The door opened, and Helena whirled to face Philip stepping in from the hall.

Startled, he paused, then with a frown he shut the door behind him. "Why, Helena! What are you doing here?"

"Philip, it is you!"

Her first impulse was to rush into his arms. She held herself in check and stood staring, now speechless.

"My dear, is something wrong?" he asked.

She had not seen Philip since he left for the Castle of Hohms months earlier. The time lapse was like an entire youth spent, but even so, she had not realized how little he resembled the image of the Greek noble she had fed within her memory. She looked at him now, almost surprised.

Something was different. The noble lift of his dark head was the same, so too was the slight frown on his aristocratic face, his elegant dress, his authority. The outward appearance remained definable.

Yet there was a perceptible change. What was it? She could not analyze now; the turmoil of her mind forbade it. Her breath came with rapid gasps.

He came to her, was prepared to speak, but then his eyes fell on the monk's robe on the marble floor. His brows pinched together, and he stooped to pick it up.

A breath of impatience escaped his lips. "Surely you did not come here wearing this?"

"Philip, I—I had to see you!"

"Helena, your whims can no longer be construed as the impulsive pranks of girlhood. Your conduct could bring us both the worst kind of scandal. Neither of us can afford to anger the bishop. My position in the palace is too important to risk."

He scolded her as though she were a silly maiden out to perform a dare. His features were taut as he gazed down at her.

Again she was taken with the change in him since their return from Nish. The displeasure in his voice brought a sinking feeling. Where was his delight in seeing her after so long an absence? Why did he not show concern for the risk she had taken? "If the guard discovers who you are, the news will reach Irene and Constantine at once. You cannot afford this kind of gossip on the eve of your debut. Why the son of the emir—" he stopped.

Helena took a step backward, her eyes searching his. "The emir? You know?"

His face suddenly crumbled into a look of despair.

"Philip—why, you already know about Antioch."

"Yes," he whispered, his voice flat. "Yes, I know."

Her hands formed into fists at her side. "Philip!"

His eyes were dark pools of hopelessness. Fear wrapped about her as she saw his impotence. She studied the finely chiseled face. This was his only response? That he knew?

"But how! How did you know?"

He threw down the monk's robe and turned away. She

waited in vain for him to react with chilling horror at the consequences. She saw his shoulders slump a little, as though bearing a heavy load. The moment came and went.

Oddly, as she waited, she felt something cool wing its way through her soul. Did she know this man?

For a moment the awful silence held them prisoners. Then she became aware that he had turned and his hands were squeezing hers so tightly she winced.

"I was informed when I arrived from St. Symeon." His mood changed to one of excitement. "Helena, my success at the Castle of Hohms has impressed the emperor. Irene has spoken to him about my request, and he has granted me the position I wanted."

What success at the Castle of Hohms? Her mind floundered with confusion between her dilemma and what Philip was talking about with such enthusiasm. And how could he change the subject so quickly? How could his mood of utter dejection swing to the high pendulum of excitement?

"Position?" she repeated.

He gave a laugh, bringing her hands to his lips as though she were some befuddled but adorable child. "Do not tell me you forgot? The position of minister of war! Basil was ill and died. I wrote you about his illness in my letters, remember?"

Yes, vaguely she remembered.

"The high position is mine."

Minister of war. Helena's memory flew back to Nish, to the arrival of Irene with the Byzantine delegation, and the dinner given in Philip's honor by Nicetas the governor. She recalled that Irene said the minister of war was ailing, and that Philip was requested to return to Constantinople to assist him. She recalled the letters she had received

272

from him since their return, telling of future accomplishments that would bring his name before the emperor. And when he possessed that authority he would astound the court with his genius.

"Helena! Do you know what my new authority means?"

His voice shocked her back to the moment. Her eyes rushed to his.

The pressure of his fingers wrapped about hers was painful. "I have opportunity to win the emperor's acclaim. I shall use the barbarian knights from the West to destroy the Seljuks! Byzantium will become as great as it was in the days of Justinian. And when I do, someday it will be me instead of the emperor who wields the scepter of power. My mother, the bishop, all of them, all of them will do as I wish. But now? I can do nothing to stop the marriage. Not when the emperor wills it to take place. The arrangements were made weeks ago."

He paced swiftly. "The emperor has plans. He will use the barbarians to defeat the Saracens, then regain control of Antioch."

He stopped and whirled to face her. "I will come for you. The time will pass swiftly. Now, a negotiated peace over the castle is to our advantage."

Stunned by his emotional tirade, it took Helena a moment to gather her wits.

Come for her! Why, he intended to do nothing to stop the marriage!

Her expression must have mirrored her outrage, for he sobered.

"You agree with the plan to marry me to Prince Kalid. You knew about the plan all along, even when you went to the castle, yet you did not come to warn me. Together we might have escaped. Instead you have celebrated your new position as minister of war with Irene and the bishop."

"I did not know until I returned. I swear it is so!" He came to her, taking her into his arms, staring down into her eyes. "But Helena, my love, try to understand my dilemma as well as yours. Can you not see? There is nothing I can do now. But I will, I promise. I intended to explain everything to you tonight at the banquet. I did not realize that Bishop Constantine would speak to you first. Believe me, I wanted to be the one to explain; I did not want you to be hurt."

"Irene knows what the position means to you. She schemed to give you the position before she told you the price you had to pay. And you! You are willing to accept it at my expense!"

"Helena!"

"And you concern yourself with the naive thought of not wishing to hurt me? My very life and future is at risk! Philip, you must do something. Do you not care?"

"My dear," he said swiftly, grasping her shoulders, "of course I care. Today has truly been my hell. I have nearly gone mad trying to think of some way out. But it will take time. If I rush to halt the marriage, I will lose everything I have planned for. Everything that will be for our eventual good. My dear, sweet Helena, how unfair all this is to one so young, so guileless. I could wish to solve the matter simply, but it cannot be done."

"Have they enslaved our wills? We are yet free to choose our way." She rushed to him, holding her cheek against his chest. "My darling, we are like young falcons. We can yet fly before they have trapped us. We must escape to the villa in Athens. There, we can wait for Nicholas to arrive."

He turned away with irritation. "Nicholas! He can do

nothing. It was a mistake to take you to the Danube in search of him."

He looked at her. "And it is useless to flee like frightened birds to Athens."

"Irene wishes to be rid of me, just as she schemed against my mother. And you will let her."

"She is doing what she believes is best for you and for Byzantium."

"She schemes for her own advancement in the Sacred Palace. She is using you, her own son, even as she intends to use me to buy peace with Antioch. Do you think she would labor to promote you if she did not benefit? That she is your mother means nothing. Go to her, Philip. Tell her you will not stand by and allow her to destroy us."

"If I had the authority to stop it, I would do so immediately, but a contest of wills now is reckless. I must wait until time is in my favor. When I can, I will come to Antioch for you."

No, this could not be happening to her. This could not be Philip speaking this way. A man who loved a woman would not stand by and allow her to be sent away. Where was his righteous indignation? Was she a mere trifle to secure his ambitions in the court of the emperor? Where was the courage of a man who would rather face arrest than see the woman he loved given to another?

"What am I to understand? That I am to sacrifice myself to secure your position before the emperor? How clever of her to compensate for our loss by offering you the position of minister of war. So she told you when you arrived? Was it before she announced my wedding?"

"Helena, please." Miserably he turned, walked toward the open terrace, and stood looking across the garden toward the sea.

She waited. The strained silence was driving her mad.

When he said nothing, she whispered, her voice breaking, "Are you saying that you will let me go?"

He whirled, his face haggard. "Shall I draw sword against the emperor? Is that what you want? What will gallantry accomplish but my rotting away in a dungeon? Would it make marriage to Kalid more bearable, is that it?"

"It is not the emperor I wish you to stand against but Irene. She has beguiled even him; she is evil. She bribes the guards with potions and deceives the emperor's wife with her magic."

She saw a flash of raw temper in his dark eyes. "You sound like a foolish peasant, piping about toads and frogs. Her stargazing and herbs mean nothing."

"Foolish?" she walked toward him. "You do not think her words foolish. Was it not her star gazing that first captured your mind as a child? Do not forget I was there also on those nights in the chamber. I saw the look on your face when she told you over and over that the stars would make Philip a crown. And she would be your wise teacher."

His lips thinned. "Do not mock me."

"Oh, Philip, I do not mock you. But do you wish truth or deception?"

"Is it so impossible that I should be emperor one day? What do you know of the gods and what they have destined for their offspring?"

"The gods! Ancient Greece no longer exists." She laid a hand on his arm. "Philip—"

He pulled away. "Irene did not have your mother sent to the dungeon. She tried to spare her, but your mother worked against her. For your safety, you must not resist Irene."

She was surprised by the urgency in his voice.

276

"Philip, you are afraid of her."

His expression grew wearied. "We would both do well to fear her. She has the means to see us exiled."

"So be it. At least we shall have each other. With you beside me, I would not care where I lived. I do not want to lose you, Philip."

He grabbed her. "We will not lose each other. Someday I will have power. And when I do," he said through gritted teeth, "I will send for you."

Her throat constricted. "Only someday, Philip? And what of now, this moment?"

"What would we do if we ran away? Wander the hills of Greece like vagabonds? Constantinople is in my blood, Helena. I care for you, but do not ask me to throw away my future in a moment of emotional weakness."

She turned, holding wearily to the marble statue of the emperor. "I assumed I meant more to you."

She looked at him; her voice had lost its energy. "You love nothing. You have only your dreams, and they are not real.

He shook his head with frustration. "Not so. I meant every word I ever spoke to you. Can you not see that my hands are chained?"

"If they are, she has done it to you, but you have let her. Your dreams, will they satisfy when you have them, Philip? Have they satisfied the emperor?"

He sighed and looked out at the sea. "Peace, where is it found? I do not know . . . I can only promise to come to you when I am free."

His eyes came back to hers, pleading. "In weakness there is slavery. In strength there is freedom."

"Is the emperor free? Is he strong? He must secure barbarians to fight for his throne," she said contemptuously. "Nor does he even trust them. He fears even his own people."

"Give me time, Helena. I will make it up to you. I will make you Empress of Constantinople!"

"Empress?" she gave a laugh. "Do you think I want to rule Byzantium? You have but one love, your pursuit. And though you were emperor, you would never sleep well for fear of plots to remove you."

"You make light of me. But it will not be so. I vow to come to Antioch. I will make you forget the folly of our youth."

Helena shook her head and to her dismay tears stung her eyes. "Nay, if you can give me to the Seljuk now, then a thousand tomorrows in your embrace mean nothing. No, I do not wish to be empress. I wish only to be loved, by you, at any price. For such love, Philip, I would gladly exchange the crown of empress, though it were mine."

"You will change your mind. You will see. Youth is but a fickle dream. When you are empress and stand beside me with all Constantinople at our feet, you will forget Antioch. You will discover, as I already have, that the method taken to travel the long road will mean nothing once you arrive at your destination."

"A sip of Lady Irene's wine has intoxicated you. Her stars have blinded your eyes. Nay, it will not do. And to think I believed I could turn to you in time of danger. That I believed you could love me. Constantine was right about one thing. Sadly so. You are ignoble, my dear Philip. Completely ruthless."

Stung, he took a step toward her, his face white, then he stopped. His dark eyes hardened.

"You will live to regret your words."

He turned and left the chamber by way of the garden stairs.

Numb, Helena watched him disappear down the marble steps into the lighted garden. She sank weakly onto the cushioned settee.

Her cold, shaking fingers touched the emerald medallion about her throat. Philip had given it to her on the night in Athens when they had pledged their love and spoken of marriage.

With a little cry of despair, she tore it from her throat and flung it to the floor. "It is he who will regret this hour!"

How long she had sat there, she did not know. A slight noise in the next chamber behind the brocade drape caused her spine to stiffen.

Who was in the chamber? A slave?

She turned her head, and her breath stopped.

The drape was pulled aside, and a warrior stood there, his shoulder leaning into the arch, a slight, familiar smile on his lips.

The blood rushed to her cheeks, and she rose slowly to her feet. Tancred Redwan.

CHAPTER 26
Philip's Chambers

✤ In a moment of horror she realized he had overheard every word Philip and she had spoken. She could imagine the gossip and laughter he could spread if he chose to amuse the haughty young men who spent their time hanging about the wine shops and the Hippodrome. "Helena of the Nobility threw herself at Philip's feet, but he declined."

His eyes went to the floor where the emerald medallion had landed with a little crash.

"You!" she gasped.

He stepped forward and bowed deeply at the waist. "Yes. Your servant," he said silkily.

"Barbarian!"

"I believe we have met before. The name is Tancred."

"How dare you sneak about Philip's chamber, snooping!"

His blue-gray eyes beneath the coal-black lashes were amused. "A thousand apologies, Lady."

He did not look the least apologetic. "Your apology is

rejected, barbarian. What are you doing in Philip's private chambers?"

"For this one night . . ." and he gestured his hand about the luxurious room, "I am a guest. And tomorrow? I shall decide if I will stay and serve him. I may decide to stay longer than I first intended. Ah, Constantinople, city of marvels! There is so much for a barbarian to learn from the civilized Greeks. Courage, for example, gallantry, and of course, honor. But as for my presence in the Noble's chambers, I might ask you the same."

He indicated the monk's robe on the marble floor. "Your clever disguise shows ingenuity." He laughed softly. "But I shudder to think what your eunuch bodyguard thought of this. How did you get Bardas to agree, or need I ask? No doubt you bullied him into cooperating."

She glared at him.

Calmly he stooped and picked up the pendant, swinging it like a pendulum. His gaze came to hers.

"Yours?" he asked innocently.

In a few quick steps she was before him, snatching it from his hand. "Only a loathsome Cretin would eavesdrop behind the chamber drape."

He mocked a wince. "Once the Noble began his gallant speech, I could find no appropriate time to make my awkward presence known."

"I doubt that."

"And the longer I waited, the more impossible it became, and the more interesting."

Interesting, was it?

"You hid deliberately!"

"I would not say deliberately. I was waiting for Philip on the divan. But I confess, when I heard you mention Prince Kalid, I was tempted to continue listening."

"Then you admit it!"

"I fear my curiosity outweighed my gallantry." He smiled. "But surely a damsel wise enough to at last see the baseness of the Noble's heart can grant me her pardon?"

Again she felt the rush of flame to her cheeks as his eyes flickered with cynical amusement.

"What you may think of Philip is of no concern."

"You forgive him so quickly. My opinion? He is not worth a moment more of your thoughts."

"I should call the guards. I should have you arrested. Your insolence in not making yourself known is beyond pardon by the gods!"

"As a seeker of the truth, your rebuke weighs upon my soul with unfathomable regret. Truly? Is there no way to earn the forgiveness of these temperamental gods?"

"No," she retorted flatly. Her eyes narrowed.

"A pity. Unlike the Noble, I would journey a thousand pilgrimages to gain your favor. Where shall I go? Tell me. Jerusalem? Perhaps to Mecca? Perhaps to one of the thousand churches in Constantinople? Or even to the temples of the Mystery Wisdoms? However, since I also am a possessor of a certain church relic, perhaps it is best if I—"

"From past experience, I realize you lack civilized manners, barbarian, and I see that you possess a cynical tongue, but do you also make light of God?"

"Does the name *Tancred* taste like poison to your lips? As for God, it is He whom I seek, as Nicholas will tell you. But I have yet to discover anyone in the barbarian West or in all of Greece who can tell me clearly how to discover Him."

"Your insolence, 'sir knight,' will surely awaken His discovery of *you*."

"Then I shall not sleep well. But then, neither will you. I know the man they wish you to marry. Other than being weighted down with pride and jewels, he has little to offer."

She paused. He knew the Moslem prince?

"When is this grandiose wedding in Antioch to take place?"

The thought brought a sickening qualm. "I shall not go to Antioch! But if the nefarious scheme of my aunt and the bishop were to know fulfillment, I would journey there soon. In the next several weeks. First, Kalid will discuss the matter of the Castle of Hohms with the emperor."

He straightened. "Kalid is here, in Constantinople?"

Her sulky eyes scanned him. His interest went beyond her dilemma to the prince himself. Why?

"I believe I saw him with Bishop Constantine. By now he is at the emperor's banquet. Is Kalid a friend of yours?" she asked accusingly.

He ignored her question. "If you hope to outwit him, you will find it a challenge. What are your plans?"

Plans? she thought wildly. Now that Philip had dashed her hopes, what could she do?

She swept past him to stand before the open colonnade, feeling the breeze from the fragrant garden. The colorful lanterns on the caiques bobbed up and down in the water.

"If I had any plans, why should I tell you? You may inform Lady Irene."

"And why would I do so? Unlike Philip, the barbed bait your aunt offers does not entice me. Nor am I so base as to betray a woman."

No, she did not think he would. *Oh, Philip, why can you not see the truth?*

She turned away, afraid he would see the pain in her eyes.

"It seems to me you are hardly in a position to reject a

sympathetic ear," he said. "You are, I take it, rather
friendless at the moment. Unless you prefer the company
of the Seljuk."

"I have not said that I prefer yours, sir knight."

"Then you make a mistake."

She turned her head, her eyes coolly meeting his.

Tancred looked from her to the silver platter of fresh
fruit on the marble table. "But before you hasten to judge
me as bold, I should explain. Unlike Philip and the Seljuk,
I do not have the slightest wish to be the seignior of the
Castle of Hohms. Nor do I intend to become involved in
the battle with the Turks to rule Jerusalem. I shall be in
Constantinople for only a short time. I have my own ambitions, and I concern myself more with my own head than I
do with Saracens."

He lifted the platter containing purple plums, red
pomegranates, and bright orange apricots. He studied
them intently, as if trying to decide which he preferred.

"However," he said smoothly, choosing a plum, "gallantry demands I offer advice."

He looked at her with a hint of a smile. "Possessing the
sublime conscience of a Norman knight, whose valor is
beyond question, I could not sleep well unless I did some
act of honor to save you from this odious Prince Kalid. For
the sake of Nicholas, of course."

Her lashes narrowed. She tried not to notice how well
he wore his blue cloak trimmed with silver. Although the
idea goaded her, Philip would do well to possess even a
small portion of the determination of Tancred Redwan.

"And how, sir knight, does it come to pass that you
know Kalid so well? You have not yet answered."

His smile was disarming. "Oh. Did I not tell you? We
are old acquaintances, he and I. He is known in the House
of al-Kareem at Palermo."

She did not know who al-Kareem was, but Tancred was at ease in discussing him.

"Being a Norman, you are also friends with Saracens?" she asked caustically.

"I have little choice. Al-Kareem is my grandfather."

Helena masked her surprise but found she could not keep her eyes from searching for evidence of his Moorish ancestry. His handsomeness was beyond dispute, and she touched the pearls in her hair to distract his gaze from holding hers. There was more to Tancred than she had first thought.

He lounged against the arch, watching her. "Kalid is an avid breeder of some of the finest Arabian horses. I bought one of his prized mares from a trader in Cordoba."

She remembered what Constantine had told her about a wedding gift and said with a rueful smile, "I too, am a lover of horses. Perhaps this is my consolation. A string of Arabians are offered to me as a wedding present from your friend."

"A worthy gift," he said lightly. "An inducement to gain your peaceable journey to Antioch." He smiled. "But I hardly think you can be bought with horses of fine blood. As for Kalid being a friend," he set the platter down abruptly, "that is debatable. He and I are on unfriendly terms at the moment, one more reason I am tempted to foil his endeavors."

She, of course, was one of those "endeavors."

"Are you offering me your sword?" she asked boldly. "If so, for how much?" She smiled. "Several Arabian horses perhaps?"

A brow lifted, and his gaze swept her. "Neither can I be bought with horses of fine blood. However, you did

lend me Apollo. I would like to think it was out of friendship. I never forget a woman's generosity."

Helena hoped her expression did not show the
thoughts racing through her mind. He was not only
strong and adept with the sword, but she also found his
company stimulating. But she would not be foolish
enough to let him guess that she did. She had the impression that Tancred could be a far more dangerous risk than
Philip.

She turned and walked to the white Corinthian column. Taking hold of it, she looked out at the sea.

Yet, Tancred might prove to be her one chance to escape Bishop Constantine's watchful spies. Could she hire
Tancred to help her escape?

"As for castles, I have the only one I care about," said
Tancred. "I do not wish to collect more."

She was uncertain what to believe about him. "And
where is your castle, sir knight, in Sicily?"

"So you remember."

"A man's boast is easily remembered," she said airily,
walking about the portico. "But if you indeed have a castle, then why are you here in Constantinople? What of
your family?"

"As I said, my mother was a Moor. My father a Norman lord. He found her when the Normans conquered
Palermo."

"She must have been very beautiful."

"She was. And I? I am in your city to accomplish two
important tasks. First, to find the assassin of my half-
brother, Derek Redwan."

She turned from the column and showed her surprise.
"Assassin!"

He walked toward her but stopped some distance
away. "The second reason is to learn from the great store-

house of libraries. One day I wish to study at the medical school of Jundi Shapur. You have heard of it? But far be it from me to utterly destroy your belief in my barbarian spirit," he mocked lightly.

Medical school? Assassin? Castle?

Helena smiled. "I do not see you as a physician."

"I am also a man quick to see opportunity for increasing my abilities as a scholar. I may wish to stay in the palace to find solace in visiting the royal library."

"What? You can read?" she asked innocently.

His mouth curved. "I read and write well. I am for hire as a translator should you know of anyone who is interested."

She managed a smile. He could be quite amusing. "You may add conceit to your other list of abilities. Is there anything you cannot do?"

"Why waste time discussing what a man is not?"

She smiled. "I shall think about your skills. And you may retain Apollo until you buy yourself a horse. As for the royal library, you ask a hard thing. But if it is true, as you say, that you are a guest of Philip, he may arrange such a visit. The emperor will wish to please his guest."

He held her gaze. "And what do you wish, Lady Helena?"

He used her name for the first time, and she noted a hint of seriousness to his voice that brought a sober moment between them. She did not answer.

"You have journeyed far on your quest to find your brother's assassin. You have trailed him here?"

"I have word from a dependable source that he is in the East. Until I find him, I cannot return to Sicily. But perhaps we are all on a long journey to discover truth. Yet who is to say who charts our course?"

"Not the stars, surely," she said, thinking of Philip. The thought brought a fresh pang.

"We both agree," he said quietly.

"You have come to the right city if you would find knowledge. And the assassin who killed your brother?"

"I shall find news of him here as well. His name is Mosul from Palermo. He is a cousin."

"Mosul I do not know. But should I hear anything of him, I will send Bardas to let you know."

"You are generous."

She looked at the emerald pendant she still held in her palm, and it glimmered green. She closed her hand into a small fist. "You have quarters in the city?"

"If you wish to locate me, ask for a Moor by the name of Zakeem. You will find him in the Venetian quarter on the Golden Horn, near the Avenue of the Booksellers."

She took in the chain mesh, remembering his skills as a warrior. The journey from Wieselburg proved that he could be trusted with a sword. But he had said he was not for hire . . .

The night was warm, and the moon had risen over the waters. There was a lapse of silence in which they stood without moving, looking at each other. The breeze touched the hem of his cloak. Under his gaze, she said suddenly, "I must bid you farewell. If caught here, my aunt will seek to bolt me in my chambers."

He said nothing, only watched her. Helena turned and went down into the cool shadows of the fragrant garden. She glanced back. He had come to the edge of the pavilion and stood there looking down at her.

"Mistress," came a hiss from the shrubs.

Helena turned swiftly toward the voice. The broad face of Bardas wore a scowl as he looked out from the vines. "Is not that the Norman barbarian, Redwan?"

"Bardas, how dare you spy on me?" she whispered.

Yet she was grateful he had been in the garden in case she needed him.

"Did not Nicholas warn me before I left the West not to let you out of my sight?"

"Never mind. How much did you hear?"

"Enough to know that Lady Irene controls Master Philip," he grumbled. "And that this Norman mercenary is clever. We may need a strong sword, but we do not need this barbarian for a friend. I truly doubt if he knows Nicholas. I would not trust him."

"At the moment we need every friend we can find."

"The barbarian is not fit company for your nobility."

"I make my own decisions, Bardas. By now you should know well enough. Come, we must hurry lest Irene send guards to look for me."

Bardas strode ahead, hand on his sword hilt. "I know the look of a mongrel."

She smiled ruefully. She knew that Tancred was anything but uncivilized. "He claims to be a count."

Bardas remained skeptical. "A woman of your position confronts many dangers, but this Norman is by far the worst. He is a professional soldier. I also have a premonition of his foul character."

She was not listening. "Find out everything you can about him. As soon as you take me to the banquet, I want you to go straight to the bazaars and the Venetian quarter on the Golden Horn. He has a friend named Zakeem, a Moor from Sicily. Let it be known that I shall pay a fair reward for any reliable information on Tancred Redwan. Ask also about another Moor named Mosul and about Segneur Rolf Redwan at the Castle of Hohms."

"Involvement with the Norman will bring trouble."

"Am I not in trouble now? Who else can I turn to? Do as I have bidden."

"Very well, but I doubt if Nicholas knows him."

"Perhaps, but I am no longer certain of it. We may be wrong. And if we are, I wish to be on friendly terms."

She felt the eunuch's suspicious gaze and glanced at him with dignity, confessing, "I intend to hire him."

He stopped. "I have learned that Master Philip intends to speak to him tomorrow about service in the Imperial Guard."

She must not be thwarted. "Then I shall outbid Philip."

"Ah, the Norman is clever. He is not to be bought easily. You play with risk. Master Philip will hire him to meet with Bohemond. The emperor insists on a promise of Bohemond's fealty before his army is allowed to enter the city."

"But Nicholas comes with the Normans. And if Tancred does ride to meet Bohemond, I intend to go with him."

"After our experience with the Rhinelanders? Surely you would not ride into the camp of the Normans?"

Helena showed no fear although her heart was pounding. She drew her cloak about her. She would not think of that now.

"Better to risk another journey than board a Byzantine vessel to the port of St. Symeon and Antioch. If I do not escape, I will become the bride of Prince Kalid."

"Master Philip will surely come to his senses and appeal to the emperor."

Would he? Her heart knew a wrench of pain. How could Philip dismiss her so easily? Would he confront his failure and move to break the emotional chains that Irene and Constantine bound him with?

"No more arguments," she said wearily. "I can take no more tonight. We need the sword and wit of Tancred Redwan. At the moment, he is the only one I can turn to. And you, my faithful Bardas, will help me to buy his services."

Bardas shot her a glance. "Suppose he refuses to be bought by you or Philip?"

Helena remembered Tancred's smooth insistence that his sword was not for hire. His determination would prove difficult, she was certain of that.

"There must be some way to convince him, and I will."

CHAPTER 27

In Lady Irene's Chariot

✢ As Helena and Bardas neared the Sacred Palace, guards emerged from the shadows to encircle them. Helena knew a moment of fear, and Bardas reached for his sword.

"Sheath your sword, Bardas. No harm will come to her if she cooperates."

The familiar voice belonged to one whom Bardas dare not challenge. A giant of a warrior stood near the road between two guards holding torches. He was ebony, muscular, and as elegantly shaped as if chiseled from marble. He boasted the colors of the Imperial Guard, his rich purple cloak edged with gold.

"You heard me. Sheathe your sword."

Bardas frowned. "Philip the Noble will not like this."

"Philip is not in command. Would you thwart Lady Irene's will?"

Bardas hesitated and glanced at Helena.

"Do as he says, Bardas," directed Helena.

Bardas whispered, "I am sorry, mistress."

"Remember what I told you," she murmured, reminding him of Tancred.

Bardas stepped back into the darkness, and Helena was left standing alone. The majestic warrior stared at her. His face was expressionless.

"A chariot waits for you, Lady Helena."

He motioned to Bardas. "You are free to go. Do not cause trouble upon pain of death."

Bardas gripped his drawn blade. "I do not go without my mistress."

Helena put a silencing hand on his arm. "Who bids me?"

"Lady Irene." Rufus walked toward the road. As he did, other soldiers stood silent guard.

"I do not like this, mistress."

"Go, do as he says."

"And leave you?"

"It is not wise to thwart her now."

Bardas reluctantly scanned the guards, then left, stepping into the darkness.

The personal guards serving Irene appeared on horseback, clothed in fine cloaks, followed by a chariot with sleek horses. Irene sat in the chariot.

"My dear niece, you will join me?"

"Do I have a choice?"

"None. Unless you wish to spend the weeks before your wedding to Prince Kalid in a dungeon. And that would be a pity. We have so much to do to prepare you for your journey to Antioch."

Helena masked all fear. She permitted Rufus to escort her to the chariot, which then moved down the street ahead of the guards on horseback. Rufus drove the team of white horses with skill, the muscles in his ebony arms gleaming under the torchlight. Lady Irene wore shimmering silk under a fur cape. Somehow Helena imagined armor would fit her better.

"Am I now your prisoner, my aunt?" she asked.

"You made a fool of yourself with Philip."

Helena settled back in the seat, staring straight ahead. "Word travels quickly."

"If one wishes to survive in the palace, spies are necessary. I know everything Philip does. He is a charming son but too gullible. Constantine watches him, of course. He must be protected from foolish errors, such as suddenly becoming gallant and demanding Prince Kalid fight for you. One never knows what Philip will do from day to day. I must say, I was surprised that you went to his chambers. You met the handsome Norman there. I suppose you tried to hire him?"

Irene was too cunning to deceive. Helena said nothing.

"It is Philip who will hire Tancred, at my request. He is important and useful at the moment. But never mind Tancred."

Irene settled back, drawing her fur cape about her shoulders. "I have effective ways to deal with both you and Philip."

Lady Irene's golden hair was woven about her head like serpent coils and matched perfectly the silk tunic of spun gold. She appeared delicate, almost a golden goddess. Only the hard gray eyes gazing on Helena revealed the nature of the woman within.

Helena noticed the medallion about her throat. Irene was never without it. It caught the light and glinted, showing the insignia of the ancient Babylonian zodiac. She had successfully instigated a tale among those she nurtured within the Sacred Palace that she possessed the power of the ancient tower priestess. Helena could feel her aunt's controlled fury. "You little fool, do you have so little pride that you could throw yourself at Philip's feet? Not even that act of abject humility will alter your destiny. As for the handsome Norman you hope to hire, do you not know he too is important to the emperor?"

Stung, Helena looked at her. Momentarily she wondered what the emperor would wish from Tancred Redwan. But the insult over her visit to Philip overruled all else.

"I do not throw myself at the feet of any man, including Philip."

"No? Then what were you doing in his private chambers?"

"That concerns Philip and me."

"Your concerns, child, are mine and the bishop's. And Philip is also under our jurisdiction, or have you forgotten he is my son?"

"I forget nothing. Including your determination to make him please your every whim."

"Do I hear the whine of jealousy? Can it be? But enough of your accusations, my pet. It is you who are under question. You hid in his bedchamber like a common slave girl. Do you realize the embarrassment I could receive as your guardian? The first night of your debut! And with Prince Kalid at the banquet."

"It is difficult to conceive of any action taking place in the Sacred Palace that would embarrass you. Does not the entire nobility know you are the mistress of Constantine, who masquerades as bishop?"

Lady Irene drew her hand back to strike Helena, but she moved back against the seat. "Am I a slave that you raise your hand against me?"

Irene halted, white faced and eyes blazing. For a moment of silence they stared at each other. Her aunt's strength seemed to reach out to wrap its cold tentacles about her.

Helena knew that Irene bullied anyone who succumbed to her in fear. Her one chance of survival depended on outwardly standing her ground.

"You will not master me, my aunt. I am the daughter of nobility, and I will not be treated as baggage to satisfy your whims. If I went tonight to speak with Philip, there was no harm in that. And any gossip ablaze will soon die."

Irene recovered her icy dignity. "As painful as it sounds, Philip will not marry you. Constantine must have made that clear. You must accept the truth and get on with your future. There are more important plans for you and for Philip. Believe me, I find no pleasure in sending you to Antioch. It was a marriage of necessity. One the emperor wishes. Nothing will be allowed to alter your course. It is written in the stars."

"The stars or your intrigue? A pity that Philip does not believe me when I tell him how you and Constantine are using him for purposes of your own. Is that in the stars also?" she mocked.

"Helena, I do not enjoy being cornered. I must, to survive, be heartless. When will you learn you are no match for me in the palace? Did you learn nothing from your mother's mistake?"

The stabbing remark brought a wince of pain. Irene saw it. "Remember well. Dungeons are dark places."

Helena did remember, and it was all she could do to stop herself from physically shaking. The thought of a dungeon, dark, cold, and infested with scurrying rats, was enough to drive her to unreasonable panic.

As a child she had been placed in that dungeon with her mother. The time she had been there was not long, perhaps a few nights or weeks. Those memories of her mother's arrest for treason awoke Helena from sleep with vivid nightmares. Always there came her mother's cry of innocence. Helena had eventually been confiscated by Irene.

Nicholas had been unaware of what happened until spies informed him. On his return, Irene tried to convince him that she had done everything to save his brother's wife, but Nicholas had not believed her. Irene had visited the dungeon the day of her mother's supposed death, and he suspected poison. There was no proof, and it was this that kept him from openly accusing her. But Bishop Constantine had moved against Nicholas, having him banished from Constantinople.

Now Helena knew her mother was alive. The question was, did Irene think so? Had she truly gone there to poison her, only to learn that some unnamed personage had come to her mother's aid? Who then had sold her into captivity?

"I know what your plans are," Helena whispered. "You intend to become the emperor's mistress. What will you do? Use your magical powders on the emperor's wife first?

"One day the emperor will see how you deliberately enslave others with your potions and stargazing. When he does, it will be you who is arrested for treason!"

"If your wild accusations are meant to hurt, they only show your folly. For your sake," Irene hissed quietly, "you do well to keep your lips silent. If necessary, I will see that your youth turns to old age before you ever walk free again."

A chill crept over Helena, but she refused to cower. "You will not frighten me the way you did my mother. Scheme against me, and I will counter every move you make."

"Then you are a worse fool than I imagined. You cannot survive in Constantinople without me. You are but a babe."

"I have not been sitting in Athens spinning tapestries, my aunt. I too know the art of intrigue."

"Indeed? Will you also intrigue against the emperor and contest his iron will? Do so, and I need not lift a finger to silence you. He will do it for me."

The emperor? Helena was set back.

"My pet," Irene said more calmly, a little smile on her lips, "it is not I who refuses to give you to Philip. As Constantine told you, it is the emperor. Have you forgotten the Seljuk threat? The emperor fears the Byzantine Empire could be swallowed up by the Turks. Do you know how badly he wishes to control Antioch? Why do you think he has called for the barbarians in the West to come and fight the Turks?"

Helena had concerned herself as little as possible with the thought of war, but she knew that the unruly mobs following Peter the Hermit were all dead.

"What do I care about barbarians and Turks?"

"Regardless of what you think, I have come in peace. I do not wish to see you in the dungeon, Helena. As your aunt, it is my responsibility to see you married for profit and with a future. The emperor agrees."

Helena almost believed her. She laughed suddenly. "How warm and motherly of you, Irene. But you need not throw up your mask for me. Save your masquerade for the emperor's wife. It is political profit you seek from my marriage, not my security."

Irene smiled triumphantly for the first time. "I have wisely convinced the emperor of the expediency of your political marriage for the good of Byzantium. In a short time you will be sent to Antioch."

Remembering the black eyes and the arrogant, hawk-like face with its short, well-trimmed beard, she went cold.

"I need not tell you how pleased the emperor is with my negotiations with Antioch," said Irene proudly. "I have his highest regard. Soon anything will be in my asking, and that, my dear, includes a strong future for Philip in the Sacred Palace. Philip understands. He realizes some sacrifices must be made to attain our goals. You will soon be accused of treason if you do not cooperate fully."

"You cannot get by with this. I am loyal to the emperor, he must know that—"

Irene interrupted with disdain. "The emperor knows nothing of the sort. He remembers your mother."

"Absurd! My father and mother were loyal. My father served him for years until his death. You and Constantine have fed lies to the emperor!"

"Enough. I advise you to cooperate and to please Prince Kalid. It may be that he will spare your friends when he takes control of the castle. If you continue to resist, you will be under lock and key until you are brought by guards to Antioch. Is that what you wish?"

Of course it was not, and Helena grew silent. If she was locked behind her chamber door until the journey to Antioch, how would she meet Nicholas?

Unexpectedly, Lady Irene smiled. "That is better, dear. As for Nicholas, it is said the Norman army from the West nears Constantinople. I know Nicholas is among them. But do not think he will intercede for you. Constantine will take care of Nicholas. And do not think to send Bardas to the camp searching for him either. I will have your slave watched."

Helena's mind raced. She had no choice now but to cooperate with her aunt to remain free. If she were to escape, she must hire Tancred Redwan.

"Very well, you win for now. I will go to Antioch. But I will not stay. Someday I will escape."

Lady Irene shrugged. "What you do in the distant future is entirely up to you."

The chariot stopped in the courtyard of the summer palace, and Helena was dismissed.

Irene watched until Helena was escorted by the guard inside the pavilion, then she turned toward Rufus. He stood by silently. Irene was proud of the caliber of warriors she had manipulated into her personal service. She smiled to herself. She had a better guard than even the empress. Rufus was a tiger on a chain, her chain.

As Lady Irene waved abruptly to him to drive on, she didn't notice how his dark marble eyes fixed on her. A small, almost hidden dislike flickered within their depths.

His service to Lady Irene was forced. From the moment she had found him in service to Seigneur Rolf Redwan at the Castle of Hohms, Irene had maneuvered to acquire him for her purposes.

Rufus would have left her service long ago, except that his son's prized position as a translator in the royal library depended on her favor. Rufus discovered that Lady Irene had power to bring success or ruin to nearly everyone. Because his son was left to her favor, he obeyed her wishes. But in his heart, he thought her the embodiment of evil.

"Where is the Norman, Tancred Redwan?" asked Irene.

Rufus presented himself as the picture of undaunted loyalty. "He awaits the Noble in his chambers, madame."

"See that he is flattered. Have gifts sent to him. Philip is to promise him anything for his service. Offer him whatever he wishes, position, gold. Spare nothing. He is useful to Philip, therefore to me."

Rufus had heard much about Tancred from Seigneur Rolf Redwan. He said tonelessly, "The Norman is no doubt like his uncle at the Castle of Hohms, Lady. He will not take well to flattery, nor can his loyalty be bought."

She shot him a sharp look. "Are you accusing me of flattering Seigneur Rolf Redwan?"

Rufus knew that she had once tried to hire him into her service, but he had turned her down, enraging her. "No, madame. But Tancred Redwan could prove dangerous. He may in the end, my Lady, be more trouble than he is worth."

"At present, his assets outweigh the risk of having him in my service. Find out how he can be bought."

"No offense is intended, Lady Irene, but I do not think he can be."

"You know him?"

"I know his uncle. Redwan's father was a mighty warrior named Count Dreux Redwan. He was killed in battle in Rome defending the Latin pope. His uncle, Rolf Redwan, you already know to be a strong seignior guarding the castle. I believe he became Tancred's adoptive father according to family custom. Tancred is well educated in Latin, Greek, and Arabic, and I have heard his uncle say he is acquainted with medicine. He is also a proven warrior."

She leaned forward in the chariot. "He speaks Arabic?"

"His mother was a Moor from Sicily."

"Interesting indeed. Count Dreux Redwan from Sicily. . . where have I heard that name spoken, and only recently?"

"I do not know, Lady."

"Find out. I want to know what brought him to Constantinople. Then report to me at once."

As the chariot clattered down the cobbled street, Irene

thought, *That name, I have heard it tonight. Was it from an informer? There was some word of a Norman named Walter of Sicily sending spies to Constantinople searching for a nephew. And did not his search have something to do with a family assassination?* Lady Irene stored the information in her mind. The knowledge would become a tool to prod the Norman into doing as she wished.

CHAPTER 28

The Baths of Zeuxippus

✥ The famed Baths, said to be built on the exact spot where Hercules yoked and tamed the fiery steeds, were located only a short distance from the Hippodrome.

After Tancred gave himself over to their warm, scented luxury, he relaxed on a marble bench. Unexpectedly, a slave wearing a long crimson robe entered, followed by several others, each bearing a magnificent gift on a silken pillow.

The chief slave bowed low. "Oh, magnificent one, in the name of the emperor, Philip the Noble offers you this gift.

"Oh, favored of the emperor, warrior of renown, great Norman of the auspicious West, my master requests you to accept these meager gifts as the beginning of a long and profitable friendship."

The first slave spread out a tunic of black brocade woven with gold thread, and a second displayed a hyacinth blue cloak with gems. The third slave offered a jeweled dagger and a sword with a jeweled scabbard. The fourth produced a magnificent Byzantine costume. The last gave two bags of gold besants. Again they bowed and motioned toward the colonnade.

"Oh great Norman, our master, Philip the Noble, comes now to greet you."

Tancred followed the slaves' gesture and heard a pleasant but stilted voice. "Ah, you have come, friend Tancred! I hope you are being refreshed?"

Philip stood between two armed guards. The young Greek noble was tall, artistic of face and slender of build, and carried himself with the pride of an emperor. He came across the pavilion wearing a Byzantine costume of brilliance. The semicircular cape was of light purple wool, the lower hem edged in gold and studded with precious gems. His black tunic reached to his knees, and he wore hosiery of the same purple, with soft buskins covering his ankles. The familiar face was haughty, so was his polished manner. Even as he tried to show warmth, he reeked with Byzantine arrogance.

I wonder what he wants from me? Tancred decided to play along with Philip's game for purposes of his own.

Philip tossed his cloak over his shoulder and sat down on the marble bench opposite Tancred. A slave hastened to fill his glass with wine; others brought in lavish bowls of fresh fruit.

"The emperor has heard of you. I have been sent to extend his greetings."

Tancred's expression did not change. If the emperor was aware of him, it would have been through Philip and Lady Irene who hoped to win over his service. The emperor was too concerned with the soon arrival of the Western princes and their armies to take note of a lone mercenary. Tancred could tell nothing of his feelings over the explosive meeting with Helena in his chambers on the eve of the banquet. Soon after Helena had left that night, Tancred too had departed the Noble's chambers. He looked into Philip's remote dark eyes, masking his contempt for a man who could relinquish the woman he wanted to the arms of a Seljuk prince. Philip's ascetic face showed little.

"The emperor has also requested you remain in the Sacred Palace in service to him."

"In what capacity?" Tancred asked.

"As liaison between the emperor and the approaching Norman army from your own Sicily. I assure you, the pay in gold will be well worth your efforts on his behalf."

Tancred saw the opportunity before him. If he was in the service of the emperor, he would have greater liberty to move about the Sacred Palace, granting not only access to Helena, but time to gather information on the whereabouts of Mosul.

"Your feudal master, Prince Bohemond, has been seen swiftly advancing into Byzantine frontiers with a strong army of knights. We would have you meet with your master to speak of his fealty to the emperor before he is admitted inside the walls of Constantinople."

Philip's use of the term *master* rankled Tancred. "You may tell your emperor that my sword and my services are mine alone. I am vassal to no master."

Philip gave an abrupt laugh. His dark eyes flickered over the warrior. "To be so unencumbered is indeed noble. Yet the kind of freedom you speak of is not easily maintained. There must be masters and slaves."

"I assume you are so convinced because you are a master. A slave would be prone to a less rigid philosophy."

Philip shrugged. "For you it is easy to say. For me? I could never leave the service of the emperor—it is my life."

"Such dependency can prove the death of one's soul.

Take my advice, leave while you still have the will to choose your destiny."

Philip's dark eyes mocked his free spirit. "Soon this magnificent city will own your soul, even as it does mine. And you will be content to have it so. As for me, I could not leave if I wanted to. There are expectations that must be met. One must sacrifice if he is to become what the gods have destined."

Tancred watched Philip empty his wine glass. He was sure the Byzantine sacrificed little of his true ambitions out of duty.

"It is my belief that said gods do not destine. It is our ambitions that chart our paths."

"So that accounts for my thorny way!" Philip mocked. "You see ambition as something evil?"

Tancred stood. "Ambition is like a sword. It can render justice or murder the innocent."

Philip smirked and held out his glass for the slave to refill. "I see you are also a philosopher."

"And you, a noble with his future glory written in the stars. You were born for power and glory."

Philip recognized the irony in Tancred's voice and arched a brow. "You flatter me, Norman. But yes, I believe in the stars. Lady Irene is gifted with the spirits of the gods. She has seen my future."

"She has made it most intriguing, I am sure."

Philip's smile was unpleasant. "We understand each other, Tancred. I suspect you also are a man of ambitions. But perhaps yours lay in the Redwan Castle in Palermo?"

Tancred was alert. Could Philip have discovered about Derek's assassination and believed him guilty?

"But you Normans also have a thirst for new lands to conquer. The Byzantine secret service, which I soon hope to direct, knows well the history of the Norman warriors."

"A bloodthirsty lot, to be sure," said Philip carelessly.

"For two years in the frozen mountains north of Greece, Bohemond fought us."

Tancred's eyes twinkled. "Yes, my father fought beside Lord Bohemond."

Philip too smiled. "And Emperor Alexius was the military commander at the time."

"Then I see why he is uneasy with the approach of Bohemond's knights."

"The emperor has never forgotten him."

"Nor Bohemond your emperor."

"The emperor is rather nervous about so many Normans beneath the wall of his city."

"Does he expect them to take Constantinople?" asked Tancred, wryly.

Philip smiled with aristocratic disdain. "Humility among the Normans is a grace in want. Who is to say the thought has not crossed his mind?"

"Who indeed!"

"The emperor would put nothing past Bohemond. It is for this concern he wishes to hire you. The Normans are not many days hence. He wishes you to ride to meet them. Who best could understand the secret intentions of the Norman lord but you?"

Tancred thought of Nicholas. Since Zakeem had already informed him that Nicholas would be in Bohemond's company, a visit to the Norman camp was already in Tancred's plan. So too, a meeting with Bohemond could be arranged, since the prince was friendly with his adoptive father Count Rolf Redwan. But Tancred would not become a Byzantine spy for the emperor. He also believed it was Philip who would advantage most from any information Tancred might discover from Bohemond.

"What else does the emperor desire of me?"

"To begin with? Nothing more dramatic than to learn the ambitions of Bohemond. Does he come in peace? Will he publicly swear his fealty to the emperor? Or does he come with an army in pretense, intending to lay claim to Byzantine territory presently occupied by the Turks?"

Philip motioned to a slave, who produced a purse. He took it and tossed it to Tancred. "There will be ten times this if you stay."

Tancred weighed the purse in his palm, as if it were his only consideration. "A sizable amount."

"That, friend Tancred, is only the beginning."

"A good beginning builds a strong friendship. The task for which you would hire me does not seem so difficult," he said evasively. "I should be able to accomplish it within a fortnight."

"Then you will accept?"

"Tell your emperor I accept. I shall meet with Bohemond before he arrives. We shall talk of his quiet entry into the city to see the emperor."

"Have him come with ten knights only. Accomplish that, and we will be much in your debt. We have scouts along the route he travels. When word arrives that he is within three days journey of Constantinople, I will send for you. Until then you are to remain on duty in the Sacred Palace assigned to the Imperial Cavalry."

Tancred thought of his mission to learn news of Mosul. So far, not even the ring of his grandfather had unstopped the tongues of the dumb, despite the nights spent roaming the bazaars. Yet, he expected al-Kareem's informer to arrive soon from Aleppo. If Zakeem sent word that the informer had arrived, Tancred would need to leave the Palace at a moment's notice.

He also expected Helena to contact him. Except for the eunuch, she had no one else to turn to until the arrival of Nicholas.

Philip raised the goblet. "Your success, my Norman friend. And the emperor's!"

Tancred smiled and lifted his goblet. "Hail to the emperor, always victorious, always fortunate!"

Philip turned to leave.

"One thing more, if I may," said Tancred. "It may be weeks before the Normans arrive. I need to occupy my mind while at the Sacred Palace. I would seek access to the great Royal Libraries. Is this possible?"

Philip's surprised gaze scanned him. "One of my slaves will see to it at once. At the library ask for Joseph the translator. He is the son of Lady Irene's bodyguard."

Tancred watched Philip leave the bath house.

Well done, he thought.

CHAPTER 29

The Armory of the Varangian Guard

✣ "Ah, Master, it is so, Kalid knows of your cousin Mosul. That is not all. The spy at the bazaar insists al-Kareem's informer was assassinated while trying to leave Aleppo."

The news from the bazaars was dark. The death of his grandfather's trusted informer convinced Tancred that his presence in Constantinople was now known to Mosul. Mosul now had the advantage.

The armorer, a powerful man of Scandinavian ancestry, kept a courtyard where soldiers met to practice with all sorts of weapons. Hired Normans of Viking ancestry belonging to the Emperor's famed Varangian Guard, were often present, as were other soldiers and bodyguards.

Today Prince Kalid was there, having not yet left for Antioch. As he practiced with his scimitar against an Egyptian, he saw Tancred arrive with Zakeem. But Tancred pretended to prepare for sword practice. Kalid dismissed the Egyptian, then unhurriedly found his way to Tancred.

"Enough of swords, my distant cousin! I see you have arrived to fight with the infidels. You would have a better chance to run the Seljuks out of Jerusalem if you were able to handle their weapons."

"Well said, Kalid. We meet again. And what brings you to Constantinople?"

Prince Kalid's smile was wolfish as he handed him the scimitar. "I have always been a seeker of truth, even as you."

Tancred took the scimitar and tried the balance. He ran it through the various steps of style.

Kalid's black brow lifted. "Only a true Seljuk could do better. And how is my famed mare?"

Thinking of Alzira, Tancred said, "She was stolen."

"Stolen! And you allowed this cursed thief to escape your blade?"

Tancred smiled faintly. "Not for long, my cousin. He will yet pay. I thought you might have seen my mare and the thief who rides her."

He lifted a hand helplessly. "I? Am I a man who keeps company with thieves?"

"You keep company with assassins. You know I search for our cousin Mosul. Where is he?"

Kalid chuckled, but his black eyes were cool as they measured him. "You attribute things to me that are far beyond my ability. I have not heard from our Moorish cousin. I have only recently come from Aleppo."

Aleppo . . . had it been Kalid who ordered the informer killed? Tancred held the scimitar still. "I wonder if you speak the truth, Kalid."

The black eyes sparked, but the smile remained. "You would not be calling me a liar?"

"Forgetful, perhaps?"

"Did you come here to prod my memory?"

"To warn you, Kalid."

Tancred could see that he pretended innocence. "Warnings about Mosul?"

"And the woman."

"There are many."

"There is only one I concern myself with. Helena."

"Ah! So that is it. She *is* beautiful, is she not? I do not blame you for becoming envious."

His smile hardened. "And what happened to the lovely Kamila, our cousin? Have you wearied of her so quickly?"

Tancred knew that Kalid had once hoped to take Kamila to Antioch as his bride. But like Mosul, she had shown no interest in either of her distant cousins, but only in Tancred. He hoped to turn Kalid against Mosul.

"Kamila is dead." Kalid's smile vanished.

Tancred stated, "Mosul killed her."

Kalid made no move, nor did his expression change, but Tancred sensed the inward rage. "I want Mosul," said Tancred. "He killed two people I cared about. He knows I am here in Constantinople. Tell him I call him a coward. Tell him I wait with the sword. If he is a warrior, let him come to me, or else I will go to him. But let him come forth as a warrior."

Kalid remained silent and unreadable.

"As for Helena of the Nobility—she is the niece of a friend," said Tancred. "I would not see her in Antioch."

Kalid's face flushed. "You make one threat too many."

"Not a threat, Your Excellency. Only the suggestion that you find another bride."

Kalid smiled. "And if I do not take your suggestion?"

"It remains to be seen. I go to visit my uncle. You know the Castle of Hohms is in his command. It may be that while I am there, I will also need to pay Antioch a visit."

Kalid met his gaze evenly. "Then, come. You will find trouble enough."

"I will come. Reconsider the Byzantine damsel; I should hate to use this scimitar against a distant cousin who bears the blood of emirs."

Tancred handed the blade back into his hand, and walked away with Zakeem.

Prince Kalid looked after him, his eyes cold.

CHAPTER 30

The Royal Library

✤ In the weeks that followed, Tancred waited for the arrival of the Normans. While visiting the famed library in the Royal Portico, he met young Joseph, a handsome lad who looked more like an Ethiopian prince than a studious translator.

"I would have access to the Scriptures."

"In Greek or Latin?"

"Both. Is it possible to pay for a Greek translation of my own?"

"Not easily, Count Redwan. But for the son of my father's friend, I can arrange at least a New Testament."

Tancred measured him with curiosity. "Your father knows Seigneur Rolf Redwan?"

"He once served him at the Castle of Hohms."

"You do not appear pleased he now serves Lady Irene."

Joseph glanced toward the big ornate doors. "I can speak little here. You have asked for a translation," he said changing the subject. "I shall have it for you this afternoon. If you wish to study now, there is one here in the library."

"I would also see a map of the environs of Antioch. Do you have one?"

"Yes, an excellent one. Please sit. I shall bring both the Bible and the map. You may stay as long as you wish, I will be working late."

Joseph was right. The map was one of the finest he had seen. Tancred removed a piece of parchment from his satchel and sketched the city of Antioch, including each of the twelve gates. He remembered as he worked that Antioch was where the apostle Paul had gone with Barnabas to teach the first Gentile church. It was also in Antioch that Paul had received his commission to begin his first missionary journey to Cypress, Thessalonica, and Berea. Now, with the map done and the Greek New Testament in hand, he sat down with the small booklet he had taken from the Jewish girl Rachel in Worms. He searched from Matthew to Revelation until he found the verses the booklet quoted. It was from the early section of the epistle to the Romans. He compared the Latin translation of the booklet with the original Greek. Seated at a desk, he read the entire epistle. Then he went back to consider the section of words in the booklet. He made careful comparison, changing some of the Latin translation into the original Greek.

The words were a balm to his soul, a light in his darkness.

And not being weak in faith, he did not consider his own body, already dead (since he was about a hundred years old), and the deadness of Sarah's womb. He did not waver at the promise of God through unbelief, but was strengthened in faith, giving glory to God, and being fully convinced that what He had promised He was also able to perform. And therefore "it was accounted to him for righteousness." Rom. 4:19–22.

Tancred stopped. *What is 'imputed'? Righteousness?*

He read on, wondering. "If we believe on him that raised up Jesus our Lord from the dead; who was delivered for our offenses, and was raised again for our justification. Therefore being justified by faith, we have peace with God through our Lord Jesus Christ: by whom we also have access by faith into this grace wherein we stand, and rejoice in the hope of the glory of God."

He read the words again and again.

"For when we were yet without strength, in due time Christ died for the ungodly. . . . But God commends his love toward us, in that while we were yet sinners, Christ died for us. Much more than being justified by his blood, we shall be saved from wrath through him. For if when we were enemies we were reconciled to God by the death of his son, much more, being reconciled, we shall be saved by his life."

Then Christianity is not a religion of human works attempting to satisfy the holiness of God, he thought. Perfect righteousness was a gift to all who placed their faith in Jesus Christ. Tancred thought of the teachings of the Koran, where human works was the means to attain righteousness. But according to the Bible, mankind could neither remove sin nor open the bolted door into paradise through self-effort. Christianity was unique, Tancred decided, and marveled. *All religions except Christianity are man's efforts to make peace with God. But Christianity is God's work to reach man! My sin is exchanged for the righteousness of Christ at the cross.* And what of the religious masters? *All have died,* he thought. *All remain in the grave. But God raised Christ from the dead, bearing witness that Jesus alone is the true Son of the Most High God.* As Tancred contemplated the message of Christianity, his heart warmed toward Jesus Christ. "Lord, I told the Byzantine Noble I had no master. But I find it the greatest of honors to bow to You, the only true Leige. You Christ, are worthy. Despite my love for my Moslem grandfather, al-Kareem, I turn from lesser lords who are mere mortals. In finding You I have found the Truth I sought. My search has ended. With your disciple Thomas I cry: 'My Lord and my God.'"

The library doors opened and Rufus stood there, his broad shoulders boasting the colors of the Imperial Guard. His solid chest was bare; the massive muscles rippled. His black trousers fit snugly and were hemmed in gold. His sword rested in a jeweled scabbard.

Tancred stood, ignoring his scabbard lying on the table across from him.

Rufus's black eyes glinted a response. "There is no need for that," and he gestured his head toward Tancred's sword.

"I know your father, Seigneur Redwan at the Castle of Hohms."

Tancred closed the Greek New Testament. "Sit. You look as though you are driven by the devil himself."

"You are not far from the truth. I cannot stay. Another time. Out of respect for your father, I bring you information."

Tancred sized up the man. Something told him that he could believe this giant warrior.

"Yes?"

"The Moorish cousin you seek is at Antioch."

"How do you know this?"

"Lady Irene is asking among her informers about you. Those who serve her in Constantinople and elsewhere are many and dangerous. As yet, she does not have this information. I have come straight to you. But I cannot keep it from her for long. I tell you now, that you might leave at once."

"Why does she seek information on me?"

Rufus's eyes hardened. "She wishes to control you for her purposes, even as she controls others. You must be cautious."

"I am in your debt."

"One thing more. If you go to Antioch, you risk your life. Prince Kalid knows of your cousin Mosul. He will warn him."

"And Mosul? Does he serve Prince Kalid?"

Rufus said evenly, "No, he is the chief bodyguard to the Seljuk military commander, Kerbogha."

Tancred had heard of him. He was a strong and clever fighter of the Turkish forces. If Kerbogha united with the other Seljuk commander known as the "Red Lion of the Desert," the Western knights would confront a formidable foe, equal to anything Bohemond and Count Raymond of Saint-Gilles could throw against him.

Tancred made up his mind quickly. He would ride to meet Bohemond to warn him and to perform the service for which Philip had already paid him in gold. He would meet with Nicholas and tell him of Helena. And then with Zakeem he would ride to the Castle of Hohms and Antioch.

Somehow he must get inside the walled city of Antioch before the Western forces arrived. Kerbogha would never surrender the city. There would of necessity be a long siege. He must find and confront Mosul.

END OF BOOK ONE

GLOSSARY

abbey: a group of buildings comprising a monastery

abbot: the head of a monastery

arrow loops: slit-like openings on a tower that permit the firing of arrows with full protection

bailey: a courtyard surrounded by soldiers' quarters, stalls for horses, and food storage rooms

conical helmet: worn over a hood; the helmet's shape and the smooth metal protect the wearer from cutting or thrusting weapons

craven: a Norman trial to establish guilt or innocence

donjon: a dungeon-like tower

Durendal: a name for the sword of Roland in the epic poem "Song of Roland"; a symbol of knightly swords pledged to the service of God

gonfalon: a banner that hangs directly from the shaft of a lance, just below the lance head

Great Horse: a specially bred warhorse that can endure heavy weight and the clash of battle. It responds to leg commands so the knight can fight with both hands

halberd: a weapon consisting of a battle-ax and a spear

heraldry: a family insignia worn on the helmet or shield or appearing on the gonfalon

jess: a soft leather thong attached to a falcon's leg

keep: the stronghold of the castle, used as a watchtower and arsenal. The thick walls are laced with arrow loops. Usually there is a well beneath it. Storage and eating rooms are above, and sleeping quarters are on the top level

mace: a favorite weapon of warrior-priests, it was sanctified and carried in ceremonial processions; an implement made of wood, with quatrefoil-shaped head that is carried slung on a loop on the right wrist

morning star: a type of mace; a round ball studded with spikes, attached to a handle by a chain

Patriarch: head of the Eastern church at Constantinople

scimitar: a curved, single-edged sword of Eastern origin

Seigneur: the trusted commander of a castle, a term of respect

seignoir: the feudal lord of a manor

"Song of Roland": an epic poem about Charlemagne's Christian victory over the Moslem Moors of Spain; an early model of knightly chivalry.